TWELVE STORIES

ALSO BY GUY DAVENPORT

Commentary

THE INTELLIGENCE OF LOUIS AGASSIZ
THE GEOGRAPHY OF THE IMAGINATION
EVERY FORCE EVOLVES A FORM
A BALTHUS NOTEBOOK
CHARLES BURCHFIELD'S SEASONS
CITIES ON HILLS: EZRA POUND'S CANTOS
THE DRAWINGS OF PAUL CADMUS
THE ILIAD: A STUDY GUIDE
THE ODYSSEY: A STUDY GUIDE
THE HUNTER GRACCHUS

Fiction

TATLIN!
DA VINCI'S BICYCLE
ECLOGUES
APPLES AND PEARS
THE JULES VERNE STEAM BALLOON
THE DRUMMER OF THE ELEVENTH NORTH DEVONSHIRE
     FUSILIERS
A TABLE OF GREEN FIELDS
THE CARDIFF TEAM

Poetry

FLOWERS AND LEAVES
THASOS AND OHIO

Translations

CARMINA ARCHILOCHI
SAPPHO: SONGS AND FRAGMENTS
HERAKLEITOS AND DIOGENES
THE MIMES OF HERONDAS
MAXIMS OF THE ANCIENT EGYPTIANS
THE LOGIA OF YESHUA (WITH BENJAMIN URRUTIA)
SEVEN GREEKS

12 STORIES

Guy Davenport

COUNTERPOINT

"Tatlin!," "The Aeroplanes at Brescia," "Robot," "Herakleitos," and "1830" were previously published in *Tatlin!* (Charles Scribner's Sons, 1974). "The Bowmen of Shu," "The Chair," and "Fifty-Seven Views of Fujiyama" were previously published in *Apples and Pears* (North Point Press, 1984). "Colin Maillard," "Juno of the Veii," "A Gingham Dress," and "Badger" were previously published in *The Drummer of the Eleventh North Devonshire Fusiliers* (North Point Press, 1990).

Library of Congress Cataloging-in-Publication Data

Davenport, Guy.
   [Short stories. Selections]
   12 stories / Guy Davenport.
   I. Title.
  PS3554.A86A6 1997
  813'.54—dc21   97-28155

ISBN: 978-1-88717-844-0

Composition, book & jacket design by Wesley B. Tanner / Passim Editions

Printed in the United States of America

COUNTERPOINT
2560 Ninth Street Suite 318
Berkeley, CA 94710
counterpointpress.com

For Bonnie Jean

Contents

TWELVE STORIES

Tatlin!

Tatlin, the ironic Tatlin, is exhibiting Constructivist works at the People's Museum of Decorative Arts. Lenin's face gazes from posters beside every entrance. Lenin's face is among the exhibits inside.

From the ceiling hangs a flying machine. It looks like nothing so much as the fossil skeleton of a pterodactyl. To those who have seen Leonardo's sepia designs for a Tuscan ornithopter, that is what it looks like.

Lenin raising his fist against a background of rippling red flags is what we see when we enter the first room of exhibits.

Then the glider, its wings spread from wall to wall.

Someone has seen Tatlin himself, going from one door to another, dressed in his worker's one-piece suit which opens and closes with two rows of metal teeth which lock together when he slides a bobbin along them.

His eyes are sardonic, intelligent, blue.

The catalog says that the machine is for workers to fly in, like a bird.

Around the glider there are blueprints of its parts, and drawings of it in different stages of assembly, front view, side view, cross section. Much of the lettering on the plans is at right angles to the horizontal, so that we have to tilt our heads to read.

This is no place to continue talking about M. N. Ryutin's remarks

1

concerning Comrade Stalin, mimeographed and running to many pages, said by people who knew to foreshadow a change.

Konstruktivizm, someone says, is no longer the right word for the style of Tatlin, yet the catalog explains that Konstruktivizm is Marxizm-Leninizm in art, the common visual experience of the Socialist Workers' State.

There are interesting drawings of sinuous parallel lines which part from each other around diagrams of the glider, like the grain of wood around a knot. These are air currents. There are arrows to indicate the direction of flow.

A photograph of Lenin signing papers at a desk hangs above an exhibit of Konstruktivist chess sets and bowls. How hard he had worked!

The flying machine looks like a big bird stripped of its feathers and flesh. For a body it has a mesh cradle, or a sled with a strange array of struts, with straps and levers, in which a man is to lie. One can see where he is to pedal, where his arms will fit to manipulate the wings.

Tatlin, Comrade Korneliy Zelinsky says in the catalog, has been with the Revolution since the very first October days.

A brooding bust of Lenin backed by deep shadows watches the flying machine.

It is called *Letatlin,* the Glider. The name of it curiously incorporates its maker's name, as if destiny had conspired.

It is neither *aeroplan* nor *samolyot* but a bird's ossature with syndactyl wings for a man to fly in. There are minds of this sort, Khlebnikov liked to say, that backtrack to the archaic, as if Clémont Ader had not lifted his *Avion* shaking like a dragonfly above a French meadow in the wild wet spring when Tatlin was twelve, or Wilbur and Orville Wright skimmed above the sands at Kitty Hawk when he was eighteen, a journeyman sailor aboard the *Aleksandr Suvorov.*

We must shatter the glass wall that Socrates and Aristotle placed between nature and the sweet lechery of an inquiring mind.

Herakleitos had seen the complementarity of all things wrestling each other like athletes red with dust, had seen all things except time

lapse into their opposites without any loss of energy or matter, dancing from shape to shape.

Had not Niels Bohr found his hooked atoms in Demokritos?

Khlebnikov had days when he lived among Solutrean flints and the reindeer lords of Hylea. Sculptors went to school to the stele carvers of Honduras. Picasso was prehistoric, Corbusier was articulating a grace of window and wall that was abandoned after the clay villages of Anatolia. Brancusi was Cycladic, Yoruban, Acheullean.

Tatlin had gone back to Daedalos.

Tatlin is professor of Ceramics at the Institute of Silicates. He is also a painter, an engineer, a theoretician.

He designs many things. Furniture, clothing, utensils of all sorts, a whole new style of art. Buildings, monuments. And the flying machine. There are two sailors looking at it and grinning.

A woman in flat shoes, a decorated woman wearing the Order of Lenin, Second Class, Hero of the People, is looking at it. She has pursed her lips. She has leaned forward an inch. She holds her elbows.

Lenin's face on an eight-foot poster stares through the flying machine.

Nowadays this historical old building with its Italian walls and waxed floors is the Pushkin Museum. Rich red drapes have been hung at the tall windows, so that the light inside is amber. There are touching relics of the poet and his Russia, many books bound in red and gold. There are many paintings both Russian and European. There are the poet's yellow gloves.

The Ukrainian needlework inspired by Agitprop is gone, the Suprematist posters all zigzags and half circles, the portraits of egotistical poets executed in violent colors and the sudden angles of Futurizm. These are gone.

All is as grand as a Romanov Easter egg, and one enters the cultured precincts with respect, a little sad, full of awe.

The first thing you see is a picture of Lenin raising his fist against a stormy sky.

O red October days!

The *planyór*, the glider, has an openwork lathe chassis the profile of which is the exact shape of a maple seed. There is a V-strut in the center, and toward the round end, the head of the glider, there is another strut. This second strut is also a V-strut seen head on, for the bottom of the chassis is a single dowel which divides at the sternum of the glider's chaste anatomy, just above its craw, and forks backwards, leaving the top of the chassis open like an envelope into which one is about to put a letter. Between these two struts rise the high elbows of a heron's wing. These flap through a system of pulleys set in motion by the aeronaut's feet.

It is a diagram of the flight of a bird translated into lithe wood of great resiliency. The webbing between the ribs of the wings is oiled silk.

The aeronaut is to wear a one-piece zippered suit of two-ply poplin, lightly quilted, such as Tatlin has on today. He is also to wear laced canvas shoes, like those of a bicyclist, goggles, a helmet that straps under the chin, and gloves that snap together at the wrist.

——What is the glider for?

—— It is for everyday use.

Tatlin is showing the glider to the press. The man from *Izvestia* is holding his notepad to his chest and adjusting his steel-rimmed spectacles.

——Regard the bent wings, Tatlin says. I believe that you will find them to be aesthetically perfect.

——Exactly, says the man from *Izvestia*.

A portrait of Lenin gazes at the white Muscovite sky beyond the museum windows in an ecstasy of sincerity.

——You must not think of my glider as a utilitarian object, nor as a work of art. You would not think of the hydroelectric station on the Dnieper as sculpture, yet it is. Its use is obvious, heroic. My glider is for the people. It is a socialist artefact, both art and utility.

——The people of the Ukraine will be particularly interested in the Letatlin Glider. One can sail for hours over the treeless fields, the tundra.

— It is, Tatlin says over a *blyudyetchko* of sage tea, an air bicycle.

Zelinsky writes this down.

Above them in a sepia photograph Lenin is signing papers at a desk.

Comrade Marya Ivanovna, of *Pravda,* straightens her back and presents herself to the artist-inventor.

— It is very beautiful, she says. Very beautiful indeed.

Tatlin narrows his eyes.

— *Pereat mundus*, he says, *fiat iustitia.*

ST. PETERSBURG 1905

Father Gapon had arrived, the icons were lifted up, the bass drums struck.

The march could begin.

A man on the corner of the prospekt nodded to a man on the opposite corner. He was Colonel S. V. Zubatov, director of the secret police. The wind of the January dawn had stung tears from his eyes. There was frost in his moustache.

The march could begin.

Father Gapon wore the tall hat of his calling, but under his alb and surplice he wore workers' clothes.

— *The Lord have mercy upon us!* he cried. *Christ have mercy upon us!*

There was a roar from the people dark behind him.

— *Vstavai proklyat'em zakleimënnyi!* a single voice deep as a horn shouted into the falling snow. *Ves' mir golodnyx i rabov!*

From his window Maksim Gorki could see thousands of workers, students, women. The Bolsheviks had brought their red banners that whipped like flame and blood among the gold of the icons.

The dawn was white.

Father Gapon raised his hand and stepped forward. A French horn that had been polished until it flashed carried the melody of the Tsar's Hymn like a lark flying up from a wheatfield.

The band was flanked by men carrying above their heads as high as they could reach icons the indifferent golden eyes of which stared into the thin fall of snow.

Two men bore between tasseled poles a color lithograph of the Tsar and Tsarina in the imperial stoles of the Romanovs.

The hymn that rose like a thunder of roaring water was droned by too many voices to be either coherent or measured. After the first four blocks of marchers, filling the street from side to side, the Tsarist hymn lost the defining glory of the drums and the lyric brass of the horns, and became the noise of a shoaling river.

Never had so many people sung together on the earth before, not even when the population of a city cried for two hours together, *Great is Diana of the Ephesians! Megalé he Artemis Ephesion!*

Whole boulevards of Paris had sung the *Marseillaise,* and Cromwell's helmeted infantry had trod behind their pikes shouting psalms, and the Spartan phalanx cloaked in red to the heels had intoned in high solemn voices the dread paion to Apollo the Healer, but these were mere battalions moving to the common heartbeat of the bagpipe, the thin rattle of the tambour, the crash of long knives against shields on which were painted in gold and green the serpent Zeus and the cock Asklepios.

The icons came through the snowfall gleaming, long-fingered Christs Pantocrator, Cyrils, Christophers, Elijahs, Boris and Gleb on their horses. Madonnas embracing their infant Christs cheek to cheek moved spattered with snow beside the gilded wooden crosses on poles and the vermilion flags of the Bolsheviks.

A copy of the petition which Father Gapon rattled in his fist was already in the Tsar's hands. It asked that the war with Japan be stopped, that the Russian people be allowed to elect representatives who would speak for them in a congress, that the people be granted what their dignity under God demanded, the right to lead their lives as conscience and wisdom dictated, unimpeded by an arbitrary power.

The Winter Palace when they reached it lay silent and sealed, its Florentine colonades stippled with snow, its high roofs fading from sight in the falling snow.

—The Tsar! Father Gapon shouted. Let the Tsar come to the door! The square, parade, and promenade before the palace filled with people, a thousand, two thousand, shawled and with the smoke of their breath before their faces. The icons and the flags and crosses floated with a carnival gaiety above them.

In the front rank, Father Gapon and his fellow priests and a line of women knelt in the snow.

—The holy father! every voice cried out. The Tsar!

All the bells of all the cathedrals of St. Petersburg began to ring, for the day was the Sabbath, and though the churches would be empty of all but the rich, the loud iron and dark bronze of the bells shook the frozen air with their call.

The fury of voices and the music of the bells muffled the first volley of gunfire, which tore into the people from their left, scarcely noticed.

The blue smoke of the rifles hung still and bitter in the air.

A woman had been shot in the breast. Two women held her by the elbows as she slid to her knees screaming, blood filling her lap. A young man in a student's blue coat fell backwards, his hands thrown above his head. A steel worker, blinded, turned around and around in his tracks, calling for his wife.

—What is the matter? Father Gapon shouted. Do they see the Tsar coming over there?

The volleys were being fired from the north end of the palace, one every five seconds. Front rank fired, brought weapons to port arms, about faced, took two steps, and about faced again, to reload. The second rank took two steps forward to become the first, and at the command of *Fire!* from an aristocratic voice like tearing silk, fired.

A cobbler through whose neck a bullet had ripped and who was drowning in his own blood crawled between stampeding legs, trying to hide.

The horses of the Cossacks pranced through the tall oak doors of the courtyards, which opened all at once. The horses were frightened and had to be reined in cruelly. Formed into jagged lines, the Cossacks drew their sabres.

——Stay clear of the blood, a captain commanded left and right, or your mounts will slip in it. *Charge!*

TERASPOL

It is, Osip Mandelstam would say in later years, the quality of sunlight on a wall.

He was speaking of civilization.

When Vladimir Yevgrafovich Tatlin was ten he spent a summer at Teraspol with Mikhail Larionov, who was fourteen and had a hint of fuzz above his upper lip.

Vladimir Yevgrafovich did not like his father, who beat him, and he felt nothing at all toward his stepmother. His father, an engineer, moved from city to city on trains with green windows through which cinders flew and rotten smoke.

At Teraspol there were cobwebs in the barley, wasps at the panes, and cats in the knitting baskets.

Mikhail Fyodorovich's grandfather was a sailor, chewed plug tobacco, had been born and raised in Archangel, and talked a great deal about ice.

He was Dyedushka Larionov.

Dyedushka Petrovsky, a farmer, was Mikhail's mother's father. He had a meal in the middle of the night, to keep starvation at bay. Breakfast was at dawn, when the mist was still in the chestnuts. He took his tea from a wineglass, sipping it with a hiss between his teeth.

There was another meal at ten, a lunch at noon, tea at four, supper at six. Then, when the fireflies were thickest and the dew began to agitate old man Petrovsky's rheumatism, the household, except for the kitchen detail, folding dough in long pans and forking pickled eels from stone jars, went to bed. At midnight they were up again, sleepy and hungry.

——We could starve in our sleep, Grandfather Petrovsky said.

His hair was tied in a red bandana, and under his blue shirt one could see his flannel nightclothes. Cold borshch and black bread, vodka and tea sat in the lamplight like a Dutch still life.

Vladimir and Mikhail slept in a goosefeather bed in an attic room under the long eaves that were carved like the dragonflame in the icons of St. George.

There was a barn out beyond the chickenyard and the pasture gate that had been abandoned for a newer one and which now stood in a forest of giant sunflowers. Honeysuckle and briar had taken over its sides, looping into its cool stalls at night and out again by day. Wasps had built paper nests on the roofbeams. Gleb the cat went in for mice and crickets.

Vladimir and Mikhail edged through the thicket of sunflowers on rainy days to find things, old bits, bottomless wooden pails, snakes, baling wire, lizards.

An old grain room that had lost most of its outer wall was somehow a fine place to go. The great paniers and rough, warped leaves of the sunflowers made a jungle on one side. The other walls were worn white and smooth, dusty with meal and bran, thick with cobwebs. A pale green cool light fell through the sunflowers.

It was here, Tatlin would remember all his life, that he had his first vision of the design of rooms, long before the cabins of ships and obligatory neatness of the sailor defined for him the rules of interior space. And when Mandelstam spoke of civilization as the quality of sunlight on a wall, thinking of the gardens of Fiesole and of the rusty gold, freckled honeycomb light on a wall along the poppy fields at Paestum, he remembered this old grain room in the barn at Teraspol.

He and Mikhail had found in a parlor album pictures of Japan, and had read about paper walls, rooms without furniture. They read about the succinct arrangement of stunted trees, the ritual placing of crockery, scrolls, whisks, screens, and folded clothes.

Tatlin swept the old grain room's floor and walls with a besom he brought from the big house. He swept it even cleaner with a goose feather, moving rills of fine dust onto a shingle.

—Our Japanese room!

They placed near a corner a stone washed in the trough, and by it they placed a bottle into which they stuck a single blue cornflower. A bench once used for the milkpails became a table for the center of the floor.

They sat crosslegged and bowed to each other from the waist.

In the big house he liked the coziness of the feather beds, the tall narrow windows, the twilit corners with their icons and candles. One walked softly. Someone was always taking a nap. Nor must one run across the verandah, for there were always people in wicker chairs around a wicker table, sipping tea and reading aloud from long periodicals the pages of which they cut with a bone knife.

They played wild west among the cows, drew ships and balloons with wax crayons, went berrying with the cook, and stood on the end of the horse trough, harpooning whales off the coast of Iceland.

But that summer Tatlin had to give up his nameless rapture, which no one must see. This was his secret, his resource, his peculiarity, accessible to none.

Alone, he got from their hiding place a collection of pieces of cardboard cut into the shape of leaves, blades, parallelograms, triangles, ovoids. Kneeling, he took one up and passed it before his squinting eyes, chirring softly. Of a thin halfleaf shape he made a buckboard, adding haughty, mane-tossing horses, thin red wheels, lens springs, a lady and gentleman, a dog trotting behind, dashing snow, a rising wind.

Ahead, a train. Another piece of cardboard became the cabin of the locomotive. Another, the rolling drivers. He hissed, for the steam, and whistled the sweet long notes that came with a curve.

In a valley lay the jumping artillery of an army, smoke puffing in balls from the cannon. A young officer, this sliver of cardboard his sabre, stood under a tossing flag, shouting commands.

The carriage, the locomotive, the army.

He heard steps, and slipped his cardboard pieces into his shirt. When his stepmother was at the door, Vladimir was looking out the window, his hands behind his back.

The Lapp king upon his reindeer and a hawk upon his fist might flash into nothing at the click of a doorhandle down the corridor, but he could be alone again, in time.

In his second year, which he remembered only as a tree remembers in the adjusted spiral of its response to sunlight a limb that has been stripped from it as a sapling, his mother died of tuberculosis.

Fourteen years before, Tsar Aleksandr II had been blown from his carriage by an anarchist's bomb to die screaming against a wall. And the anarchists had chosen the month of March again, when, he was told later, his mother had been buried in a fierce spring snow, to assassinate Aleksandr III. They were to use grenades filled with pellets of strychnine.

The assassins, among whom was Lenin's older brother Aleksandr Ulyanov, were arrested in their cellars and hanged.

A piece of cardboard could become anything. That was the good of it. The lean parallelogram could be an icebreaker, the barrel of a revolver, an adze, a kite, a submarine.

The sunflowers at Teraspol recovered a memory, from where or when he did not know. He woke one morning after a long train ride that had lasted for days. Out his window he saw above a majestic row of sunflowers the carved orange and blue second story of a wooden house.

Gylea, they called this part of Russia, far from Russia proper.

He remembered low mountains all green, and sheep. Under an overcast sky they were white, black-shanked, black-muzzled, but under the bright sun dun and barbaric, green-tongued, green-eyed.

The shepherds wore filthy embroidery.

He saw his first fig tree, and the flat blue of the ocean beyond the roofs. Every yard had sunflowers.

Mikhail brought the history book to the old grain room, and explained the woodcuts. They swept the room daily. The first thing they did when they came to it every afternoon was sit crosslegged and bow to each other.

Vladimir stayed at Teraspol on into the mists of September, the birches thin and quivering above the fallen yellow of their leaves, splinters of frost growing from the ground in the night.

Then the birches shed their last blond leaves onto shallow snow. Vladimir Yevgrafovich convinced himself that if they went out into the first torrential snow, past the lowing cows shambling to the barn at noon, past the rye stubble fast going under, they would see wolves at the edge of the wood.

—You know them, he said, by their shining eyes.

They saw cold birds in the forks of branches, and a hare kicking snow as it bounded, but no wolves.

—Listen! Mikhail said.

Grandfather Larionov was calling them from the summerhouse, the white fretwork of which was invisible in the pouring snow, so that he seemed to be standing in a magic hole in the weather.

—The post has come, he shouted. The Tsar is dead.

THE SEA

The flint Baltic to which a bog mist clung like smoke to a peat fire gave way to the chopped silver and gentian straits of Norway. The German sea was oily, a great water rolling as if it were cumbersome to itself, its black swells roughened by a wind of light.

—Up starboard forward! cried the junior deck officer, down port aft!

The French coast was gray, the Spanish yellow and green. At Gibraltar they saw apes and sad Englishmen. They bought pipe tobacco as strong as a mouthful of acid.

In the Sryed'izyémnaye Mórye, blue as a summer sky, they took off their heavy black sweaters and wool caps and rolled the sleeves of their flannel shirts to their biceps. The Gdansk sailor Klaus stripped altogether, wearing only a *cache-sexe,* the *Badenhose* of the German swimming clubs.

By the time they reached Istanbul they were as brown as Tartars and Tatlin's sketchbook was full of shaggy, windy-haired merchant seamen. Here Sergei with legs like calipers stood with his collar over his ears, the quartermaster reading the chart, Foma rigging tackle.

On shore he saw how changed he was. His chest had fleshed out and grown a fine down. He walked with tilting hips. His hair was pale Romanov gold. The calves of his legs defined themselves, his shoulders were square, and his hands had become blunt and hard. His nose in the mirror was excellent, but his upper lip was too long and his chin academic. In profile he looked like an intelligent fish.

There was fire in the light of Istanbul. Every form, old wooden fence, long wall, and dusty green garden tree took its tone from a gentle light that was the counterrealm of the icy brightness and sullen twilight of Petrograd and Moskva. Russian colors were bitter, flat, touched with blue. Tatlin saw yellows in Turkey that his eye could taste like honey on the tongue.

Everywhere here was the light for which in Russia he waited and longed, a particular light on weathered windowsills, doorframes, beechbark, tabletops, or steps upon which morning silver changed to the brown of afternoon and lay with a failing glow that seemed to be the essence of time. It was the congenial light of late-summer windows, the light on rocks in forests, the sweet light in yards with fig trees in the Hylea. Civilization was the art of building walls for such rich light. *Italy*, as Mandelstam said. *Istanbul*, Tatlin would say in later years.

Sancta Sophia was the mother of all the churches of Russia, even stripped as it was of every icon and cross, its tall saints and Fathers and Christs Pantocrator covered over with the fanatic calligraphy of Islam. The lamps on their long chains hanging high as a mainmast made him sway with wonder.

The gardens of Istanbul were greener than any Russian green. He had been on the verandah of the Larionov's blue house over which kudzu and gourd and wisteria grew, making a green interior of summer air, and once in the forests on the road to Moskva, a wonderment after the Ukrainian prairies, he rode in the green tunnel of trees all giants of their kind, but nothing Russian was like the Brazil of these Turkish gardens.

Greece after Turkey was naked. He walked among the heaped stone of the Acropolis, and watched black goats grazing in the agora.

He was seventeen when he went to sea. He hid his shyness under a mask of tomfoolery and became the ship's clown. He danced with limber legs to the kontsertina, gave imitations of the quartermaster, and

sang bawdy capstan ballads falsetto. *Bot kak!* he would say in the voice of a peasant, and fart.

Before they had consigned their cargo of galoshes at Brest and Lisbon, Tatlin had had his nose bloodied, learned that his *pyetúkh* was extravagantly long, and discovered the novels and stories of Leskov.

He learned the names Lenin and Marx.

His body hardened under the demands of seamanship, his eyes became bluer, his hands calloused and skilled.

He learned the wind, the laws of tension, the advantages of constant order, the clarity of the minimal.

When, in his classes at the Institute of Design and Ceramics, he said *Consider wax and tars and resins, vosk, dyógot, kamyéd,* he spoke from the sailor's fund of exact knowledge of materials.

Every force evolves a form, he taught. Sea and wind had shaped the ship.

Shape answers use. And then use modifies shape.

Gulls flew just behind the aft deck, crying *Tatlin! Tatlin!*

1913

The zeppelin Reichsschiff L2 rose six hundred and fifty feet from its Ankermast at Johannisthal Flughafen into the Berlin October blue.

Tatlin watched it grow a white ball of fire veined in scarlet from its forward engine car. The fire broke and spread, leaving as it stripped the zeppelin's long fuselage the black web of its skeleton to nose up in the rolling, wrinkled white smoke bulging with round fire.

The airship buckled and exploded again as it fell, and exploded a third time as it smashed into Berlin.

It was The Hohenzollern Year. Because Kaiser Wilhelm preferred folksongs to Wagner and Strauss, Berlin rang with bazouki and balalaika, tambourine and autoharp. Larionov had taken him to hear a band of Ukrainian singers. They were off to Berlin to make a fortune in the German parks and *Kabarette.* Tatlin was weary of the sea. He could play the kontsertina. He joined them. It was like running away with the Gypsies.

They crossed Poland in a third-class carriage that bounced like a buckboard and shook like a trawler in a crosswind.

The Tsar and Tsarina had preceded them in ten armored Pullmans. The Imperial train had ridden into Berlin between two miles of the Reichswehr in quintuple ranks along the tracks.

They saw the Kaiser on a white horse prancing through the Brandenburg Tor. He wore the uniform of the Death's Head Hussars.

Berlin was as crowded with rhetorical sculpture as Saint Petersburg. The Germans waddled like geese. It was against the law to walk more than three abreast on the wide pavements, to swing a cane or umbrella, to whistle, to sing, to dance the tango.

They stared at automobiles, students with sabre cuts down their cheeks, women in hobble skirts.

They tried to give concerts on the streets and were threatened with jail by the police. A café hired them. Their wildest songs did not change the expression on German faces. One evening a poet tried to talk with them about their native land. He mentioned endless fields of grain. They nodded. Troikas. Many troikas, Tatlin said. Black bread, embroidered kerchiefs, fat landlords, remote and lonely crossroads.

Tatlin wore blue sunglasses, as at sea.

Who were the Futurist painters and poets of Germany?

Kulturbolschewismus!

The Ukrainians were shocked at the decadence of Berlin. The chaste Maryenka was outraged by such insinuations as she could make out. *But they are pigs!* she said. Tatlin and Pavel Fyodorovich were told by a monocled and chinless officer that they couldn't hold hands while walking down the street. *Pigs!* Maryenka said.

Their café manager told them excitedly that the Parks Commissioner had heard of them, the Ukrainian Folksingers, and that they were to play in the park along the route of the Kaiser's *ricorso*. Next to God and the Army, the Kaiser liked folksinging best. He owned a troupe of Cephalonian singers. He was an expert in a knowledge of national costumes.

They played in the park, flanked by the police. Their balalaikas trilled, Tatlin's kontsertina jounced through mazurka tempi. They sang of the miller's daughter who couldn't sleep in the full of the moon.

The Kaiser stopped on his white horse. His moustaches turned up like a swallow's wings. He seemed to wear three capes of different lengths. He listened with great seriousness. He signalled to an aide-de-camp, who sprang into a salute. The Kaiser pointed to Tatlin.

From deep within his uniform the Kaiser extracted a gold watch which he detached from its chain and handed to the aide-de-camp. Then he waved and rode on.

—His Imperial Highness gives this token of his esteem to the blind Ukrainian folksinger, said the aide-de-camp, handing Tatlin the Kaiser's gold watch.

Not a word of which Tatlin understood.

—*Spasíbo*, he said with dignity.

PICASSO

He sold the Kaiser's watch and went to Paris. The streets of the gray, civilized city ran between plane trees and walls. The houses behind the walls seemed to him to be consulates. The air smelled of garlic and urine, of tobacco and horse manure.

—The beehive! a Bohemian told him at a café. They will know at the beehive, *la ruche.*

It was No. 2, Passage de Dantzig, near the slaughterhouses in the Vaugirard district. There he would find many Russian painters, painters of every nationality, *la vie tzigane.*

It was the strangest building in the world, a twelve-sided pagoda of wood.

A staircase zigzagged up the center. Each landing had twelve doors leading to twelve studios, which were wedge-shaped. Above each door inside was a bed. He heard Italian, English, French. Somewhere a woman was crying and shouting. A mandolin on the floor above, the word *cubist* in Yiddish on the floor below.

— There is a man from Vitebsk two flights up, he was told, who paints horses playing violins and hands with seven fingers.

He was painting a cow dancing in the sky when Tatlin found him, a handsome, merry Jew with wads of curls and beautiful eyes.

— Segal, he said, waving Tatlin in. Here in France I must spell it this way.

He pointed to a signature on a canvas: Chagall.

— I would like to spell it Chagalll, but the French are very particular and say that it is not a thing to do. Do you hear the poor cows? They slaughter them just over there. That is why I paint so many cows. You are a painter?

— A painter, an engineer, a sailor, a strolling musician. You paint a bit like Larionov.

Chagall's studio was full of eggshells, soup tins, feathers, Russian embroidery, fishbones. Reproductions of El Greco and Cézanne were tacked to the walls. The paintings all seemed to have been done in Vitebsk.

Over a glass of tea he said he had come to meet Picasso.

— So, Chagall said, batting his eyes. By who can I send you Picasso? Cendrars, he bent down a finger. Archipenko, Léger.

A mooing of cows outside, a chair kicked across the floor upstairs. Chagall bent down more fingers.

— A minute, he said, skipping out the door.

He came back with a man who might have been his brother.

— We are in luck. Meet Chaimke Lipchitz. With Picasso he is like a member of the family.

— Everything is Russian just now in Paris, Lipchitz explained. Everybody talks Diaghilev and Nijinsky. Igor Stravinsky, the protégé of Rimsky-Korsakov, is by everybody proclaimed a genius.

5 rue Schoelcher.

He had just moved here. He had been down to Céret in May and June, Lipchitz said, with Juan Gris, whose cubist pictures the Mademoiselle Stein from America was beginning to buy. Braque, the other master, and the poet Max Jacob had gone to Céret with Picasso. He liked people. He was a lonely, even furtive man who could paint for ten hours at once, but he was always hungry for people. Had Tatlin seen Guillaume Apollinaire's book on the Cubists which had just been published?

— In Petersburg there are rooms full of Picasso, of Matisse, of Gauguin.

— Yes, but you are years out of date.

A wolfhound barked. The concierge wiped her hands on her apron and looked at them over her glasses. He could see sculpture through the studio windows, classical heads bevelled and faceted in the Cubist manner.

A short man with broad shoulders, a dash of hair across his forehead, black eyes round as a seal's. His voice was rapid, pitched high. Tatlin could understand nothing.

Lipchitz translated.

He was cutting paper and pasting it onto boards. Wallpaper, newspaper, construction paper. Here was a paper guitar with wrapping cord for strings.

— He eats my studio with his eyes, Picasso said to Lipchitz.

— Tell him, Tatlin said, that I understand what he is doing.

Picasso shrugged his shoulders.

— This is what sculpture should be.

He was looking at a compote of ice cream complete with spoon modelled in plaster and painted with mauve and pink dots.

Picasso was jubilant. He shook Tatlin's hand.

— Just the other day, Lipchitz explained in Russian, the Mexican painter Diego Rivera called that little piece silly, pretentious, an outrage. I myself agree with the Mexican.

— Ask Picasso if I may become his pupil. Tell him that I am a sailor used to housework and will sweep his floors and clean his brushes.

— No, no, Picasso said. Waste not a minute. Go do what you want to, what you can. Get a lifetime of work into a week. Plan nothing: make.

1917

By the dawn's early light one could make out the trapezoid of the *Avrora*'s gray profile in cold mist, her three stacks streaming smoke in the north wind from Finland, her nervous lanterns, the bright arc of windows on the bridge, and her mainmast, on which a flag was rising. It was red.

The black water at her stern was turbulent. The *Avrora* was swinging broadside.

Her officers could hear gunfire on the mainland. They knew that the Smolny Institute where girls in identical white pinafores learned chemistry and French now bore Schneider mitrailleuses on its steps. The red flag floated from its cupola.

Citizen Nikolai Romanov was somewhere on a train.

Men lay on the fenders of Packards moving toward the Winter Palace. Streets leading into the prospekt to the palace were sandbagged and guarded by the Bolsheviks.

It was said that Aleksandr Kerensky would defend the palace on his white horse.

Streetcars full of troops, red flags whipping from their windows, passed down the Nevsky. People stood dazed on corners and looked up and down the street from doorways.

It was cold, the dawn white and slow.

No one could guess what would happen. Kerensky had put women in the inner rooms of the palace near the great halls.

The outer rooms were guarded by cadets from the academy, boys in their teens. Military professors with their hands behind their backs were their officers. Company by company, room by room, they stood by rifles as tall as themselves, grinning, solemn, lugubrious, pious, afraid.

No Russian would fire on women and boys. The battle would happen at the conference table instead, Kerensky with folded arms, Lenin raising his fist.

Dawn reddened the *Avrora*'s standards. Semaphores clicked on shore, on deck.

——*Quadrant!* cried the gunner's mate. *Chetárye dyévyat' odín tri!*

The guns of the *Avrora* rose.

——*Deflection! Vósyem' syem' dva!*

The guns of the *Avrora* rode to the left.

——*Fire at my command!*

——All power to the soviets!

——*Fire!*

The first salvo pitched geysers of gravel and ice from the parade ground, halved a wall of the park, and shore the chimneys from the gardener's house.

The second salvo went into the tall windows of the Winter Palace which had just begun to flash silver in the dawn.

LIGHT

Listening on his cane-bottom chair in the cream and gold salon of the Shchukin town house to Gottschalk's *Caprice for Two Pianos,* the conceited players with hair à la Liszt sitting in cocky poses as different from Rubenstein at the keyboard as an electric doorbell from a grand duke's porcelain knocker, Tatlin reflected how little he liked Mayakovsky.

A canvas by Matisse above a vase of gilded leaves held his gaze: a woman with rich brown hair, folded hands, a green blouse, dark and placid eyes. In among the intelligent women and red dancers of Matisse hung gloomy Picassos. Morosov owned better paintings by the master, a Cubist Vollard through which the ghosts of Cézanne, Euclid, and Bach had passed while it was on the easel.

The butlers were handing around tea and a liqueur that smelled of aniseed and marigolds. The piano concert had pranced to a halt.

——*Bog Poldnya!* a professor said, looking about him as he stood to make certain that he had the room's attention.

One hand behind his back, the other lifted in a loose gesture, he recited Ivan Alekseyevich's poem in which a girl and her sister watched black goats on red rocks in some Sicily of the Russian imagination. A blue bay, rocks baked, an olive's dry shade. The god Pan like a swarm of buzzing flies came down.

Tatlin could not follow the intricate image of knees, skirts, strong arms, nipples, and camomile, but he joined in the applause.

—*V gorakh Sitsilii* . . . the professor began again, with more about dust, gold, and stone.

Larionov wrote on his paintings to indicate that he was the most unsophisticated of artists. After he had worked through his imitations of the French from the pure Impressionism of Camille Pissarro to the Fauve period of Derain, he began to paint as if he could not paint at all. He gave up perspective, proportion, chiaroscuro, and any style more advanced than that of a child.

He was doing his military service of nine months. On weekends he brought canvasses to be shown at the Bubnovyi Valyet, The Jack of Diamonds.

Mikhail, Aleksandr Vesnin said, had discovered vulgarity in the army.

In the Kremlin, Tatlin corrected. He has been on bivouac in the nice woods north of the city, but mainly he does squad drill in the Kremlin, pulls guard duty, and paints. It is better to go to sea between sessions of art school. Sealight gives you an eye.

Tatlin painted an old sailor. An oval of light ochre did for the face, a russet rectangle for the beard. The crumpled cap he treated as if it were dented tin, and its bill was a black sickle naively outlined in white. A blue dot for each eye, a triangle for the nose, the mouth omitted. The peajacket, high-collared, he painted blue, the hands, rope burnt, knot knuckled, red.

He applied the flat, stretched aesthetic of the icon to long-uddered nudes. He put a shallow bend into all straight lines.

Painting was the first spirit to be freed in the new world, the giddiest and most elated of the whole revolution. And in gratitude the new painting depicted the spirit itself. Like Matisse Tatlin had painted in bold outlines, blue or red or green, asking of lines only that they have verve. Like Cézanne he painted light as flakes of color.

This wild boldness was a childhood, a drunkenness of style, a dance. It would grow up, it would take forms never seen, it would

become an articulator of the new world, its bones and nerves and muscle.

He remembered his rhombs and trapezia and rectangles of cardboard that he used to pass before his eyes as a child, chirring softly, making them become airships and buildings, Captain Nemo's submarine and Robinson Crusoe's umbrella of skins. That's what Picasso's constructions in paper were: a vocabulary of forms, a model of harmonies and relations. Art must die and be reborn in everything.

TSIOLKOVSKY

Tatlin when he had begun to design the Letatlin air bicycle gave a lecture on Tsiolkovsky at the Ceramics Institute.

Konstantin Eduardovich Tsiolkovsky was perhaps the greatest Russian man of science, he began, and eyes looked at eyes among his students. Professor Tatlin thought Khlebnikov a poet greater than Pushkin. *Búdytye vnimátyelyni!*

On 17 Syentyabr 1857, during the reign of Tsar Aleksandr II, Tsiolkovsky was born in Izhevskoye, a village in the Spassk Okrug of Ryazan Gubernia. His father, a cold and distant man, was a forester. Invention was in the family blood, for Tsiolkovsky's father designed a threshing machine and taught his sons to build models of houses and palaces. The young Konstantin Eduardovich had a very happy childhood. He learned the dignity of labor and the joy of making things. His mother was a jolly woman: the opposite of his *red* father, whose integrity of character was respected by his superiors and inferiors alike.

Tsiolkovsky built huts of sticks in the Spassk forests. He was a champion roof walker.

His pet cockroach he put in a little gondola made of paper which he tied to a kite. Thus the theoretician of the dirigible, the rocket, and the aeroplane began his love of the sky as man's destined highway.

When he was eight his mother gave him a small balloon, a collodion balloon filled with hydrogen, a great rarity in those days. The roach *Tarakán*, like Mendeleyev in his aerostat observatory, was now hydrogen borne.

He was a passionate reader, the young Tsiolkovsky. He invented in his imagination a miniature world and pretended that he was small enough to inhabit it. It is a great advantage to think to scale. In later years Tsiolkovsky would have to be content with models of his inventions.

One of his favorite daydreams was to cancel gravity and act out the joy of leaping telegraph poles.

When he was nine Tsiolkovsky caught a terrible cold from sledding down a mountain. The cold developed into scarlet fever and left him deaf.

He had to quit school, an awful deprivation for one who loved both books and companions. The silence into which he entered made him a lonely, melancholy man. *My deafness*, he once said, *made my life uninteresting. I longed to hear human speech.*

All his later life he tried to recall a single event between ten and fourteen, the years when his young mind still could not accept a soundless world, and never could. *The dark sadness*, he called those years.

At fourteen he began to be Tsiolkovsky. He built a carriage with sails, and even learned to tack against the wind.

He taught himself arithmetic. He learned to use an astrolabe and measured with one of his own construction the distance between the Tsiolkovsky house and his father's fire-tower: twelve hundred feet. For the first time he had verified a theory.

So gifted was this young provincial that his father and mother sent him to Moscow. This was a mistake. His deafness, poverty, and unfamiliarity with city life blocked his way to a career. He lived off brown bread and water, going to the baker's every third day. With the rest of his money he bought books, quicksilver, retorts, sulphuric acid.

It was in Moscow that he first conceived of leaving the earth and entering space. Centrifugal force, he thought, was the way. A cell containing a man, an oxygen supply, and scientific instruments would zip off into space if a rod rotating on its roof swung heavy balls at a very great speed. That would not work. He thought then of pendula at the

end of a stable rod. When they were set spinning, surely the craft would rise and go off into space, perhaps toward the moon, perhaps to Mars. Nay, to the very stars.

He wandered around Moscow all of a night delirious with the idea of travelling into space in his machine propelled by centrifugal force. By dawn he knew it would not work. But he spent the rest of his life finding other means of getting into interplanetary space.

He began to study the air, its currents, density, elasticity. He took up organic chemistry to find the proper fuel for a rocket, for it was now in rockets that he placed his hope for travel into space. He learned the higher mathematics. He became one of the most thorough and resourceful of engineers. He pondered the earth's motion, the nature of centrifuges, balloons, birds.

His trousers were so stained and burnt by acid that boys in the street asked him if rats had eaten his pants, but of course he could not hear them. His hair grew to savage length: he never looked in mirrors. He read *Fathers and Sons*. What can he have thought of Bazarov? He read Pisarev, who taught him how to put his ideas in order.

After three years of starvation and intense study, he passed the examinations by which he obtained a post as a country school teacher in Borovsk, Kaluga Province. He was a very good teacher. A man who cannot hear a student's question makes everything clear to begin with.

His apartment in Borovsk flashed with lightning and boomed with thunder. A visitor picking up a spoon to taste some jam Tsiolkovsky recommended as particularly toothsome was knocked sprawling. Electricity seemed to be in the very walls. A toy octopus which the unwary examined made your hair stand on end and sparks fly from your fingers and shoes.

He discovered the kinetic theory of gases and wrote a paper for the Academy in St. Petersburg. They wrote him back that the theory had been known and elaborated for a century.

He submitted a second paper to the Academy: *The Mechanics of a Living Organism*. Sechenov the physiologist read it and had Tsiolkovsky elected a member.

In 1883 he began to record in a journal the behavior of objects free of gravity and resistant forces: objects in, for instance, the cabin of a space ship. Here momentum, moment of momentum, and kinetic energy would remain constant. A moving object would move until it hit something. A still object would never move until pushed. A house in space, he noted in February of 1883, would never crumble under its own weight. A man could stand on a needle without its piercing his foot. A man could hold a locomotive in his hand. A man throwing a ball in space would move one way, the ball the other.

Therefore a space ship would move in the total vacuum of interplanetary nothingness if it sprayed a stream of gas from a nozzle at its stern.

By 1903 he had a coherent theory of space travel, and had written the formula for the escape velocity needed to move from the earth's gravity:

$$V = w\ln \frac{m_0}{m}$$

Thus the century of freedom and enlightenment was only in its third year when a village schoolteacher in Borovsk gave man the power to step onto the gray dust of the moon and to plant the red flag in what may prove to be the Pleistocene forests of Mars.

In 1885, at the age of twenty-eight, Tsiolkovsky began to design a cast-iron zeppelin. As schoolteaching took all of his day, work on this project had to be stolen from his duties. He rose at dawn, to have time before school, and worked until late into the night.

His work resulted in the voluminous *Theory and Practise of the Aerostat* and the more popular *Elementary Studies of the Airship and Its Construction*, together with a summary for rapid consumption that was published in *The Aeronaut* in 1905, a magazine which was as important in its way as Lenin's *Iskra*.

These theories were sent to Department VII of the Russian Technological Society, which body declined to grant Tsiolkovsky funds to build a model, as it was their opinion that a dirigible was impractical, owing to its being forever at the mercy of the winds.

In Borovsk Tsiolkovsky built a model of his dirigible with wrapping paper, and supplied its hot air with a brazier on its underside. Sparks from the brazier burnt in two the string by which Tsiolkovsky secured his model. The free dirigible sailed grandly over Borovsk before it set itself on fire and crashed onto the shoemaker's roof.

After his dirigible, Tsiolkovsky turned to the aeroplane, which had been invented by the Russian engineer Mozhaisky. It was Tsiolkovsky's idea to give the aeroplane a metal fuselage, and to streamline it by making it follow the shape of a bird. This was in 1894. He was thus far in advance of the Wrights, Santos-Dumont, or Voisin.

To study the coefficients of air resistance on various models of his aerostat and aeroplane, Tsiolkovsky built the first wind tunnel.

Tsiolkovsky's report to the Academy on airflow, friction, and stress, matters in which he was a pioneer and about which he had learned a great deal from experiments with his wind tunnel, went unanswered.

Pyotr Nikolayevich Lyebyedyev proved the existence of the pressure of light, and succeeded in measuring such a delicate weight. He lived like a monk, so great was his dedication to science. He paid for all his equipment out of his own pocket. Ilya Mechnikov did his work in France, so indifferent was Russia to scientific advancement. Sofia Kovalevskaya, the brilliant mathematician, taught in Sweden, as Russian universities did not think it proper for a woman to lecture.

It was reading Jules Verne that inspired Tsiolkovsky to invent the space rocket.

SNOW

Tatlin rattled the sifter of his porcelain stove, turned the damper up, pulled on his heavy brown sweater, settled down by the tall window against which snow was boiling like an insubstantial surf, a sea of weightless hexagonal crystals blown from Finland, *snyeg*, always *snyeg*, and opened his Leskov to *The Tale of the Cross-Eyed, Left-Handed Gunsmith from Tula and the Steel Flea*, imagined the museums of England with their cast-iron-strutted plate-glass ceilings allowing pink sunlight to fall together with the delicate shadows of nightingales upon Mr. Babbage's brass-and-walnut calculator, cases of minerals, butterflies, samurai swords, Islamic coins, tertiary fossils, Merovingian bees, T'ang horses, Andaman wicker shields, and the tanned and stuffed corpse of Jeremy Bentham in its wide-awake hat, stock, and alpaca coat. *Snyeg*, always *snyeg*.

Picasso's hands were square, Catalan, as modern and *kybist* as the motor of a Packard. He drew from the shoulder outwards, the line commencing deep in his back. He drew like the cave painters from whom he was descended, he was Cro-Magnon, he was the child of the Aurignacian bull draughtsmen who painted with their whole body, lunging by rushlight at their magic pictures, red bison, bistre cows, ideograms in tar black of their souls' thatched houses by Celtic rivers silver with salmon spawn.

—*¡Señor Tatlino!* he had said, an artist has an eye, a hand, and balls.

Lipchitz had translated. Picasso had no theories, no manifestos, no party, no club. *I do what comes to hand.*

Tatlin was shown canvasses in the African manner, faces like masks, slit-eyed, chisel-nosed, bottle-top-mouthed. He saw Cézanne's geometry brought boldly into dominant play, and then into a kind of metaphysical music whereby the graphic information of a portrait was treated as so many shards of light and chips of shadow.

Snow tumbled in the branches of the larch.

He took down Khlebnikov's *Sinie okovy, Blue Chains*. The title, one of Velimir's strange richnesses, recalled the Sinyakovs of Kharkov, who dressed up like dryads and Theokritan shepherds and walked in the woods at Krasnaya Polyana, young Boris Pasternak among them, and David Burliuk, who was now in New York.

> *Smeley, smeley, dusha dosuga*

he wrote of the girls, five sisters,

> *honey of dark gold her loosened hair*

he wrote of Nadezhda, and somehow in an image that grew into a black and yellow butterfly and then into a flowering of the sky, into wind, into a field of barley, into Pushkin and Lensky on a road, and finally into a windflower clinging to the foot of a passerby.

The sea, the poetry of Khlebnikov, the prose of Leskov, and the films.

Dark. The cone of light from the projector leaps into being across layered smoke, carbide and latakia. The projector ticks and squeaks.

The machinegun shakes like a constipated dog. It is a Sokolov.

A general knits his cupped hands to receive the foot of the Tsarevich dismounting from a horse. He walks away like a woundup toy.

A crowd staggers in trembling light on the screen.

—Lenin!

Men with picks and shovels hack at a tomb. Lenin grins. Lyef Vladimirich Kulyeshov in a cloth cap. Lenin shakes and trembles. Kulyeshov grins.

Dirt from the tomb goes into the air, a spray. The crowd trembles. Religion, says the card, is the opium of the people.

Pigeons. Blurred pigeons erase themselves in the air. They peck, shaking. A lieutenant staggers out, feeds the pigeons, trembles.

An Austin armored car. Sabres.

Khlebnikov. The brindle, burn, and shake of light across the summer Voronezh.

In a Scythian tomb of yellow ice they found the dust of a standing horse that wore still a high-antlered mask upon his skull. It was saddled with red barbaric rugs.

Górod i khram, and peasants who entice the elf into a shoe. *Tri sestry,* and death in the thistle and in the white loaf of the moon.

He reread *The Gadfly* of Ethel Voynich and drank sage tea.

CLASSROOM

Lissitzky and Moholy-Nagy took Konstruktivizm to Berlin in 1922. The Revolution will follow, Tatlin told his students.

Looking at them sideways out of the corners of his eyes, he talked through pipesmoke of Severini, Boccioni, and Balla. In the metaphysical Italian mind beauty and utility had fused. He discussed the ideas of Mach, speed, sound. Only we Russians could hear this music, he said. Our response was more eloquent than the Italian source. Natalia Goncharova saw the harmony of cogs and levers. Malevich painted his *Knife Grinder*. Russian painting became vibrant, dynamic, *skorii, zhivoi*.

Naum Gabo made sculpture that twanged like a plucked bowstring.

Malevich, Tatlin said, prefigures the future. I am the future. Malevich is a kite, I am a glider.

Malevich was right to insist that if man lives among harmonious lines, abstract examples of balance and just proportions, he will live with a sense of design and apt degree. But we must follow him with a system of harmonic advantages.

A house is a vocabulary. A city is a language. Each made thing is a constructivist statement that continues in time. Petrograd is a novel in the vernacular with baroque official passages, military treatises, and religious fantasies.

Venice, by contrast, is music. It smells of cantaloupes, coffee, wine, hemp, wet stone. There is nothing there rotted by snow or split by frost.

They are sister cities, Venice and Petrograd, built on island marshes in the sea. They are navies of city blocks.

Railroad tracks were first used for launching ships. The locomotive, a modified steam-pump for draining mines, was crossbred from the carriage and Watt's steam engine. There is a biology of machines. Wed the bicycle to the kite and you have Blériot's aeroplane, but not without the bionic principle of the dragonfly. Even the locomotive retains the gallop of the horse.

A table is a quadruped.

The centaur is the first machine. The Egyptian combinations of animal and man were simply masks. The centaur is not metaphor or actor but a resolution of cooperating forces into an ideal structure.

A house is a ship turned upside down.

Puni has glued a plate to a tabletop and called it a construct: the

cubist guitar. He can go further. He can identify the full moon in the sky as a cubist guitar.

In the third year of the Revolution Tatlin, Shapiro, Meyerzon, and Vinogradov issued a manifesto for the work ahead.

The ground on which we work is not of a piece. The painter, sculptor, and architect have been lost in romantic individualism, giving a personal expression to an art that ought to be public and communal. The painter has degraded his art and lost sight of his duty. He has decorated private homes, nests of the selfish. The architect has designed monotonous rows of Yaroslav Railway Stations.

Yet by 1914 certain artists had anticipated the Revolution of 1917. We accepted material, volume, and construction as the foundation of our art.

We therefore distrust the eye and subdue its sensuality with mathematics.

Malevich is an Old Believer, a cunning God-possessed Slav, a mad Platonist descended from the Byzantines, a mediaeval geometer. We agree that art is a model for living. He is a blueprint, I am a saw and hammer.

Tatlin designed a suit of clothes all in one piece for workers, snug and trim for warmth and safety. He designed a stove, chairs, socks.

AFTERNOON

The rocketship *Tovarishch Tikhonravov* stood in the silent and infinite black of space. Inside, Polkovnik Bazarov has pulled his floating self along the brass handrails to the aneroid barometer, the reading of which he punched into a paper tape with a silver clipper, rolling the tape forward into the information mill of the Babbage Difference Engine whose walnut levers and mica registry windows gleamed in the perennial noon of dustless interplanetary light.

An Edison phonograph cylinder played the *Internatsionál*.

Polkovnik Bazarov swam to the telescope mounted in the glass nose of his ship. A tilted prism projected the visual field onto gridded paper pinned to an easel. Here Bazarov measured with calipers the dark Platon crater. It was larger by a millimetre and a fraction. He consulted his slide rule and made a log entry.

He was approaching the moon with a speed which on earth would blur the vision.

Here there was no sensation of movement at all. He moved like a spider under water. The gyroscope spun in silence.

The earth through the port windows was marbled green and blue, its seas black and shining. Cyclones of weather botched the outlines of continents, as if a map had been strewn with curls of wool. He could distinguish Africa and the bright Indian ocean.

The hen Marya jumped onto his knee. He chucked the wattles of her comb.

The dragonfly wings of the ornithopter hung from the ceiling. *Constructs* in paper and plaster, in cut tin cans and string, shingles and thumbtacks, stood around the room. Plans for a workers' library lay on the drawing table.

The hen Nadezhda roosted in the dowels of the ornithopter's fuselage, bird in bird.

It was Tsiolkovsky he was reading: a voyage to the moon.

To the red dust of Mars.

EVENING

Khlebnikov, the enemy of time, speaks through a red megaphone in the voice of Zangezi.

—*Tramvai pyot'!*

The ghost of Khlebnikov trembles in a fall of yellow leaves. His head is on upside down, as in a canvas of Chagall. There is an aria somewhere near, birds, the wind in telegraph wires, a radio, a stone mouth that has opened to emit Italian song.

—*Lyud 'i! Uchityes' novoi voinye.* People, learn a new war.

Mikhail Larionov had painted the wall: a soldier milking a cow, a brown moon, a peasant girl smoking a pipe.

The American Harry Smith was playing *The Maple Leaf Rag* on the piano, an African composition by Scott Joplin of baroque *da ca-*

pos, a melancholy lilt, and a spry wit that defined the brisk republican
walk of Newport and Chicago whereby a gentleman with a malacca
cane tucked under his armpit raised his panama to a lady in tulle and
gingham and they both gave a smart kick backwards, rolling their
hands in little circles.

O to hear an American jug band!

The long summer Petrograd afternoons thinned into dusk with
the slowness of a season changing.

They talked about Ethel Voynich, Jack London, Isadora Duncan,
Gurdyev, Ouspenski.

Khlebnikov talked of the mathematics of time, Ivan Puni of Berlin
and Paris, Tatlin of materials: pine, birch, tin, glass.

THE TOWER

Tatlin's monument to the Third International was to have been a
cylinder above a cone above a cube within a spiral half a mile tall.

We must grasp nature, Cézanne said, as *cylinder, sphere, cone.*

Cézanne + Lenin = Konstruktivizm.

The cube, of glass and steel, was to have revolved once a year, the
cone every month, the cylinder every day.

In the cube he placed lecture halls for scientists and poets, gym-
nasiums for Spartakiada, Agitprop offices, assembly rooms for the
soviets, cinemas, a great hall for the international Communist con-
gresses.

Tatlin specified that no room of the cube was to be a museum or library. All must be kept kinetic, fluid, revolutionary.

In the cone were the offices of executives, commissars, secretaries,
directors.

The cube was the voice of the tower. Every day at noon a chorus
sang the *Internatsionál:*

> *Vstavai proklyat'em zakleimënnii,*
> *Ves' mir golodnyx i rabov!*
> *Kipit nash razum vozmushchënnii*

> *I v smertnii boi vesti gotov.*
> *Ves' mir nasil'ya mi razrushim*
> *Do osnovan'ya, a zatem*
> *Mi nash, my novii mir postroim,*
> *Kto bil nichem, tot stanet vsem.*

From the cube came news bulletins every hour, broadcast by megaphone over Red Square. A screen outside the cube showed films at night, and a board of electric lights constantly changed pattern: now the hammer and sickle, now the ear of wheat, now the face of Marx, Lenin, Engels, Fourier, Tchernikovsky, Cézanne, Trotsky, Saint-Simon, Rousseau, Ruskin, Mayakovsky, Blanqui, Khlebnikov, Raspail, Hegel, Tsiolkovsky, Stalin.

A projector using the gray Moscow clouds for a screen placed the motto of the day in the sky.

Lenin + electricity = Socialism.

Property is theft.

Proletarier aller Lander, vereinigt euch!

The dictatorship of the people is the will of history.

From each according to his abilities, to each according to his needs.

Die Religion ist das Opium des Volkes.

The First International was founded by Marx and Engels in 1864, the Second in 1889 by an international congress of socialists and republicans, the Third, called the Komintern, in 1919, by Lenin. To this coalition of all the Communist parties in the world Tatlin designed his tall monument, from which a thousand red flags would whip and ripple in the free Russian air.

It was at once a building, a sculpture, a painting, a poem, a book, a moving picture, a *construct*.

In the radio and telegraph station of the tower news of all the international movements would arrive and be instantly broadcast to all of Moscow. The landlords of Peru are hanging from the lamp posts! The red flag flies over the Louvre! The usurers of New York have been lashed from the Stock Exchange by heroic mothers and noble youths!

The steel spiral rising from a garden to the clouds was supported by tetrahedral struts. In one model of the monument, Tatlin added a second spiral. Within the spirals a central axis held the cube, cone, and cylinder. The axis leaned like that of the earth itself, at a phallic tilt, like the thrust of Tsiolkovsky's rockets leaving the earth for the moon.

The Department of Fine Arts commissioned Tatlin to design the monument in 1919. He designed it swiftly, with the inspiration of the revolution, boldly, deftly. A wooden model was ready for exhibition in 1920. It was shown at the VIII Congress of the Soviets. Another, smaller model was driven on the back of a truck through the streets of Leningrad.

The spiral said natural growth, history, evolution, turbulence, flight.

Boullée's Cenotaph for Isaac Newton, five hundred and forty feet high, was round like the atom and like the universe. It symbolized the age that began with the Ionian physicists and ended in the nineteenth century.

Tatlin's monument was to the people, and flew upward. It was the tilted flagstaff from which the bloody flag of revolution flowed. *O bandiera rossa! O rote Fahne! O drapeau rouge!* O Feuerbach!

It was a hundred metres higher than the Tour Eiffel.

The spiral will be the course of voyages to the moon, for to launch a rocket from the turning earth in its orbit to the turning moon in its orbit, one must bore through space as honeysuckle climbs a post.

The molecule of Kossel and Levene's deoxyribonucleic acid, which may well be the unit of life, is a spiral wrapped around a spiral.

The shape of the Renaissance was the dodecahedron with its pentads of triangles, a closed order, the starfish and the Tuscan star, the webbed dome, the long perspectives of quincunxes in floors, ceilings, orchards, battalions, the triangulations of Mercator's maps, the sextant, the theodolite.

1919 began the age of the spiral, Goethe's spiral, Descartes's

vortices, the propeller, the banked upward course of the aeroplane, the spin of shells from rifles, the drill of the oil well, the dynamic coil of the spring, the lyric upward lift of revolutionary history, the whirl-wind.

A static allegory raised her antique torch over America. The triumphal arches of France were but the imperialistic gates of caesars and dictators.

Tatlin's monument to the Third International was a swirl as of music and an upright thrust rising into place like the red flag pushed forward by the suffering hands of the poor and the oppressed.

It was alive.

From apartments designed by Le Corbusier and Frank Lloyd Wright Muscovites would look every evening at the rotating screen to see images filmed by Dovchenko, Eisenstein, Shklovsky, Kylesho.

Shostakovich, Stravinsky, Prokofiev from the loudspeakers.

Lenin, with lifted chin and raised arm:

——*Pomyanítye moe slóvo!*

Lenin in his plaid cap came to see the model of the monument.

Nikolai Punin stood beside him, his blue eyes shimmering with intelligence behind his spectacles as clean as rain. He wrote in a small notebook as Tatlin talked.

——It is an image of the revolution, this tower. It is its monument, its raised fist, the splendor of its aspiration.

Tatlin was dressed in his sailor's pea-jacket, his engineer's cap. He smoked English tobacco in his pipe. He and his assistants, Sophia Dymshits-Tolstaya, T. M. Shapiro, and I. A. Meyerzon, had worked for months to make the scale model of wood, wire, and glass.

He explained to Lenin that the actual building would be of steel and glass.

——It is the master fusion, Viktor Shklovsky said, of the new technology and the revolutionary sensibility.

Lenin said nothing at all.

LETATLIN

Naum Gabo and Moholy-Nagy had gone into the west, taking along the spirit, perhaps the ghost, of Konstruktivizm. But there was Lenin's tomb: it was Konstruktivist. Viktor Borisovich told him in a low voice that nothing, nothing could save Osip Emil'yevich. Zamyatin was in Paris. Mayakovsky had blown his brains out. Stalin's doctors had murdered Gorky. They had denounced Akhmatova, Kyleshev, Bulgakov.

Tatlin picked up his hen Maryenka and set her on his lap. His trousers were shapeless, his shoes tied with knotted jute. He stroked Maryenka's speckled ruff.

The hen Adelaida roosted on the struts of the *planyór*.

In the wheat, lions. In trees, the angels of God.

Vremya! Svyet!

We saw Ulisse among the birds. Sharp he was, black he was. In his keen beak hooked out over his red beard his cunning ran like electricity in a wire.

The ball bearings of his ankles rolled with a fine click and we saw the engine of his heart bright as watchworks. He spoke in the Greek, rushing through words as long as the legs of herons, trilling like a nightingale, clashing bronze sounds against iron, keeping to the rhythm of a galloping horse in a windless summer. Figures bloomed in his speech, outrageous and daring.

There were brilliant rivets in his wrists and hips, cold tears in his ravished discourse. We thought of the rocks of the Morea, of the blind caryatids of the Erechtheum, of the long knives of the Arcadian shepherds.

Puppets hung in trees. *Dedalo!* cried the old women.

We saw Daidalos at the outer wall of time, near the meridian, walking against the aether. One great wing was outside time, the other inside.

It is Dedalo we have hung in the trees. He and his boy Ikaro were aeroplanes in the days even before the shit-of-a-dog Turks. These dolls in our trees are Dedalo and Ikaro, *ifrit* who are kin to the stork and the hawk.

Where now were Panait Istrati and Nikos Kazantzakis and their flowered Balkan shirts, their sage tea, their lonely eyes? How they said *Lenin* with a determined fist! Kazantzakis wore around his neck an ancient Greek coin and Istrati looked into all the corners of the tower room, where behind the dowels and laths of various unbuilt models of the Letatlin were nests with eggs, twigs for kindling, jars of sunflower seeds.

Their eyes are blue from looking through the sky. That is Dedalo with the big testicles, Ikaro with the small.

Elias and Minas paralyze our tongues and cross our eyes, but it is the truth we speak!

— How very lovely and strange, Kazantzakis said, that I should come from Crete where the birdman Daidalos made his flying machine to Russia only to find you, Comrade Tatlin, dreaming again that archaic dream.

—*Fantastíchyeskii!* Istrati said.

—Archaic, yes, Tatlin said, but it is an idea that has been added to over the centuries. Da Vinci had most of the elements in hand. He knew that a man in a flying machine must be free from the waist up to balance himself as in a boat, so that he may shift his center of gravity and that of the flying machine as it tilts in a change of resistance.

To da Vinci I have been able to append the elegant study of flight made by the genius Tsiolkovsky, who analyzed the three positions of wings in birds, bats, and insects. He also understood what *to fly* means. A pigeon, for instance, flies very little of the time he is aloft. He flies very hard to take off, and he needs strenuous wing movements to keep in proper relation to currents of air, and he needs to brake with a rather fierce flutter when he alights. But the rest of the time he is merely gliding. The wind keeps him in flight so long as he knows his advantages.

Bird blood is hot, very hot, which means that a bird's flight is more demanding than a man could ever endure. And a bird's bones are hollow, almost weightless.

All I have done is build the most ideal and *bionic* model of a bird, and put in a man's intelligence and such a leverage that a man can with training learn to imitate the quick bursts of energy needed to get into the air and to get down and to stay aloft by riding the air.

Men in aeroplanes, you see, are not flying. They are merely sitting in a machine. They are, true, steersmen of much alertness and skill. But man must keep translating his models back into the primal reality.

I am returning the instrument panel back to the head from which it came, and the motor back to the lungs and heart of which it is a model.

Can you imagine the beauty of the young people of the first generation to fly the Letatlin ornithopter as casually as they now ride bicycles?

— Build it, Comrade Tatlin! Build it!

1953

Tatlin stroked the ruff of the Wyandotte hen that sat on his lap. He had been explaining to Viktor Shklovsky over tea what Velimir used to say of politicians: that they are all mad. Men spiral upward within their capabilities. A genius has no interest in controlling people with anything so crude as power. The artist has true power. The intellectual may hunger for power as his ideas prove to be weak, but he is for the most part content to live in his mind.

— Fairly bright men go into business, the army, the university. The incapables left over either drift into the lassitudes which are the wakes of other men's power, or they become politicians.

He felt that he was boring Viktor, who kept looking at the bundles of dowels standing against the walls and in the corners, the skeletal wings of the air bicycle, boxes with chickens in them.

But it didn't matter. They were talking for the comfort of it, to fill the ambiguous vacuum of their elation.

The old roach was dead.

The air of the room was vile with the stink of cabbage soup, the

droppings of chickens, two of which sat on the bed as if in the cool dust under sunflowers in a country yard, the sour reek of cigarettes.

—It was Khlebnikov's revolution, our revolution. Then it was Lenin's, then Stalin's.

The *Nekuda* of Leskov in a plum cardboard binding was streaked with chicken shit.

The window was dirty. Marya, the Mongol bantam with silky feathers gold and brown, hopped into Tatlin's lap. He inspected her beak.

—They've been having the pip.

It was snowing in the birches below. Beyond the tumbling clouds, over there, was the Kremlin.

As level and high as a crane above the Ukrainian wheat the Letatlin plane would glide in liquid flight. The aeronaut, sensing an upward current, would pedal with a lyric fury, fitting his long wings into the upflow, and then, breathing like a lion on the bound, would slip down the wind at so shallow an angle that miles of green wheat would stream below him.

He sees a village and brakes the eagle span to drop down in an easy swoop.

For seven years he had taught materials and structure at Inkkuk, for twenty years he taught ceramics in Moscow. Now he had won a rest and time for research. He, the designer of the greatest tower in the history of technology, now lived in the tower of a monastery. Models of the ornithopter stood against mediaeval pilasters. His chickens nested in his boxes of drawings.

There were pouches crumpled with wrinkles under his eyes. His face had sagged into wattles under the chin. His hands shook.

He liked the monotony of it all. He sometimes walked in the Friedrich Engels Garden where old women sat in their shawls by the zinnias, or under green catkins in the spring.

Everything, Velimir used to say, changes into its opposite in time. Nikolai Romanov was the last of Byzantium, but not the last of Hylea, of the Mongols of the plain. And Burliuk used to lift his guitar ecstatically inches above the cylindrical meat of his thigh smooth under black Baltic cloth. A wedge of Mongolia, his nose. That music was personal, human, as rich as Khlebnikov's poetry.

He had starved, the divine Khlebnikov. One month he was riding through Saint Petersburg on a lorry proclaiming himself President of the World, another he was dead. He was spared seeing what they did with our poetry. That gay sense of parade and wild color became red flags, a fire of flags, a wind of crimson flame, poppy, scarlet, blood, vermilion, carried by ranks of gymnasts past Lenin's tomb, by the Komsomol, by the Red Army, by the Communist Party of the Ukraine, by the Communist Party of Lithuania, by the Young Pioneers.

Fifty boys had run through the streets of Kishinev shouting *The Futuristy are here!* Some lovely scamps shouted *The futbolisty are here!* They were in the hire of Burliuk, Kamensky, Mayakovsky.

But the world would have the air bicycle, something to show for the years of effort. It would be a disaster of the spirit were man to become mechanized in his movement. Convenience was the monster of Europe and America, the machine should never have made man casual and passive. The automobile was the carriage of the aristocracy all over again. He would give man a new horse, a Pegasus. The state had not yet understood. When in 1930 Koroyov designed the Krasnaya Zvezda glider, they made on over that. They had rewritten the history books to say that Lenin ordered all Soviet aeronauts to follow Tsiolkovsky. Zhukovsky believed in Tsiolkovsky. Tukhachevsky believed in Tsiolkovsky. Tupolev believed in Tsiolkovsky.

He, Tatlin, was the true follower of Tsiolkovsky. They would see.

Dvoeverye, doublethink. See this, but think that. Zinoviev, Kamenev, Smirnov to the Urals. Mandelstam to the Arctic Circle.

On the awful desolation of the far side of the moon lies the crater Tsiolkovsky facing away forever from the milky sapphire of earth into the black emptiness and fiery stars of space the limits of which are the same as those of time.

There are but two craters which bear names on the outer half of the moon, the Tsiolkovsky, the Jules Verne. A third crater large enough to be fancied as in the Renaissance a sea has been named in the higher style of Soviet pedantry the Mare Muscovensis.

Tsiolkovsky, whom Lenin encouraged.

—And he is dead?

—Iosif Vissarionovich Dzhugashvili is dead.

—Will they mummify him and place him beside Lenin in the tomb?

—The only example of Konstruktivist art in Russia.

—In public.

They sat in a kind of grief, a kind of joy, stunned.

—Will they publish your books, build my tower, open the jails?

—It is only Stalin who is dead.

—Aren't we all?

Viktor left. He could pick up each hen in turn, calling them each by name. He could choose what to read by the lamp, for he read the same pages over and over: Khlebnikov, Tsiolkovsky, Leskov. He could ponder the glider strut by strut, and with a soft chirr and dance of hands, imagine it agile as a bat over rivers, lakes, fields.

The Aeroplanes at Brescia

Kafka stood on the seaway at Riva under the early September sky. But for his high-button shoes and flaring coat, his easy stance had an athletic clarity. He walked with the limberness of a racing cyclist. Otto Brod, with whom he had spent the morning discussing moving pictures and strolling along the shore under the voluble pines and yellow villas of the Via Ponale, lit a cigar and suggested a light beer before lunch. A wash of sweet air from the lake rattled a circle of pigeons, who flapped up into a shuttle of gulls. A fisherman in a blue apron reclined on the harbor steps smoking a small pipe. On a staff over a perfectly square building rippled the Austrian flag with its black, two-headed eagle. An old man knotting cords in a net strung between poles watched them with the open concern of the Italians. A soft bell rang in the hills.

——Good idea, said Kafka. It will get the taste of Dallago out of our mouths.

His eyes, when they could be seen under the broad brim of a black fedora, seemed abnormally large. To the natural swarthiness of his square face, rough of bone, Italy had already added, Otto noticed, a rose tint.

The *ora*, the south wind blowing up from Sirmione, had begun to scuff the dark blue of the lake. The old Venetian fort between the Città Riva and the railway station seemed to Kafka to be an intrusion into the Euclidean plainness of the houses of Riva. It reminded him of the *schloss* at Meran that had disturbed him not only for being vacant and blind in its casements but also because of the suspicion that it would inevitably return in his most anxious dreams. Even without his intuition of the mute claim of this empty castle to stay in his mind as a presence neither welcome nor explicable, it was always terrifying to know that there were things in the world empty of all significance and yet persisted, like heavy books of the law which mankind in a stubborn reluctance would not destroy and yet would not obey. The castle at Riva, the *Rocca,* the Rock, was a barracks housing the new conscripts, but the castle at Meran, the Brunnenburg, was a great shell. Suddenly he heard a telephone ringing in its high rooms, and made himself think instead of the morning at the Bagni della Madonnina and of Otto's polite but equivocal replies to Dallago the poet who had apologized by rote man's oneness with nature. What a fool, Otto had said later, on their walk.

The cubes of Riva, white and exact, were an architecture, Kafka remarked, the opposite of the lobes and tendrils of Prague. And there was truth in the light of Riva that was, as a poet might say, the opposite of the half-truths of the cut-glass sunlight of Prague, which had no fire in it, no absolute transparency. Instead of tall slabs of squared light in just proportions, Prague had weather of a dark and glittering richness.

Otto replied that the light here was pure and empty, creating a freedom among objects. The very shadows were incised. It is an older world, he added, and yet one to which the new architecture is returning. Concrete is but the Mediterranean mud house again, and glass walls a new yearning to see light sliced as in the openness of the Aegean landscape. The newest style, he said, is always in love with the oldest of which we are aware. The next *Wiedergeburt* will come from the engineers.

Max Brod, whom they had left writing at the *pensione,* was already at the café, and was holding above his head a newspaper for them to see.

—They are going to fly at Brescia! he shouted, and a waiter who might have been bringing a seltzer to the Tsar of Bulgaria, so grave was his progress, looked with uninterrupted dignity over his shoulder at Max, who to him was but a Czech and probably a Jew, stamping his feet and rattling *La Sentinella Bresciana* in the air.

—Aeroplanes! Blériot! Cobianchi! *Die Brüder Wright!*

—*Due bionde, piacere,* Otto said to the waiter, who was relieved that the Czech's friends did not flap their arms and dance on the terrace.

—Incredible, Otto said. Absolutely incredible luck.

Kafka laughed outright, for Max was as of the moment as he a brooding postponer, and their friendship had always been a contest between the impulses of Max and the circumspect deliberation of Franz. It was a comedy that popped up everywhere between them. They had been in Riva a day, Max had spent a month convincing Franz that he must come to Riva on his vacation, and here was Max dashing them off on the second morning. But, as he quickly said, he could not question the call of the flying machines, which none of them had seen. They were well worth giving up the sweet quiet of Riva.

Otto took the newspaper from Max and laid it out on the table.

—Brescia is just at the other end of the lake, Max explained. We can take the steamboat to Salò, and get a local from there. It's three days off, but we'll want to be there at least the day before, as Mitteleuropa will have arrived in droves, with their cousins and their aunts. I've written the Committee there in the second paragraph. Naturally there is a Committee.

—By all means, Franz said, a Committee.

At its head, in gilt chairs, sat Dottore Civetta, Dottore Corvo, and Mangiafoco himself.

—I told them that we are journalists from Prague, and that we require accommodations.

In the last analysis, Kafka sighed, all things are miracles.

There was a steamboat the next morning. They boarded it and marvelled at the antiquity of its machinery and the garishness of its paint.

Only six years ago, Max had told them the evening before at the café, under a sky much higher than the skies of Bohemia and with stars twice the size of those of Prague, two Americans had chosen the most plausible combination of elements from a confusion of theories and constructed a machine that flew. The flight lasted twelve seconds only, and scarcely five people were there to see it.

By a fat wheatfield under the largest of skies an intricate geometry of wires and neat oblongs of stretched canvas sat like the death ship of a pharaoh. It looked like a loom mounted on a sled. It was as elegantly laced, strutted, and poised as the time machine of H. George Wells. Its motor popped, its two screw propellers whirred, bending the lush American weeds to the ground. Fieldmice scurried to their burrows in the corn. Coyotes' ears went up and their yellow eyes brightened.

Were they like the Goncourts, inseparable brothers, Orville and Wilbur Wright? Or were they like Otto and Max, twins in deference and simple brotherhood but essentially very different men? They were from Ohio, nimble as Indians, but whether Democrats, Socialists, or Republicans Otto could not say.

The editors of the American papers, taken up with duelling and oratory, paid no attention at all to their flight. The strange machine flew and flew before any word of it appeared. Icarus and Daedalus had flown above peasants who did not look up from their bowl of lentils and above fishermen who were looking the other way.

The Brothers Wright were the sons of a bishop, but, as Otto explained, the sons of an American bishop. His church was one of dissenters separated from dissenters, a congregation with a white wooden church on a knoll above a brown river, the Susquehanna perhaps. One could not imagine the dreams of Americans.

If one flew over this community in an aeroplane or drifted over it in a balloon, there would be school children below planting a tree. Buffalo and horses grazed in grass so green it was said to be blue. The earth itself was black. The houses, but one story high, were set in flower gardens. One might see the good Bishop Wright reading his Bible at a window, or a senator driving his automobile along a road.

The young Orville and Wilbur had constructed mechanical bats, Otto said, after the designs of Sir George Cayley and Penaud. For

America was the land where the learning of Europe was so much speculation to be tested on an anvil. They read Octave Chanute's *Flying Machines;* they built kites. The kite was their beginning, not the bird. That was da Vinci's radical error. The kite had come from China centuries ago. It had passed through the hands of Benjamin Franklin, who caught electricity for the magician Edison, who, it was said, was soon to visit Prague. Men such as Otto Lilienthal had mounted kites and rode the wind and died like Icarus. The Wrights knew all these things. They read Samuel Pierpont Langley; they studied the photographs of Eadweard Muybridge. That was the way of Americans. They took theories as pelicans swallowed fish, pragmatically, and boldly made realities out of ideas.

But the morning's paper, which had come up to Riva on the steamboat, reported that the Wrights might fly in Berlin rather than at Brescia. It hinted of a rivalry between them and the American Curtiss, whose improvements on the flying machine were in many ways far in advance of theirs.

Villages on the lakeshore were stacked, house above house, as in a canvas of Cézanne, from the waterfront to the hilltops, where the church was the highest of all, ringing its bell. In the old city at Prague under the wall he had felt among the alchemists' kitchens and the tiny shops of the smiths in the old ghetto the alien wonderment he felt in Italy, as if an incantation had been recited and the charm had worked. Had not one of the gulls at Riva spoken a line of Latin?

The lake was as vast as the sea.

Otto, who wore a cap and belted jacket, did turns around the richly obstructed deck of the trembling steamboat. Max and Franz sat on a folded travelling rug by the wheelhouse. Otto and Max, it occurred to Kafka, might seem like two princes from an Art Nouveau poster for a Russian opera to those who did not know them. This was illusion, for they were modern men, wholly of the new age. Max was twenty-five, he had his degree, a position, and had published a novel last year, the *Schloss Nornepygge*. Was this why the desolate Castle Brunnenburg in the wild Camonica hills hung in his memory like a ghost?

They seemed not to feel the emptiness of the lake at noon. They had their inwardnesses, how deeply they had never let him see, inviolably private as they were, as all men were.

Otto had been born into the new world, conversant with numbers and their enviable harmonies and with the curiously hollow thought of Ernst Mach and Avenarius, whose minds were like those of the Milesians and Ephesians of antiquity, bright as an ax, elemental as leaves, and as plain as a box. This new thought was naked and innocent; the world would wound it in time. And Max, too, had his visions in this wild innocence. A suburb of Jaffa had just a few months ago been named Tel Aviv, and Zionists were said to be speaking Hebrew there. Max dreamed of a Jewish state, irrigated, green, electrical, wise.

The destiny of our century was born in the lonely monotony of schoolrooms. Italian schoolrooms were doubtless the same as those of Prague and Amsterdam and Ohio. The late afternoon sun fell into them after the pupils had gone home, spinning tops and throwing jacks on the way. A map of Calabria and Sicily hung on a wall, as polychrome as Leoncavallo, as lyric in its citron gaiety as the chart of the elements which hung beside it was abstract and Russian. Sticks of yellow and white chalk lay in their troughs, and the geometry drawn by them was still on the blackboard, evident, tragic, and abandoned. The windows, against which a wasp rose and fell, testing all afternoon the hardness of their dusty lucidity, were as desolate and grandly melancholy as barn doors looking on the North Sea in October. Here Otto heard of the valence of carbon, here Max saw bright daggers drawn from a bleeding Caesar, here Franz dreamed of the Great Wall of China.

Did men know anything at all? Man was man's teacher. Anyone could see the circle in that.

Tolstoy was at Yásnaya Polyána, eighty and bearded and in peasant dress, out walking, no doubt, in those thin birch groves under a white sky where the sense of the north is a sharp and distant quiet, an intuition shared with the wolf and the owl of the emptiness of the earth.

Somewhere in the unimaginable vastness of America Mark Twain smoked a Havana cigar and cocked his head at the new automobiles three abreast on roads hacked through red forests of maple. His dog was asleep at his feet. Perhaps William Howard Taft called him on the telephone from time to time to tell a joke.

A sailboat passed, an ancient bearded hunter at its tiller.

Franz Kafka, jackdaw. Despair, like the crane's hunch on Kierkegaard's lilting back, went along on one's voyages. His degree in jurisprudence was scarcely three years old, he was rapidly, as Herr Canello assured him, becoming an expert in workingmen's compensation insurance, and the literary cafés of Prague to which he did not go were open to him, both the Expressionist and those devoted to the zithers and roses of Rilke.

Had not Uncle Alfred, who had been awarded so many medals, his mother's elder brother Alfred Löwy, risen to be manager general of the Spanish railways? The Spanish railways! And Uncle Joseph was in the Congo, bending over a ledger to be sure, but he could look up and there was the jungle. But then Uncle Rudolf was a bookkeeper at a brewery, and Uncle Siegfried a country doctor. And his cousin Bruno was editing Krasnopolski.

There were odysseys in which the Sirens are silent.

Without paper, he conceived stories the intricacy and strangeness of which might have earned a nod of approval from Dickens, the Pentateuch and Tolstoy of England. Before paper, his imagination withdrew like a snail whose horns had been touched. If the inward time of the mind could be externalized and lived in, its aqueducts and Samarkands and oxen within walls which the Roman legions had never found, he would be a teller of parables, graceless perhaps, especially at first, but he would learn from more experienced parablists and from experience. He would wear a shawl of archaic needlework, would know the law, the real law of unvitiated tradition, and herbs, and the histories of families and their migrations, to which stock of tales he might add his own, if fate hardened his sight. He would tell of mice, like Babrius, and of a man climbing a mountain, like Bunyan. He would tell of the ships of the dead, and of the Chinese, the Jews of the other half of the world, and of their wall.

—What silence! said Max.

—I was listening to the Sirens, said Franz.

From Salò they went by train, along with many hampers of garlic and a cock that crowed all the way, to Brescia.

The station was very night. Kafka wondered that the people milling outside didn't have lanterns. The train as it slid into Brescia was like a horse dashing through the poultry market in Prague, throwing cage after cage of chickens into a panic as it passed. Every passenger was out of his seat before the train hissed to a halt. An Austrian fell out of a window. A woman asked if anyone saw her brother-in-law outside, a gentleman and courier to the Papal court. A hat passed from hand to hand overhead. People getting off stuck in the doors with people getting on. They promised each other not to get lost, and suddenly they were outside the train. Otto emerged backwards, Kafka sideways, and Max frontwards, with his necktie across his face.

Panels of light carved in the blackness of the station disclosed vistas of Brescia the color of honey, almonds, and salmon. Red smokestacks rose above turreted palaces. There were green shutters everywhere.

Now that they were in Italy proper, Kafka's high-button shoes and black fedora which had been so smartly contemporary in Prague, his new frockcoat with its pinched waist and flaring skirts, seemed inappropriately sober, as if he had come to plead a case at law rather than to see the air show at Montechiari. The land of Pinocchio, he reminded himself, and, rubbing his hands together and blinking in the generous light of the street, he remarked to Otto and Max that here they were in the country of Leonardo da Vinci.

A hat sat on the sidewalk. A cane carried in the crook of an arm hooked a cane carried in the crook of an arm. Each pulled the other out and both fell together. Everything seemed to be the grand moment of an opera about the arrival of the barbarians in Rome

Max through some quickness that was beyond Otto and Franz, who stood together more stunned than merely hesitant to decide the direction in which they ought to move, had already bought a newspaper. Under a headline in stout poster type the whole significance of their journey was proclaimed in prose which, as Max remarked, wore a waxed moustache. Papers in Italy were not read in coffee houses but on the sidewalks, the pages smacked with the backs of hands, the felicities of the paragraphs read aloud to total strangers.

——Here in Brescia, Max read to them once they had found a table at a *caffé* on the Corso Vittorio Emanuele, we have a multitude the likes of which we have never seen before, no, not even at the great automobile races. There are visitors from Venice, Liguria, the Piedmont, Tuscany, Rome, and even Naples. Our *piazze* swarm with distinguished men from France, England, and America. Our hotels are filled, as well as every available spare room and corner of private residences, for which the rates rise daily and magnificently. There are scarcely means enough to transport the hordes to the *circuito aereo*. The restaurant at the aerodrome can easily offer superb fare to two thousand people, but more than two thousand must certainly bring disaster.

Here Franz whistled an air of Rossini.

——The militia, Max read on, has already been called to keep order at the lunch counters. At the humbler refreshment stands some fifty thousand people press daily all day long. Thus *La Sentinella Bresciana* for the ninth of September 1909.

They took a fiacre to the Committee, hoping that it would not fall to pieces under them before they arrived. The driver, who for some reason was radiantly happy, seemed to turn alternately left and right at every corner. Once they went up a street which they were certain they had seen before. The Committee was in a palace. Gendarmes in white gloves rattled their long swords and directed them to concierges in gray smocks who pointed to the heads of stairs where there were officials in celluloid collars who directed them to enormous rooms where other officials, bowing slightly, gave them frail sheets of paper on which they wrote their names and addresses and occupations. Max proudly listed himself as *novelist and critic*, Kafka wickedly wrote *journalist*, and Otto, humming to himself, *engineer*.

Pinocchio clattering down a hall with a gendarme hard on his heels was lost to sight when Kafka stuck his head around a door to see.

In a green room into which they were summoned their papers were spread out on a desk from which a bald official in a fuchsia tie welcomed them in the name of the Società Aerea d'Italia. He found the name of an *albergo* in a notebook and Max copied it down.

Pinocchio had just cleared a corner when they came outside, and a gendarme hopped awhile, and pulled his moustaches awhile, before giving full chase.

The landlord of the inn, when they got there, was a copy of the functionary of the Committee, except that he did not affect a tie. His fingers wiggled beside his face as he talked, spit flew from his lips. He rubbed his elbows, bowed from the waist, and put their money, which he knew that as men of the world and of affairs they wished to pay in advance, in some recess under his coat tails.

By asking each other in all seriousness they discovered that their room was the dirtiest that any of them had ever seen. Moreover, there was a large round hole in the middle of the floor, through which they could see card players in the room below, and through which, Max observed, Sparafucile would later climb.

Light lay flat and ancient upon the colonnade of the old forum. In the temple of Hercules, now green-shuttered and rusty with lichen, there was a winged Nike writing upon a shield.

The squares and streets of Brescia were pages from a book on perspective. One might write a novel in which every line met in a single room, an empty room in an empty building in an empty novel. Random figures could not be avoided. Perspective drawings placed gratuitous figures in empty *piazze* or mounting long steps, faceless men with canes, women with baskets, Gypsies with dogs.

What endurance there was in the long Italian afternoons! In Prague the city stirred about against the evening. Lamps came on in windows. Smoke rose from chimneys. Bells chimed. In Italy eyes hollowed in the faces of statues, windows darkened, shadows moved across squares and slid up the walls of buildings. The night was a mistake, it was fate, *sbaglio e fato antico la notte*. Da Vinci had put water in globes to magnify the light of his lamps, like Edison with his mirrors. And the Italians did not sleep at night. They slept in the afternoon, they were abed half the morning. At night they talked. They went up and down stairs. They ran in the street, like Pinocchio trying his legs.

The old Tarocchi lay on marble tables, the tray of cups beside a stone jug as Roman as a bust of Cinna. And the *Elementi Analitici* of Tully Levi-Città lay beside them with unquestionable propriety. Here was a country where Zeno's motion could be understood. Italy's monotonous sameness was like the frames of a film that moved with the slowness of sleep, so that accident and order were equally impossible. The shape of a glass and the speech of an anarchist were both decided upon millennia ago, and emerged daily, with all other Italic gestures, from a rhythm generated in the ovens and olive presses of Etruria.

In Vienna, in Berlin, the new smelled of frivolity and the old of decay, lacking the Italian continuity of things. A poster on a wall as old as the Gracchi announced in pepper greens and summer yellows a comedy with the curious title *Elettricità Sessuale*, and the old woman beside it in her black shawl and with a basket of onions might easily step into the gondola of the dirigible *Leonardo da Vinci*, which was expected to arrive at any moment from Milan, piloted by the engineer Enrico Forlanini, and sail off to market, gossiping about the priest's nephew Rinaldo, who, she had just learned at the baker's, was now the mayor of Nebraska.

A *galantuomo* in pomade and cream shoes cleaned his ears with the nail of his little finger while they dined across from him on sausages and peppers. After coffee and cigars they went to bed with a soldierly indifference. Max said that they must agree among them to remember the hole in the floor, through which they could now see a great red pizza being quartered with a knife that, as Kafka observed, was surely a gift of the Khan to Marco Polo, as each of them over the years would tend to doubt his sanity in remembering it. Before they went to sleep Otto had a laughing fit, which he refused to explain, and Pinocchio ran down the street with Mangiafoco after him and three gendarmes after them, and a woman narrated just under their window, as best they could understand her, the family affairs of one of the late emperors.

Kafka dreamed that night of Ionic columns in a field of flowers in Sicily, which was also Riva, as dreams are invariably double. There were brown rocks alive with lizards, a moth on a wall, a gyre of pigeons, a stitch of bees. The pines were Virgilian, shelved, and black. He was distressingly lonely and had the impression that he was supposed to see certain statues, possibly of statesmen and poets, wonderfully blotched by lichens and ravaged by the sun. But they were not there. Then Goethe came from behind a column and recited with infinite freedom and arbitrariness a poem he could not understand. There was a rabbit at his foot, eating a mullein.

The Committee had suggested that they take the train to the aerodrome, and they had agreed that, Italy being Italy, this was decidedly an order. What little gain over chaos they could find, Max laid it down as a principle, there they would scramble. The line to Montechiari was the local to Mantua and ran beside the road all the way, so that they had the illusion, once aboard, standing on the swaying and heaving platform between two cars, that the world in all its ingenuity was moving along with them. There were automobiles bouncing in their dust, trembling with speed, their goggled drivers keeping a strange dignity above the wild agitation of their machines.

There were carriages rocking behind horses that paced as if to the *bucca* and drum of the Praetorium, drawing Heliogabalus to the Circus Maximus. There were bicycles on which one could see characters out of Jules Verne, Antinoos in a plaid cap, Heidelberg duellists, English mathematicians, Basques whose faces were perfect squares under their berets, and a priest whose dusty soutane flared as if he were Victory bringing in the fleet at Samothrace.

No aeroplanes were in the air when they arrived.

The way to the aerodrome was like a gathering of the Tartar tribes at an English garden party. Booths and tents, all topped with flags, rose above a crowd flowing in all directions, of people, carriages, horses, and automobiles.

A heron of a German flashed his monocle and pointed the way to the hangars. A Socialist with a wooden leg was selling *The Red Flag* to a priest whose purse was deeper than his fingers were long. From a bright yellow Lanchester descended a dwarf whose bosom protruded like the craw of a pigeon. His clothes were black and pearl, with many elaborately buttoned panels and facings.

Gypsies haughty as Mongol royalty stood in a line, watched by a gendarme whose very eyes seemed waxed.

Above the bumble of voices they could hear a band clashing its way through the overture to *I Vespri Siciliani,* and suddenly a clatter of cavalry parted its way through the crowds, a brave disarray of silken horses, tossing plumes, and scarlet coats.

An old woman with a milky eye offered them bouquets of tiny white flowers. Beside a French journalist in pointed shoes stood a peasant in a great coat that had seen Marshal Ney.

The hangars were like large puppet theatres, their stage curtains drawn, Otto explained, to keep all the inventions from prying eyes. Some aeroplanes were out, however, and they stood, rather guiltily, and allowed the strangeness of the insect machines to astonish them more than they had anticipated. They are too small, a Frenchman said from behind them.

The Brothers Wright were indeed not there. They were in Berlin, but here was their rival Curtiss sitting in a folding chair, his feet propped on a benzine tin. He was reading *The New York Herald Tribune.* They looked at him in utter awe. Kafka appreciated his professional nonchalance, which was like that of an acrobat who is soon to be before everybody's eyes, but who for the moment has nothing better to occupy him than a newspaper. He was satisfyingly an American.

Then they saw Blériot.

A man with calm, philosophical eyes stood with folded arms and legs spread. Twice he broke his meditative stance and strutted from the door of his hangar to the engine of an aeroplane on which two mechanics were working. The mechanic bending over the engine kept reaching back an empty hand, its fingers wiggling, and the other mechanic put into it a wrench or screwdriver or wire brush.

——That is most certainly Blériot, Otto said. Because that is his airship, the one in which he flew the Channel.

Max remembered later, at dinner, the anecdote of the father and son on horseback who came upon a painter at work in a field. *That is Cézanne,* said the son. *How in the world do you know?* the father asked. *Because,* the son replied, *he is painting a Cézanne.*

It was indeed Blériot. He wore a snug cap with ear flaps that tied under the chin, like the caps of the medieval popes. His nose was *cinquecento,* a beak befitting a bird man. He kept darting forward, standing on tiptoe, and watching the fingers of the mechanic.

The Bleriot XI was a yellow dragonfly of waxed wood, stretched canvas, and wires. Along its side ran its name in square letters of military gray: ANTOINETTE 25 CV. Otto offered the information that its motor had been built by Alessandro Anzani. Its power was clearly in its shoulders, where its wings, wheels, and propeller sprang at right angles from each other, each in a different plane. Yet for all its brave yellow and nautical wire-work, it was alarmingly small, scarcely more than a mosquito magnified to the size of a bicycle.

Near them a tall man with thick chestnut hair held his left wrist as if it might be in pain. It was the intensity of his eyes that caught Kafka's attention more than his tall leanness which, from the evidence about, marked the aeronaut and the mechanic. This was the age of the bird man and of the magician of the machine. Who knows but what one of these preoccupied faces might belong to Marinetti himself? This was a crane of a man. The very wildness of his curly brown hair and the tension in his long fingers seemed to speak of man's strange necessity to fly. He was talking to a short man in a mechanic's blue smock and with an eye-patch. From his mouth flew the words *Kite Flying Upper Air Station, Höhere Luftstazion zum Drachensteigenlassen.* Then the small man raised his square hands and cocked his head in a question. *Glossop,* was the answer, followed by the green word *Derbyshire.*

Further along another aeroplane was being rolled from its hangar. Before it an aviator walked backwards, directing every move with frantic gestures.

Otto squared his shoulders and approached a man who was obviously both an Italian and a reporter.

—*Informazione, per favore,* he said with a flamboyance Max and Franz had thought he used only upon the waiters of Prague. The reporter's eyes grew round and bright.

—*Per esempio?*

—*Chi è il aviatore colà, prego?*

—*È Ruggiero. Francese.*

—Ask him, Franz said, if he knows who that tall man is with the deep eyes and chestnut hair.

—*E quest' uomo di occhi penetrante e capigliatura riccia?*

The reporter did not know.

Nothing seemed ready to fly. They wandered to the bales of hay which separated the flying field from the grandstand where society sat in tiers under a flag-hung canopy. It all looked like the world's most crowded Impressionist painting. In a wicker chair the heavy Countess Carlotta Primoli Bonaparte sat under a blue parasol. She was the center of a flock of young ladies veiled in blue and pink.

Were the three Bourbon princesses here, Massimilla, Anatolia, and Violante? To move from the long steps of the Villa Medici, now scattered with the first leaves of autumn, from the tall trees and noseless herms and termini of their walled Roman gardens to the hills of Brescia, was it simply an outing to which they were invited by male cousins all moustaches and sabres? Yet D'Annunzio was said to be here, who had published this year a *Fedra* and a *Contemplazione della Morte*, titles which reminded Kafka of mortuary wreathes, and had they not heard that he was taking flying lessons from Blériot?

They saw Puccini. He was leaning on the barricade of straw that protected the grandstand. His face was long and his nose a drunkard's.

The profile of a lady with a perfect chin and gentian eyes was blocked from Kafka's view by the top hat of a gentleman in bassets, and then, as Max was trying to show him a boy in a sailor suit walking on his hands, he discovered that all the while he had been thinking of the interior of high grass, the mouse's world.

Blériot was going to fly. Arms waved. Mechanics slapped their pockets. Blériot, with a nonchalant pivot in the swing up, was suddenly in his machine, holding the lever by which he was to guide, a kind of upright tiller. Mechanics were everywhere. One wondered if they knew what they were doing or if they were frantically preserving their dignity. Blériot looked toward the grandstand but obviously did not see it. He looked in all directions, as if to assure himself that the sky was still there, and that the cardinal directions still stretched away from him as they always had.

Kafka realized with a shiver somewhere deep under the lapels of his coat that nothing extraordinary was happening as far as Blériot was concerned. He had seen the wrinkling crawl of the Channel thousands of feet beneath him; he had seen farms and rivers and cities stream below him as casually as one watches fields from a train window. He had the athlete's sureness and the athlete's offhandedness. Perhaps only in the awful light of the extraordinary was there real calm in human action. Nothing he might do was superfluous or alien to the moment.

A mechanic was at the propeller, grasping it with both hands and standing on one leg for leverage. He pulled downward with a fierceness. The machine waggled its wings but the propeller didn't budge. Another mechanic took over, and this time it spun, kicked, and froze in another position. One after another they spun the propeller. The engine spit and whined, dying in its best efforts. They brought spanners and screwdrivers, a can of oil, and began work on the engine. One could feel the excitement in the grandstand wilt. Talk sprang up. Otto did not take his eyes off the beautifully trim yellow machine.

The propeller was stubborn, and worse than stubborn, for it stalled after a few hopeful whirrs as often as it refused to spin at all. Blériot's heroic indifference was wearing thin, though even the most comely Italian ladies could be made to understand that the fault was in the engine. A long-beaked oil can was brought from the hangar by a running mechanic. Another took it from him and poked it here and there in the engine. A mechanic brought what was probably a part for the

engine. A part like it was unscrewed, taken out, and compared criti-
cally by three mechanics, who talked softly, as if in a dream. The
Princess Laetitia Savoia Bonaparte watched them with purple eyes, as
well bred as if she were at the opera.

Blériot climbed down. Leblanc swung up to replace him. Otto
opened and closed his hands in sympathetic help. He remarked that
Blériot had crashed some eighty times before he flew the Channel. He
was not a man to be discouraged. In the Channel flight an English rain
had all but swamped him just as he reached the coast.

The reporter who had identified Rougier for Otto was signalling
them with his notebook. He opened it as he ran toward them, tearing
out a page, which he handed Otto with a smile of ancient courtesy.
Otto frowned over the page. The reporter took it back and frowned at
it himself. Then with the air of a corporal delivering a dispatch to a
field marshal, he gave the page back and hastened away, for something new was developing around Blériot's aeroplane.

Otto gave the page to Franz.

—There's the name of the man you asked about, he said. He wrote it
down for the *giornalista*.

Kafka looked at the name. It read, in light pencil, the kind meticulous men used to jot down fractions and the abbreviated titles of
learned journals, volume, number, and page, probably a thin silver
pencil with fine lead, *Ludwig Wittgenstein*.

—Who? Max said.

Suddenly the propeller was spinning. Blériot ducked under a wing
and vaulted into his seat. The mechanics grasped the aeroplane, for it
was beginning to roll forward with trembling wings. Their clothes
rippled. Blériot's moustache blew flat against his cheeks. The engine
deepened its voice and the propeller whirred on a higher note. He was
going to fly. Everyone exchanged glances and quickly looked back at
Blériot. The aeroplane waddled forward. It seemed to slide rather
than roll, and darted one way and another like a goose on a frozen river. Kafka was appalled by its desperation and failure of grace before
he reflected that the most agile birds are clownish on the ground.

Surely there was danger that it would tear itself to pieces before it got into the air. Now it was making a long curve to the left, hopping and sliding. Then it wagged its wings and flew up, bouncing once in the air while no one breathed.

He flew out toward the sun. Then they realized that he was making a long turn and would fly over them. A slash of light flared on his wings when they dipped.

As he passed overhead he seemed to be a man busy at a desk, pulling now this lever, now that, and all with studied composure. Heroism, Kafka reflected, was the ability to pay attention to three things at once.

It was not after all a machine for the grave Leonardo, his white beard streaming over his shoulder, his mind on Pythagoras and on teaching Cesare Borgia to fly. It was rather the very contraption for Pinocchio to extend the scope of his mischief. A random wizard would have built it, an old Dottore Civetta of an artificer who had not been heard from by his friends since his graduation from Bologna. He would have built it as Gepetto carved Pinocchio, because the image was latent in the material, and would not have known what to do with it, being too arthritic to try it himself. The fox and the cat would have stolen it, being incapable of not stealing it, and enticed Pinocchio into it, to see what trouble would come of it.

Blériot hummed in circles around them like an enormous bee. There was obviously a rumor going through the crowd. They picked it up in German. Calderara had crashed on the way to the air show. There were distressed faces everywhere. He was flying his Wright. He was hurt when he crashed. He was not hurt when he crashed. The Wright was ruined. The Wright could be repaired in a matter of hours. He would still fly, if they all had patience. He was the only Italian who was to fly, and now the Italians must watch but foreigners fly at their own air show.

He would turn up, most certainly, with a gloriously bandaged head.

The band, which had been playing idle waltzes, struck up *La Mar-*

seillaise, a tribute to Blériot, who was obviously going to fly over the grandstand. Women cowered and waved their kerchiefs. Officers threw him salutes. They could see him plainly. He did not look down.

He was going to land, they heard, only to go up again. The red windsock on its mast filled and rippled to the west. A man in a gray fedora remarked that the wind was just so, and that Curtiss was going to put down the *Herald Tribune* and fly. Bleriot was flying for practise, they supposed, for the sheer fun of it. Now they were all to fly for the Grand Prix de Brescia. There was a stir on the grandstand. Officers and husbands were explaining it to the women.

Gabriele D'Annunzio, who was wearing a cream lounge suit striped in lime and a hot rose cravat, was paying his devoirs to Count Oldofredi, the chairman of the Committee. He twirled his poet's finger above his head. The Count grinned at him and nodded, and frequently looked over his shoulder. D'Annunzio waved his arms, spread his open hand on his chest, and talked like a herald in Sophocles. Kafka noticed how thin and short he was, and how accurately he resembled a rat.

Everyone was looking up. From nowhere at all the dirigible *Zodiac* had appeared, and was drifting majestically toward the grandstand. The band began a confused national anthem. Dignified Germans leaned backwards and stared, their mouths open. Two boys leapt up and down as if on springs.

Ladies and gentlemen hastened to the bales of hay. Photographers went under their black cloths. The violent, Republican flag of the *Vereinigten Staaten von Amerika* ran up a staff and as soon as its red stripes and blue reticulation of stars rippled out into the Lombard air there was a roar more sonorous than they had heard all day.

Curtiss's propeller had caught on the first kick. The man himself was standing beside the fuselage of his machine pulling on long-cuffed gauntlets. His throat was wrapped with a scarf which streamed over his shoulder in the wash of the spinning propeller. He mounted, settled himself, and with a toss of his head signalled the mechanics to stand away.

He was across the field before they realized that his preternatural composure was going to take him immediately into the air. The wheels cleared the ground with a dreamy laziness. The prospect which they had watched all afternoon was suddenly immense, and there was a wood on a knoll which they had not noticed either. Curtiss flew over the wood, lost to view. They watched the wood intently, and then they realized that he was now behind them. His machine had arisen from behind some farmhouses. Then he was above them. The underside of his wings looked peculiarly familiar and wildly strange all at once, like a ship in harbor. And while they watched his trim biplane it was already above the wood again, small and melancholy. This time everyone turned to watch the farmhouses. Because they were waiting, the trip seemed longer the second time, but there he was, as suddenly as before, up out of nowhere.

He made five flights over the wood and around a circuit they could not see, returning each time over the farmhouses. Before he was down, word went around that he had most certainly won the Prix de Brescia. He had flown fifty kilometres in forty-nine minutes and twenty-four seconds. He had won thirty thousand lire.

The bandstand stood and clapped as Curtiss climbed from his machine. His wife was standing with a group of men, who ushered her forward. The blood was draining back into her face, and she was trying to smile.

The man named Wittgenstein was again holding his left wrist, massaging it as if it were in pain.

They heard that Calderara was definitely injured, and that his Wright was a wreck.

Curtiss was scarcely down when three machines all started their engines. The evening was coming on, a brown haze with a touch of gold. Dust blew against dust.

The crowd became restless. Rougier was now in the air, between two great wings on a sled the runners of which curled up at both ends to bear smaller wings. He seemed to have more to do than he could manage, pulling and pushing levers. But apparently he was managing beautifully, like a man for whom writing with both hands at once is natural.

Blériot was in the air again, too. Leblanc's monoplane looked redder in the air than it had on the ground.

The crowd was moving away, to get seats on the train, which could obviously take only a small part of them. By running, they got to the train in time to pry themselves aboard.

Rougier was still in the air when the train began to move. *Ancora là!* His craft droned above them like a wasp at the end of a long afternoon at harvest time, drunk with its own existence and with the fat goodness of the world.

——Franz! Max said before he considered what he was saying, why are there tears in your eyes?

——I don't know, Kafka said. I don't know.

Robot

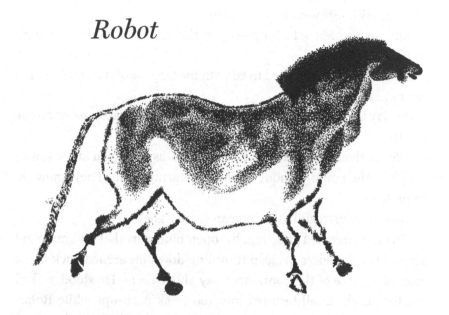

Down there the ochre horse with black mane, black fetlocks, black tail, was prancing as if to a fanfare of Charpentier, though it would have been the music of shinbone fife and a drum that tickled her ears across the tall grass and chestnut forests along the Vézère.

Coencas, tousled haired, naked, and yawning, held Robot in his arms, dodging with lifted chin his wet nose and generous tongue. The campfire under its spit of forked sticks, its ashes ringed by rocks, looked abandoned in the woodslight at morning. The crickets had begun again, and a single nightingale trilled through their wild chirr on the slopes beyond the trees.

The old priest was coming from Brive to look at the horses, the reindeer, and the red oxen. He knows more about them, Monsieur Laval had told them, than any man in Europe. More, *d'ailleurs*, than any man in the world.

Ravidat was awake, propped on his elbows in his sleeping bag. In one of the pup tents Agnel and Estreguil lay curled like cats. A leaf stuck to Estreguil's pink cheek. He had slept in a sweater, socks, and hat. Agnel's knees were near his chin.

Queroy and Marsal were asleep in the other tent under Ravidat's canvas jacket.

Since Thursday they had lived with the tarpans of the Dordogne in their eyes.

——Friday the thirteenth, Coencas said. *C'était par bonheur, la bonne chance.*

——We *felt* them on Thursday, Ravidat said, as when you know somebody's in the house without seeing or hearing them. They knew *we* were there.

——Scare me, Estreguil said, so I can scare Agnel.

Ravidat stretched kneeling, his open blue shirt that had bunched around his shoulders in sleep tumbling down his arched back like a crumpled piece of the September sky above them. He stood, naked but for his shirt, fell forward into ten brisk push-ups while Robot barked in his face, then rolled onto his back and pedalled his long legs spattered with leafshadow in the sharp morning air.

——Ravidat, Marsal said gloomily from his tent, is having a fit.

——Show me, Estreguil said.

——*Et alors, mes troglodytes,* Coencas hailed the tents, help me get a fire going.

Estreguil crawled out in silly haste. Agnel rolled behind him. Robot studied them anxiously, looking for signs of a game.

Ravidat had pointed on Thursday toward the slope across the Vézère.

——He is over there! he called through cupped hands.

The others were catching up. Coencas had whittled a staff and was whacking thistle and goldenrod with it. Marsal put two fingers in his mouth and whistled like a locomotive.

Ravidat was watching the shaken sedge across the river where Robot nosed his way. He was seventeen, long of jaw, summer brown. His eyes were glossy black discs set in elm-leaf outlines of boyish lashes. His new canvas jacket smelled of pipeclay and gunpowder. His corduroy trousers were speckled with beggar's lice and sticktights. Over his shoulder he carried his uncle Hector's old octagon-barreled breechloader.

The Vézère was low, for the summer had been dry, and the reeds along its bank were thick with dragonflies and quivering gnats.

Through a stand of scrub oak and plum bushes as yellow as butter the others filed toward him, Marsal with the other rabbit gun, Queroy with the sleeves of his sweater tied around his neck, Coencas in short blue pants, ribbed socks, a scab on one knee, brown cowlick over an eye, Estreguil sharp-nosed under a gray fedora, and little Agnel, who carried a frog.

The hum of an airplane had stopped them.

— Robot is over there on the slope, Ravidat said.

— A Messerschmidt, Coencas said. The Heinkels are much shriller.

— See my frog.

— When your hands are all warts where he's peed on you, Queroy said, we'll see your frog.

— The Stukas were so low we could hear them before we could see them, Coencas said. When a car stalled, or got hit, the people in the cars behind it would jump out and roll it in the ditch.

— They wouldn't roll *my* car in the ditch, Queroy said.

— They would, if you got kicked in the balls, like one man I saw. There were fights all the time. But when the Stukas came over the road, going down it with their machineguns *rat-a-tat, rat-a-tat,* everybody took to the fields, or woods if there were any. Afterwards, there were *burning* cars to get off the road.

Agnel watched Coencas's face with worried eyes.

— They are over there, Coencas said, pointing northwest.

Queroy spread his arms like a Stuka and ran in circles.

— Queroy is a Nazi, Estreguil said.

Estreguil was all dirty gold and inexplicably strange to look at. His hair was the brown of syrup, with eddies of rust spiralling in and out of the whorls of bright brass. His eyes were honey, his face apricot and wild pale rose over the cheeks. He had been to Paris, however, and had seen real Germans on the streets, had heard them pound on their drums. Coencas had only seen the bombers. Agnel didn't know what he had seen.

—You might have to live forever in Montignac, Marsal said. The Germans may never let you go back home.

—I'm glad, Queroy said.

—*Merde alors*, Ravidat said. Then he shouted across the river:

—*Bouge pas, Robot!*

—He's going up onto the *hectares* of the Rochefoucauld, Marsal said.

—We can cross down at the meadow ford, Ravidat said, leading the way. Marsal and Coencas joined him, and the three little boys came in a cluster behind, Agnel's frog puffing its throat and swimming with a free hind leg. Estreguil's large gray fedora was a gift from Madame Marsal, Jacques's mother.

Robot had met them halfway up the slope, splashing his tail from side to side. His feet were still too big and he still fell when he wheeled. He squeaked when he barked and he squatted to pee, like his mother, which he did with a laugh, lolling tongue, and idiot eyes. He had never in his life seen a rabbit.

He thrashed his tail while Ravidat tickled him behind the ears.

—Find us a rabbit, old boy, Ravidat said. Find us a rabbit.

Robot let out his tongue in an ecstasy and rolled his tail.

—When the Nazi tanks turn, Coencas was explaining, they don't do it like an auto. It comes, *bram! bram! bram!* to a corner. If it's turning right, the right tread stops, *clunk!* and the left keeps the same speed, spinning it right around.

He swung his left leg out.

—And when it's facing the street it's turning into, the right tread starts again. Sparks fly out of the cobbles. Keen.

Queroy turned like a tank, spraying leaves.

—Are the rabbits just *anywhere* around here? Estreguil asked. Are they hiding?

They entered the oak forest at the top of the hill. The silence inside made them aware of the cricket whirr in the fields they had left, and the cheep of finches in the tall September grass. They could no longer hear the drone of the airplane. Caterpillars had tented over the oleanders.

The hills of the Dordogne are worn down to easy slopes, and outcroppings with limestone facings slice across the barrows of the hills.

—*C'est bien ajusté le slip Kangourou?* Coencas slapped Ravidat on the behind.

—*Va à ravir*, Ravidat laughed. *Et marche aussi comme un coq en pâte.*

—*Capiteux, non?*

Ravidat leaned his gun carefully against an alder, unbuckled his belt, unbuttoned his fly, lowered his trousers, and raised his shirt tail. He was wearing a pair of Coencas's underpants cut like swimming briefs, trim, succinct, and minimal.

—They're the new style from Paris, Ravidat explained. They are called *Kangourous*.

—Because you jump in them! Agnel squealed.

—Because your *queue* sticks out of the pouch when you want it, Estreguil said. *Idiot!*

—Has your peter got bigger still? Queroy asked. His was as yet a little boy's, his testicles no bigger than a fig.

Marsal, like Coencas, was old enough to have his aureole of amber hair, but Ravidat was already a man, full bushed in black.

—Let us see, Queroy said.

They looked at the rose heft of its glans with professional curiosity, the twin testicles plump and tight, Marsal and Queroy with envy, Coencas more complacently, though he felt his mouth going dry. Ravidat admired himself with animal pride.

Agnel considered these mysteries briefly and held out his frog to a tangle of gnats dancing in the air.

—Don't hurt him, Estreguil said. Will he eat the gnats?

Coencas slid his hand down into his short pants, stuck out his tongue in sweet impudence, and bounced on his toes.

—*Attendez!* Marsal said quickly, his voice hushed.

Robot was crashing through leaves. His tenor bark piped down the slope.

Ravidat stuffed his cock back into his shorts and the frog leapt from Estreguil's hands.

He grabbed his gun, holding it against his chest with his chin while he did up his trousers. Marsal was already away among the trees. Then they all galloped down the hill, elbows out for balance.

—Up and around! Marsal shouted.

—Show me the rabbit! Agnel cried from behind them.

Ravidat and Marsal were out front, stalking to the top of the slope, sighting along their guns. Coencas, his stick at the ready, was at their backs with Estreguil and Queroy.

—Say if you see my frog, Agnel said.

—Everybody stop! Ravidat cried. Keep quiet.

The woods were wonderfully silent.

—He went down the slope, Marsal said quietly, and then across, down there, and up again, didn't he?

—If he catches it, will he eat it? Estreguil asked.

—Shut up.

Robot was barking again. They turned together.

—Show me the rabbit, Agnel said, falling backwards.

They ran around him.

—How did the dumb dog get *behind* us? Ravidat asked.

They plunged down the hill, looking, jumping for a better look, kneeling for a better look. The familiar oakwood as they ran through it became unfamiliar and directionless, as though it had suddenly lost its ordinariness.

Agnel tripped and fell, spewing up a dust of leaves. Ravidat and Coencas bounded over fallen trees, their mouths open like heroes in a battle. Marsal was more methodical, sprinting with his gun at port arms.

—Everybody still! he shouted.

Only Agnel kept padding on behind them.

—I hear Robot, Marsal said, but damned if I know where.

The woods were all at once quiet. The distances were deepening dark.

Then they heard Robot. His bark was vague and muted, as if down a well. It was beneath them.

—Holy God, Ravidat said.

—Quiet!

Marsal went on all fours and cocked his ear. Robot was howling like a chained puppy. Then he began to whimper.

—*Robot!* Ravidat called. Where *are* you? *Eh, mon bon bougre, où es tu, hein?*

Marsal began to move on hands and toes.

—He's under the ground, Ravidat. In a fox den or rabbit burrow.

—He'll come out, Ravidat said. I'll bet he has a rabbit.

—Show me, Agnel said.

Marsal was walking around the hill, signalling for the others to follow. They could hear Robot's howls more distinctly as they clambered over an ancient boulder, a great black knee of stone outcropping. They came to the upended roots of a fallen cedar.

—He's down there! Marsal said.

The cedar in falling had torn a ragged shellhole in the hillside, and the weather had melted it down in upon itself. There was a burrowmouth at the back of the cavity, down which Ravidat, lying on his stomach, shouted.

—Robot!

An echo gave back *bô! bô! bô!*

—Get out of there! Ravidat coaxed. Come up, old boy! Come up! Marsal gave a keen whistle.

—He's a hell of a long way down, Coencas said. You can tell. Ravidat took off his canvas jacket, throwing it to Marsal.

—I'm going in after him.

—The hole's too small.

—Only the hole. You heard that echo. It's a cave.

—Sticks, Marsal ordered. Everybody find a good stick.

Agnel set to, arms over his head. Marsal drew his hunting knife and began to hack at the edges of the hole.

—It goes in level, he said. It must drop later on.

Estreguil came dragging a fallen limb as long as a horse. Ravidat brought a leafy length of white oak, stripping branches from it as he dragged it up to the hole.

—Let's get this up in there, he said, and walk it back and forth.

Ravidat and Coencas on one side, Marsal and Queroy on the other, like slaves at the oar of a trireme, they pushed and pulled, grinding the rim of the hole until Ravidat said that he thought he could crawl in.

—Go in backwards and feel with your feet, Marsal said. You can climb out then if you get stuck.

His legs in to the hips, he walked his elbows backwards, calling out, *Courage, Robot! Je viens!*

A half-circle of faces watched him: Marsal's big gray eyes and tousled brown hair, Queroy's long Spanish face with its eyes black as hornets, Coencas's flat-cheeked lean face, all olive and charcoal, Estreguil's long-nosed, buck-toothed blond face with its wet violet eyes, Agnel's taffy curls and open mouth full of uneven milk teeth.

Level light from the setting sun shone on Ravidat's face.

—We ought to have a rope, Marsal said.

—It goes down here, Ravidat's muffled voice came out. There's a ledge.

He lowered his feet, loose rotten stone crumbling as he found footholds. His elbows on the ledge, he struck a heap of scattering objects with his feet. They must lie on something. He dropped.

—I'm on another ledge! his distant voice rose, as if from behind closed doors several rooms away. I'm standing in a muck of bones. It's a graveyard down here!

Earth poured on him in rivulets. An ancient dust, mortuary and feral, lifted from the bones he had disturbed. Coencas was wriggling in head first, loosening pebbles and sliding loam.

—Matches, he said, reaching down into the dark.

Then he said:

—I'm coming down!

Ravidat caught him, shoulders and arms, so that the one, his feet still in daylight, hugged upside down the other standing in dark bones. They could hear Agnel saying:

—I'm next!

Coencas pivoted down, crashing onto the bones beside Ravidat.

—We're on a ledge, I think. Feel with your foot.

Coencas struck a match. White clay in striated marl beside them, utter blackness beyond and below, where Robot whined and yelped. Another match: the bones were large, bladed ribs in a heap, a long skull.

—Bourzat's ass!

—Queroy! Jacques! Ravidat shouted upwards. Last year, when old Bourzat's ass disappeared, you remember? Here it is!

—It was just about when that storm blew this old tree over, you're right, Marsal shouted down. You're right.

—Does it stink? Agnel hollered.

Another match showed that the ledge dropped at a fierce angle, but could be descended backwards, if there were footholds.

—Keep striking matches, Ravidat said. I'm going down.

Robot had found a rhythm, three yelps and a wail, and kept to it.

—There's no more ledge. I'm going to drop.

A slipping noise, cloth against stone, and then Coencas heard the *whomp* of feet on clay far below him in the dark.

—*Robot*, he heard, *ici, ici, vieux bougre*.

—I hear Robot's tongue and tail, Coencas said upward. Everybody come on down. It's a long drop after this ledge.

Coencas lowered himself from the ledge of bones and fell lightly onto soft clay.

—We're here, Ravidat said from solid dark.

Marsal and Queroy were inside, handing down Agnel and Estreguil.

—Can we get back *out?* Marsal asked.

—*Qui sait?* Coencas said in the voice of Frankenstein's monster, and his words, full of grunts and squeals, rolled around them.

—Is the rabbit down here, too? Estreguil said, panting.

—Can we *breathe?*

—Here's the far wall.

A match showed it to be calcined and bulbous, a white billow of stone. The floor was uneven, ribbed like river sand, pot-holed, an enormous round-bottomed gully.

—I've never been so dark before, Agnel said.

—You're *scared!* Estreguil said.

—So are you.

—It keeps going back, Ravidat's hollow voice boomed in a strange blur.

—I've got two more matches.

The hole through which they had entered was a dim wash of light above them.

—Agnel, Ravidat said beside them, take Robot. *Here!* Keep steady with one hand. Hold onto Robot with the other. Coencas is going to stand on my shoulders, and push you up to the ledge. *D'accord?*

—Good old Robot! Estreguil said.

Ravidat braced himself against the wall. Coencas climbed onto his shoulders, reached down for Estreguil and Robot, pulled them up with a heave, and lifted them toward the light.

—Stand on your toes, Ravidat, Coencas said. I think we're just going to reach.

Estreguil pushed Robot onto the bone ledge. Then, skinning both knees, he clambered up himself. Agnel went up next, and had to come down again: he couldn't reach the ledge from Coencas's shoulders.

—You go up, Queroy, Ravidat said, and pull Agnel up when you get there.

Marsal went up next, showered them with dirt and pebbles, and hollered down:

—How are *you* going to get up?

—Get that long limb, Ravidat commanded. Poke it in, and you four bastards hold onto it for all you're worth.

Coencas climbed out first, using the limb as a rope, and Ravidat followed. The clarity of the long summer twilight still held. Robot was in Agnel's arms.

— We have, Ravidat said in a level voice, discovered a cave.

— Tell nobody, Marsal said. Estreguil! Agnel! You understand? *Nobody*. It's our cave.

— Find my frog, Agnel said.

— It's a damned *big* cave, Ravidat said. And Marsal and Queroy know what I'm thinking.

— What? asked Coencas. What is there to think about a cave?

At the ford Agnel fell into the Vézère. They dressed him in Queroy's sweater, and Ravidat carried him piggyback to the great spreading beech in Montignac.

— *Regardez les grands chasseurs!* the old men at their coffee sang out.

Agnel had gone to sleep, Robot sat and let his tongue hang down, and Ravidat gave a confidential nod to the Catalan garage mechanic.

What he wanted, once they were leaning nonchalantly against the castle wall across the road from the beech and the elders, was grease. Old grease. And the use, for a day, of the old grease gun that had been retired since the new one arrived.

— Grease, my goose?

Precisely. The use to which it was to be put would be known in time. Meanwhile, could it be a matter among friends?

— *Seguramente.*

And he needed it first thing in the morning.

Queroy, Marsal, and Estreguil were to come out to the cave as soon as they were out of school. They could bring Agnel. Better to keep him in on it than have him pigeon.

— Meet me, Ravidat said to Coencas, at the flat rock on the river as soon as you're up. *Va bien?*

Bien. He heard the Heinkels in the night, and the cars of the refugees going through Montignac, headed south. He thought of the armies north and west, of white flares falling through the night sky, and of the long clanking rocking tanks that would most certainly come south. An old man under the great tree had said that the French battle flags had been taken to Marseille and had been paraded through the streets there. They were on their way, these flags, to the colonies in Africa.

By cockcrow he was up, making his own bowl of coffee, fetching the day's bread from the baker, as a surprise for his mother. He left a note for her saying that he would be back in the afternoon, and that he would be just south of town, in the Lascaux hills.

On the flat rock when he got there lay Ravidat's shoes and socks, trousers, canvas jacket, blue shirt and Kangourou underpants. Ravidat himself was swimming up the river toward him. He stripped and dove in, surfacing with a whoop. Ravidat heaved himself out of the river and sat on the flat rock, streaming. The day was a clear gray, the air sweet and cool. He walked in his lean brown nakedness to a plum bush from which he lifted a haversack that Coencas had not seen. Inside, as he showed the wet, grinning Coencas, was a long rope, the grease gun, and a thermos of coffee.

—A sip now, he said, the rest for later.

They dried in the sun. The coffee was laced with a dash of cognac.

—What do you think we're going to see? Coencas asked.

—You'll see when you see.

They secured the rope outside the cave, and let themselves down the shelved clay. Ravidat lit a match and fired the grease gun: the kind of torch with which he had gigged frogs at night. The flame was greenish yellow and large as a handkerchief. Ravidat held it high over his head.

Neither spoke.

Everywhere they looked there were animals. The vaulted ceiling was painted, the crinkled walls lime white and pale sulphur were painted with horses and cows, with high-antlered elk and animals they did not know. Between the animals were red dots and geometric designs.

—Did you know they were here?

—Yes, Ravidat said. They had to be.

The torch showed in its leaping flare a parade of Shetland ponies bounding like lambs. Above them jumped a disheveled cow like the one in *Mère Oie* over the moon. Handsome plump horses trotted one after the other, their tails arched like a cat's.

The cave branched into halls, corridors, tunnels.

They found long-necked reindeer, majestic bulls, lowing cows, great humped bison, mountain goats, plaited signs of quadrate lines, arrows, feathers, lozenges, circles, combs.

All the animals were in files and herds, flowing in long strides down some run of time through the silence of the mountain's hollow.

—They are *old*, Ravidat said.

—*Tout cela est grand*, Coencas said, *comme Victor Hugo.*

—They are prehistoric, like the painted caves of the Trois Frères and Combarelles. You have not been to them?

The cave was even larger than Ravidat had thought. It branched off three ways from where he had lit the torch, and two of these passages branched off in turn into narrow galleries where the floor was not clay but cleft rock. Their echoes rounded in remote darkness.

——It goes on and on.

They heard shouts outside: Marsal, Queroy, Estreguil, Agnel. They were out of school.

——Come look! Ravidat called up to them. It is Noah's Ark down here!

They told no one of the cave for three days. On the fourth they told their history teacher, Monsieur Laval, who had once taken them to the caves at Combarelles and Les Eyzies. He came out to the cave, trotting the last steep ten metres. When they held the torch for him, he gripped his hands and tears rimmed his eyes.

——Of all times! Of all times!

He found a lamp by which the painters had worked, the mortar in which the colors were ground, the palette.

Coencas found another lamp, a shallow dish in which a wick soaked in deer fat had lit the perpetual night of the cave.

They began to find, sunk in the clay of the floor, flint blades, though most of them were broken. They found most of these shattered stone knives, thirty-five of them in all, just beneath the buffalo and the herd of horses.

——Maurice Thaon! Monsieur Laval said. We must get Maurice Thaon. He will know who must be told.

Breuil, Thaon, who came the next day, bringing a block of drawing paper, told them, is just over at Brive-la-Gaillarde with Bouysonnie, would you believe it?

Ravidat held the torch while he drew.

——I had a note from him last week. He will be frantic. He will dance a dance in his soutane. He will hug us all. The war has driven us together here, and we have found the most beautiful of the old caves.

——Lascaux, he said, as if to the horses that seemed to quiver in the torchlight. Lascaux.

The postman went to Brive on the nineteenth with Monsieur

Laval's note addressed to L'Abbé Henri Breuil, whom he had the distinguished honor of informing that in a hillside on the estate of the Comtesse de la Rochefoucauld a prehistoric cave with extensive paintings had been discovered by some local boys. Knowing the eminent prehistorian would like to inspect this very interesting site, he awaited word from him and begged him to accept his most elevated sentiments.

Thaon arrived later the same day with drawings.

—A car! the Abbé shouted. Do we have the petrol? For myself, I can walk.

They drove up the next day at the Great Tree of Montignac in the Abbé Bouysonnie's wheezing Citroën. Laval mounted their running-board and directed them to the Lascaux hills.

Robot barked them to a halt.

—Here we are! Monsieur Laval said, shifting from foot to foot and waving his arms as if he were conducting a band.

The six boys, all with uncombed hair, stood in front of the automobile. L'Abbé Breuil herded them before him like so many geese.

—Brave boys, he cried, wonderful boys.

He stopped to look at their camp, shaking hands even with Estreguil and Agnel, who had never shaken hands with anybody before.

—I am decidedly prehistorical myself, is that what you're thinking, *mon gosse?*

Estreguil broke into a wide smile. He instantly liked the wide-backed old priest.

—Oh, I'm well beyond halfway to a hundred, and then some, he said to Agnel.

Then he turned to Ravidat, who stood with Robot in his arms.

—And that's the pooch to whom we're indebted, is it?

He patted the suspicious Robot, and mussed Ravidat's hair.

They promptly forgot that this was the man who knew more about prehistoric caves than anybody else in Europe. He was simply an easy old priest with a wounded eye. His face was long, rectangular, big-eared, with strong lines dropping to comfortable pendules and creases under his jaws. A silken wattle hung under his chin. The gray bristles of his thick eyebrows rose and fell as if part of the mechanism of his meticulous articulateness.

— My eye? Prehistory got it. We've been climbing around Les Eyzies all week, Bouysonnie and I, and one of your indestructible bushes, through which, mind you, I was making my way in clear forgetfulness of my age, whacked me in the eye. I see lights in it, rather beautiful.

— But I'm forgetting my manners. This is Dr. Cheynier, who has come to help me, he said to the boys as if uncovering a surprise, and this is Monsieur l'Abbé Bouysonnie, who is an expert in primitive religions. And we're all anxious to enter the cave, if you are ready.

The first thing the Abbé's electric lamp found inside the cave was the rabbit.

It sat chilled with fear in the cone of light, its sides shivering. Marsal and Ravidat moved beside it just outside the beam, and the one chased it into the other's arms.

— We've not seen it the whole time we've been down here, Ravidat said.

— *He* was the first one in! Coencas said.

— Take him up, the Abbé said, and let him loose, and don't let the dog get him. He must be famished.

They heard Agnel shouting above.

— The rabbit! The bunny!

Light after light came on. A star trembled on the Abbé's horn-rimmed glasses. Silent, he looked. His weathered right hand was on Marsal's shoulder, as if he needed to touch the force that brought him here. A battery of lights shifted over their heads. Ravidat held the largest. Queroy aimed a long flashlight.

With his left hand the Abbé traced in the air the suave curves of a horse's back and belly.

— The colors! The tints! The gaiety of their movements! The wit of the drawing, the intelligence!

— They *are* old, are they not, Monsieur l'Abbé?

— Yes, *mon cher Laval*, no doubt at all of that.

He pointed higher, the lights climbing with his aim.

—They are as old as Altamira. Older, far older, than civilization.

A long cow faced her bull in the heart of the cave, the titan grandmother of Hathor and the cows of Africa upon whom the Nuer people still wait, burnishing their hair with her urine, imagining the female sun between her horns, replenishing the divine within human flesh with her holy blood.

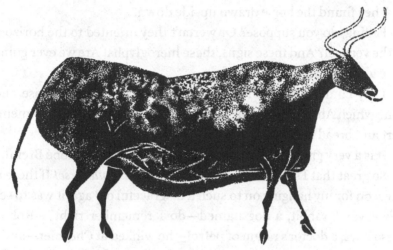

With them run, as if pacing to the music of the first voice of the world, horses, elk, bears, and a spotted animal whose only portrait occurs here and whose bones have never been found. This first voice, the discourse of waters and rain, of wind in leaves and grass and upon mountain rocks, preceded the laugh of the jackal and the voices of the animals themselves, the rising wind of the cow's low, the water voice of the horse, the trumpet of the elk, bleat of the deer, growl of the bear.

In the Abbé's left eye trembled a jangle of red. He saw the prancing horse the color of rust through a snow of fireflies.

—Thaon brought me a drawing of this.

And of a line of reindeer:

—They are swimming a river. I have seen the motif before, carved on bone.

He worked the clay of the floor in his fingers.

—The bears were going when this cave was painted. Man could enter. The Aurignacian snow owl still drifted in at twilight, for the mice. One can imagine the sound of her wings in this stillness. The red rhinoceros was too blind to venture so much dark. The world belonged to the horse, the tarpan, the reindeer. Lion was terrible, but man could smoke him out of the caves, and lion, when the encounter came, was afraid of horse. The old elephants kept to themselves, eating trees.

They found the horse drawn upside down.

—Falling, do you suppose? Or weren't they oriented to the horizon, to the vertical? And these signs, these hieroglyphs! Are we ever going to read them, Bouysonnie?

They climbed out for lunch, cold chicken and mayonnaise and wine which Abbé Bouysonnie brought in two hampers, with Camembert and bread for dessert.

—It is a very great thing, is it not? Dr. Cheynier asked Abbé Breuil.

—So great that I sit here stunned. *Absolument bouleversé!* If there is a reason for my hanging on to such a disgraceful old age, it was to see this cave. A rabbit, a dog named—do I remember right?—Robot, these boys, a doctor's ration of petrol—he winked at Cheynier—and I suppose we must even give grudging thanks to the filthy *boches* for driving me from Paris. A veritable conspiracy of Providence!

Bouysonnie smiled.

—You've *always,* my dear Henri, been just around the corner from the discoveries, when, indeed, you weren't yourself the discoverer.

—I have, the Abbé said, I have.

He turned to the boys. Estreguil, who was sucking his fingers, was embarrassed.

—I have been around. Africa, oh yes, and China even. I was in China with a nephew of Voltaire who was quite close to his accomplished granduncle in spirit and brains. The church, in fact, thinks him too very much like his uncle, in a different sort of way. We went to China to look for the deep, the *very* deep, past of man. At Tcheou-kou-tien, a village some thirty-five kilometres below Peking, just under the lovely Fang Mountains—the Fang shan—*shan* is *mountain*—we found a very old skull, four hundred thousand, perhaps five hundred thousand years old. Five hundred thousand years old! *Cinq cent mille ans!*

He looked at each boy in turn, to make certain that they were following.

—Pierre Teilhard de Chardin, that was my friend in China, the nephew of Voltaire. A tall man, all angles like a proper Jesuit. Me, I'm just a parish priest. They called us Don Quichotte and Sancho Panza, our friends in those days. A man name of Pei made the actual discovery. We went to look at the tools. I was most interested in fire, and the ancient men of Peking definitely had that. As a matter of fact they cooked and ate each other.

—Ate each other!

It was Estreguil who interrupted, and Agnel looked at him as if he knew more about the subject than the old priest.

—Most prehistoric people did, Abbé Breuil said, rolling a cigarette.

—What *are* these caves? Dr. Cheynier asked.

—Arks for the spirits of animals, I think. The brain is inward, where one can see without looking, in the imagination. The caves were a kind of inward brain for the earth, the common body, and they put the animals there, so that Lascaux might dream forever of her animals, as man in the lust of their beauty and in need of their blood, venison, marrow, and hides, and in awe of their power and cunning, thought of them sleeping and waking.

He drank back the last of his wine and held his cup out for more.

—They were neither gods nor fetishes nor kinfolk nor demons nor mere food, but something of all.

An airplane buzzed in the distance.

—The animals themselves have sometimes confronted us, you know! I mean bones, and the mammoths found frozen in Siberia, I mean the beasts themselves in all their ruin, as distinct from paintings, engravings, carvings.

Coencas was trying to see the airplane.

—Listen carefully. In the Swiss Alps, up the side of the majestic

Drachenberg, five thousand feet above the valley floor, you can find the entrance to a cave. It was in its day a hunters' cave. Inside it we have found all sorts of bones: wolf, lion, chamois, stag, even hare, who was a hefty alpine fellow in those times, before the last Ice Age locked all that world into a solid glacier and thousands of years of snow.

——The cave bear, an enormous creature now extinct, was a kind of god, or totem. They broke his bones and sucked out the marrow after they had eaten his flesh and rendered his grease and dressed themselves in his hide. But they placed his skull reverently on ledges in open caves, looking outward, sometimes as many as fifty, all looking outward with their eye sockets, formidable I assure you, especially when they are found, as in the cave of the Drachenberg, covered with ten thousand years of dust.

——Fine dust, not quite half an inch thick. It looks as if the skulls were sculpted of dust.

——The snouts of these dread cave bears are all pointed out toward the sunrise, each in its hump of dust, its mask of dust, and each with its pair of empty bear eyes under a brow of dust. The lower jaws have all been removed, so that the long yellow teeth hang more bearlike in the dark while the sun, morning after morning for twenty thousand years, found the skulls on their ledges. It was like a shop with nothing to sell on its shelves but skulls of bears.

Estreguil and Agnel put their arms around each other.

——You have, some of you, the Abbé said to the boys, been to Combarelles and Font-de-Gaume, Monsieur Laval has told me. It was I who discovered them, oh years and years ago, when your parents were infants. So you see, you have been in my caves and now I have been in yours. *Nous sommes confrères!*

——You are not, you know, the first boys to have discovered a paleolithic cave, though it seems that you have found the most beautiful of them all.

——Three strapping fine brothers discovered Le Tuc d'Audoubert and Les Trois Frères. They were in their teens when they found the Tuc, and soldiers home on leave from that other awful war when they found the cave that's named for them. Max, Louis, and Jacques de Bé-gouën they were. Their father is the Comte de Bégouën, Henri as he

must always be to me, as I am Henri to him. He has retired after a love-ly career of politics and owning a newspaper and such terrible things to a house in the Ariège, near St. Giron, though he has never really re-tired. He is, if I can put it euphemistically, a man who has never lost his taste, bless him, for the good things of this life.

——His dear wife died early, leaving him three sons to bring up. We may note that they were brought up very well indeed, if just a touch wild, young wolves even in their Sunday best. And the Count Bé-gouën, never stinting his love of good food, a splendid cellar, and a gracious lady with whom to share them, is now in his eightieth year, as hale as a prime bull.

—But I'm getting off my subject as if I were eighty myself. On the Bégouën property, Montesquieu-Avantès, the little river Volp runs right through a largish hill, in one side, out the other. What else must a boy do, I need not tell you, but build a raft of oilcans and wooden boxes, and paddle himself into that cave?

—That's what Max did, oh most decidedly. A farmer thereabouts, François Camel, had been as far up the Tuc d'Audoubert end of the mountain as where you can't go any farther unless you are a weasel, but that never stopped a boy, to my knowledge.

—They *all* went, of course, Jacques and Louis too. They got to a kind of beach and, what do you know, they came across an inscription scratched there in the eighteenth century. They had to turn back, but not for long. They came back and hacked the weasel hole until they could get into it. They found that it was a *gours*, a chimney in the rock, and up it they scampered, forty feet.

—When we turned the rabbit loose that Robot chased into the cave, Estreguil said, he ran as if the Germans were after him!

—*Tais-toi!* Ravidat said. *D'où sors-tu?*

The Abbé sighed, and smiled.

—And what did they find there? Sculpture! The very first prehistoric discoveries were of course sculpture, carved pebbles and bones, but this was modelled in clay, two bison, two bison moreover about to copulate. Close by they found the heelprints of children, such as Cartailhac would find later, also in the heart of a mountain, around the headless statue of a bear, with evidence that a real bear's head had been staked onto it. Both these sites seem to have been the occasion of a single ceremony. The animals were shaped by the light of a torch, who knows with what sacred dread, and children danced on their heels, and the cave was closed forever.

—The curious thing about this cave is that if you were to drill through the rock in the right direction you would come to the end of another cave, the Trois Frères, which the Bégouën boys found in 1916. At the uttermost recess of *it* is that strange sorcerer, or god, a man dancing in a mask with a beard. He wears antlers, a horse's tail, bear's paws. His sex is human, but it is placed where a cat's is, under the tail. He is our oldest portrait of God.

——The caves are the first draft of the book of Genesis, when man was a minor animal, not suspecting that the divine fire in his heart was unique. He was thousands of years away from the domesticating of these animals. The dog was the first. He is man's oldest friend.

Abbé Breuil lit his pipe.

——Oh, Robot knew they were down there! He is one of them. I'm afraid I've already scandalized the archbishop—he winked at Agnel—with the heresy I can't get out of my head that animals most obviously have souls, but unfallen ones, as they did not participate in the sinful pride of our common parents. Ancient man must have been in some measure envious of the animal, suspecting its superiority.

——He was right, of course, he added.

A man in blue overalls had come up behind them.

——Ramón! Ravidat called out.

It was Ramón's grease gun that had first illumined the cave. But he was signalling that he did not wish to be called to. He sat under a tree some metres away and lit his pipe. He winked at Ravidat and made himself comfortable.

——Abbé, are we going down again today?

——I think not, Thaon. I should rest my eye. It's full of lights again. Will the boys keep their guard?

——You couldn't drive them away, Monsieur Laval said. They're well set up in their camp. *Pour eux, c'est une aventure.*

——For us all, the Abbé smiled. We shall be at the Hôtel Commerce, he said to the boys, tweaking Agnel's ear and Estreguil's nose.

He shook hands with Ravidat, acknowledging his age and responsibility. His eyes indicated Ramón under the tree.

——Let no one into the cave, he said.

—That's an old friend, Ravidat explained. He is the mechanic in Montignac.

— *Tiens. Jusqu'à demain.*

As the Citroën bounced down the hill, Monsieur Laval on the runningboard, the Abbé Breuil waving his handkerchief from a window, Ramón walked toward them, his hands in his pockets.

—Madame Marsal, he said, will be sending up hot soup.

He approached Ravidat with a look that was both intimate and inquisitive.

—Is it a big cave?

—It's a right good size, yes.

Ramón looked about him. He indicated with his eyes that he wanted a word apart. Ravidat followed him.

—Wait, Ramón said. *Marsal aussi.*

He put the flat of his hand out to the others. Then he stared at Coencas, who was looking at them from under his cowlick.

—You too, Ramón said. Come with us.

Queroy, Agnel, and Estreguil drew together, left out of a conspiracy.

—Why can't they come? Coencas asked.

Ramón's face showed that Coencas had jeopardized his own eligibility.

—What's it all about? Coencas was persistent.

Ramón saw his mistake. All or none, however dangerous that seemed. He stood in his indecision, pulling his nose.

— *Igual*, he said. Gather around.

He squatted, taking cigarette paper and a sack of paper from his pockets.

—This is a matter for *cojónes*, he said in a low voice. The priests will be through looking at the pictures in the caves in a few days. That's to be seen. I shall talk with him, too. And with the others. They're all French.

He sealed the cigarette with the tip of his tongue.

—The Germans are not here yet.

He looked at each of them in turn.

—They will be, in time. There are some of us who will be ready. Do you understand?

—I think I see, Ravidat said.

—We call ourselves the *Résistance*. We are all over France. Have you heard about us, Ravidat? No? Well, you have now. You and Marsal own guns. And you know your way about.

—You are a refugee, *hein*? he said to Coencas.

—From Charleville.

—And you and you, Ramón said to Estreguil and Agnel.

—They're old enough to understand, Ravidat said.

—I want you to swear, Ramón said. One hand on your balls, one on your heart. Swear!

—So help us God.

Ramón looked over his shoulder. It was only Robot jumping at a cricket. They sat quietly, listening to the trill of the nightingales and the wash of wind in the trees.

—The important thing at the moment, Ramón said, is a place to stash ammo. I can get straight off a consignment of Bren guns, if I can find a place to hide them. Is that cave big enough?

—You can hide anything in it, Ravidat said. It's as big as a castle down there.

—If you tell the priest, Coencas said, he won't let you. He'll be afraid you'll hurt the pictures.

—*Foutre les tableaux*, Ramón said. We won't tell him, then. We'll wait until he clears out.

—He's already said, Marsal put in, that he wants to keep the cave secret. That fits in. His secret and our secret will work out the same.

—Anybody who lets our secret out, Ramón said quietly, will have to answer to the *Résistance*. And we are many.

—When do we start? Coencas asked.

—I'll tell you when the time comes. The priest will be measuring the cave. Remember his figures. And tell me all his plans. When he's gone, we can begin to move.

He stood up.

—I'm going back down to the village.

He scooped Agnel up under the arms and held him above his head.

—You know about the Germans? he said. The war? If you tell anybody about this, we lose the war. If you don't, we win.

He set him down.

—That goes for you too, he said to Estreguil, crooking his finger as if on a trigger.

—For all of us.

He set off, as casually as he came.

—*Ravidat,* he said, *vous avez la verge la plus longue. Soyez le capitaine de ces voyous!*

—*Nous sommes soldats!* Queroy said.

—*Agents, au moins,* Ravidat said.

—*Des espions!*

The moon when it rose was red and perfectly round. Robot gave it a perfunctory trombone howl, joined by Agnel, answered by an owl.

Queroy hinted that Marsal was afraid to be in the *Résistance,* that his mother wouldn't let him if she knew, and got his lip split in a pinwheel of a fight by the fire. Ravidat parted them with slaps and made them shake hands.

Estreguil fell asleep in his clothes beside Robot, who slept facing the fire.

Coencas standing in the red light pulled off his shorts and studied his dick.

—Mine's the next longest, he said to Ravidat.

—Mine is, Marsal said, crawling back out of his bedroll.

—No, Ravidat said. Robot, I think, is next in rank.

Next morning they found the figure of the hunter in the shaft at the back of the cave, a mere stick of a man, bird-headed, ithyphallic, childish. Beside him is a carved bird on a staff. His spear has gored a bison, whose bowels are spilling out. To the left of the hunter is a rhinoceros.

These signs, Thaon! *What* do they mean? These quartered squares on legs, are they houses on piles, as in the Swiss lake wattle houses, houses perhaps for souls? Are those feather shapes arrows, spears?
—Your *houses*, l'Abbé Bouysonnie said, have four legs. Could not they too be horses? Written horses beside the drawn horses?

We've got onto a wall of cats. Mountain lions, probably. One old tom has his tail up, testicles well drawn, spraying his territorial boundaries.
—The artist, Abbé Breuil added, has observed the whiplash curve you get in a stream of water coming from a shaking source. We have all seen a cat wiggle his behind when he's peeing.

Another cat has an arrow in its side, like the Sumerian lioness. These are engraved, not painted like the larger beasts.

Outside, over coffee, Abbé Breuil talked about the hunter, the disemboweled bison, and the rhinoceros.

—The rhinoceros trotting off to the left is in heat, you can tell that from her arched tail, even if you've only seen a cow or a cat ready for the male. It was the realism of the *chat qui pisse* that led me to see that. The rhythmic dots drawn under her tail are her delicious odor, I should think. She is ready to breed.

—To the Aurignacian hunter she is ready to die. Except that it is not death he brings with his spear. It is mating in another sense. Nor does this picture mean that she is to die while in heat. It means that in the painter's vocabulary of symbols to die by the spear and to receive the male are cognate female verbs.

—Reality is a fabric of many transparent films. That is the only way we can perceive anything. We think it up. Reality touches our intuition to the quick. We perceive *with* that intuition. Perhaps we perceive the intuition only, while reality remains forever beyond our grasp.

—Man is the javelin bearer, the penis bearer. Woman conceives through a wound that bleeds every lunar cycle, except when she holds the gift of the child, magically healed. The hieroglyphs of these cave painters for wound and vulva are probably the same.

Monsieur Thaon frowned.

—The hunter with arms outspread before the wounded bison is embracing the idea of death, which to him is the continuity of life. The spilling entrails are an ideogram of the vagina. The bison is life under the guise of death. Who knows what metamorphosis death was to these archaic minds?

—The hunter wears a bird mask exactly like the bird on his shaman's baton. He is therefore not a picture of a man but of that intuitive film over reality we call myth. He has assumed the character that the bird totem also represents. Together they have brought the bison down.

The terrace of the Hôtel Commerce, *cèpes paysannes*, Laval, Thaon, Breuil, Bouysonnie, *truite meunière.* Ravidat is in a chair apart, his fingers laced together. Coencas, slapping his beret on his thigh, has just come in.

—I was at Altamira, bless you, in the year 1902! the Abbé was saying. Eh! *It* was discovered by a dog, too. It was, it was! I have just now remembered the coincidence. It must have been Robot's Spanish grandfather.

—The cave, but not the paintings, which were discovered by a little girl. Her father, the owner of the property, had been going out to the cave for years, once his dog had found it, but he was looking for celts and flints. He had never once looked at the ceiling, if you can imagine. One day his little daughter came along with him, and walked in and looked up, first thing. *Papa,* she said, *los toros, los toros!*

—Cartailhac was convinced that those bulls were thousands and thousands of years old. I went down with him and began making drawings of them. I've been in the business ever since.

—One day at Altamira I was on my back drawing. They hadn't yet lowered the floor as they have now. I was working with crayons by candlelight, dabbéd all over with dripping wax, drawing the great mural of bulls, when a very large-eyed young Spaniard came in on hands and knees. He had come from Barcelona, and his clothes were, I remember, of the Bohemian cut as they said in those days.

The Abbé's eyes became mischievous and knowing.

—He said *bon jour* and I said *bon jour,* odd as it was, *vous savez,* to be of a civility deep in a Magdalenian cave. And *bon jour* was precisely all the French he had. He lay on his back, looking, looking. *Hermoso,* he kept saying, *hermoso.* He was not interested in the age of the drawings, but, *ma foi,* in their beauty. He asked, as best I understood his

Spanish, if he might touch them, and I explained that pigments that had adhered to limestone for twenty thousand years weren't likely to rub off now. But he didn't touch them. He took one of my candles and followed the bold lines of the beasts as if *he* were drawing them. There was a terrible look on his face, wonder and admiration, and a kind of worship.

——I got his name straight once we were outside. Picasso. It meant nothing to me then, of course. Such eyes.

——*Picasso*. He did not forget Altamira. His eye has never forgotten anything. The bison at Altamira were to him *très moderne*. I have always thought of him as a Cro-Magnon painter out of time.

——The painted caves in Spain are in the north, in the Cantabrian mountains. They are all across, from San Román in the west to Santimamiñe in the east, and this last is outside Guernica where the divebombers struck first in this awful war.

——And when Picasso painted his great symbolic picture of the bombing of Guernica, he made one of the bulls of Altamira dominate the design.

——But yes! said Abbé Bouysonnie. And I had never seen that at all.

——I like to think of that bull, whether at Altamira or in the angry and eloquent *Guernica,* as Being itself, in all its power and dumb presence.

And as if he suddenly found it more comfortable to change the subject, the Abbé Breuil turned to Monsieur Laval:

——What a beautiful old tree! he said of the Montignac beech that filled the *place* with its shade. They are cutting them down, you know, all over France, an obstruction to artillery sighting. A village without a tree is like a woman without hair. Some poet must write an elegy for the trees of the French villages, nay, for the trees of Europe. There was a venerable oak at Guernica, wasn't there? Some great pagan tree that burned when the divebombers came. I keep coming back, it seems, to Picasso.

——But, Bouysonnie said, Picasso does not allude to the Basque oak in his mural, does he?

——No, no, Breuil said. It is not in the prehistoric genius to depict trees. This man Picasso *is* a painter from the Reindeer Age. The *Guernica* with its wounded horse, its hieratic bull, its placing of images over images, is a prehistoric painting. It honors and grieves and stands in awe. I have copied hundreds and hundreds of these beasts until they file through my dreams. God will take me to them when I die, to the saucy Shetland tarpans whose jet manes run the length of their backs, to the long red ox and woolly rhinoceros. But perhaps the *Guernica* I see is not the one everybody sees. The painting I see is as old as Lascaux.

The Drachenberg bears, their jaws full of shadow: *We are Ursus, companions of the Pole Star, god of the Finnmark, brothers of Artemis Diktynna, lords of the forest. We are Bruin, Arkturus, Baloo. We are eaters of the honey of the bees of Han, the golden bees of Mykinai and Tiryns, the red bees of the Merovingians. Man with his gods, fire and flint drove us from the caves but put our souls on the walls along with blind bison, shrill horse, slow cow, royal salmon, wizard elk, cruel puma, idiot jackal.*

In the forecourt of the chthonic granary of souls at Lascaux two long cows shamble toward three long cows, dewlapped Indus horned cattle lowing and prancing on stiff forelegs. They are not domestic and pied but wild and brown, still in their eland grazing age. Nor are these aurochs yet Hathor nor the royal herds of Harappa. They are, bulls and cows together, female to the Magdalenian mind, creatures of the realm of woman. So were bison, ox, and mammoth. The male domain was horse, ibex, stag.

Breuil leaned on his geologist's pick and gazed.

The bison transfixed by the hunter's spear at the back of the cave is new to us. In a kind of visual pun the spear is drawn from the sexual parts downward and emerges along the bison's belly like a penis in a ventral foreskin. Men have read languages before now without a dictionary.

How could he decipher what men had forgotten twenty thousand years ago?

His eye hurt. He was old. This place was holy. To know, to know.

——*No, Breuil,* he said to himself aloud. *To see.*

Robot on his knees, the Abbé sat in the red rain of light that trembled through the shelved leaves of the great tree in the *place.* Ravidat sat at his feet in a seine of leafshadow. Monsieur le Maire in his high collar and the tricolor across his breast rolled the wine in his glass. Agnel and Estreguil stood on each side of Maurice Thaon, whose hands rested on their shoulders.

——You cannot imagine Africa, the Abbé was saying. Djibouti in the Somaliland, on the Gulf of Aden, Nizan, is it not, who calls Aden the worst place in the world? Djibouti, then, is the next worst place. Admiral Scott, you remember, when he first saw Antarctica, said, *Mon*

Dieu! What an awful place! and I wish I could have said something as fine about Djibouti but I was speechless.

The Mayor looked from Thaon to a concierge in black stockings who was standing at a respectable distance from the men. He nodded with deep appreciation of the abbé's words.

—You have lived all your life in France, *mes gosses, messieurs et dames.*

He, too, nodded politely to the concierge, who dared not acknowledge the honor except by folding her arms.

—The Somaliland is a baked waste. My American friend Monsieur Kelley once said that France smells of wine, urine, and garlic, but Africa smells of carrion, of *merde* ripened by flies as big as hornets, of rotten water silver with filth and green with contagion.

—Indeed, said the Mayor.

—Djibouti is ravaged dirt streets, shacks with blinding tin roofs, whole buildings of rust and packing cases wired together.

—*Il est poète,* the Mayor whispered to Thaon, *l'Abbé!*

—And all of this steaming rot is surrounded by white mountains, sparkling mountains of salt. Imagine that. I was there with Père Teilhard de Chardin, as in China, and with an extraordinary man, a Catalan with an almost French name, Henri de Monfreid, from the Roussillon, the half-brother of Madame Agnès Huc de Monfreid. Their father fell out of a tree some twenty years ago, strange way to die. He was Georges-Daniel de Monfreid, a painter and friend of Gauguin, whose paintings he used to buy under the pretense of selling them, to encourage him.

Maurice Thaon was laughing.

—Since when is a priest not a gossip? the Abbé asked. I'm putting everybody to sleep.

Monsieur Thaon laughed the louder. The Mayor was confused but smiled nevertheless, rolled the wine in his glass, and leaned forward attentively.

—*Et alors.* Where was I? The salt heaps of Djibouti. The stink of Africa. *Ah!* That extraordinary man Henri de Monfreid. He has been everywhere, everywhere that other people haven't been. He was the man who took Père Teilhard to Abyssinia, its awful deserts. Harar, where Rimbaud lived, Obok, Diredawa, Tajura. Prehistory is very rich around there. They found rock paintings, lovely graceful animals, hunters with bows, geometric designs all dots and angles.

Marsal came closer, sitting behind Ravidat.

——I went with them a bit later, like going to the moon. At Obok there is nothing alive. The old volcanoes are still in the week of creation, black and wrinkled. The silence lifts the hair on the back of your head. —And then we got to Ganda-Biftu, where there are four hundred metres of paleolithic drawings across the face of a cliff. We climbed up, having built a scaffold for the purpose. I drew and drew and drew, as high up on the rock as the third story of a building. Sickle-horned African buffalo, lions, antelope. And lithe men, far more realistically drawn than in our European caves. And among the buffalo, quite clearly, were long black oxen. You see what that implies. Domestication.

The Abbé stared before him, sipping his wine.

——We found more pictures, found them at Diredawa, and then outside Harar. We went to the Porcupine Cave, as they have named it, that Teilhard had seen earlier. But I saw something he had passed over. It was a calcined protuberance, wonderfully suspicious, and with no trouble at all I found a bone beneath. A human jawbone, but not of man as we know him, but of the breed of men before us, the apelike man Neanderthal. He had never been found in Africa before, and it was not known that he was an artist. It was thought that he could only arrange stones painted red ochre, and set the mountain bears' skulls on ledges as in the cave at Drachenberg.

He drained his glass and set it on the table.

——But he could draw. *Mon Dieu,* he could draw.

The first boxes of ammunition were placed in the Shaft of The Hunter and the Bison late in October, when the moon was dark. Long cases of carbines packed in grease, grenades, flares, .45s rose in neat stacks to the black shins of the prancing horses.

At Drachenberg the bears' skulls sat on their ledges hooded in dust older than Ur or Dilmun. Their muzzles all pointed to the rising sun, which fell upon them dimly in the depth of their cave in the cliff, lighting all but the sockets of their eyes.

Herakleitos

The red rooster stood on his cobalt legs and brought the sun to Ephesos. His grandfather had come from Mongolia, and when he closed his eyes he sometimes saw a mare nursing her foal under the yellow leaves of a gingko, and heard the *tap tap* of the horseskin drum that preceded the stirring of the caravan when the moon went down toward dawn.

Here there were no great snowhawks of the tundra, but the running shadows of the Anatolian storks were as fearful.

His hens were still on their roosts. His master, who threw him chickpeas and wild pulse, was up, however, and had already sent the mute slave to the baker for the splendid bread to dip in the wine that was even now on the top of the oven warming.

Bees were gathering for the honey.

The master was on the terrace, bald, spare of flesh, full bearded, wrapped in a comfortable old wool peplum with a fringe many years out of style.

Selena, the wringer of necks and the thrower of corn, was moving around the master, the loose sandals on her old feet slapping the stone floor. Up in the hills, where the sun was finding olives in the mist, the cicadas were beginning to chirr.

Now the master was saying his prayers. Selena stood still, pot in hand. And a man had stopped at the door of the court, a tall man in a traveller's cloak, with a staff and a wool sack containing papyros, stylus, three onions, and a bottle of ink.

Behind him, wide-eyed, was the slave with the bread.

The man came into the garden and stood at the edge of the terrace, where the master was sprinkling crushed herbs into his wine, basil, tarragon, and sage.

—There are gods here, too, the master said to the traveller, smiling.

Selena grabbed her elbows, dipped her knees, and licked her lips. She did not know who the stranger might not be. These acknowledgments were sufficient for his dignity, and if he were nobody, her politeness was ambiguous enough.

Then she shifted her eyes, and the slave came forward with the bread.

—*Khaire!* the traveller replied, lifting his staff.

—*Kalemera,* stranger. Will you honor me by sharing my bread and wine?

—If indeed, said the traveller, I have followed my directions and come to the right place. Would you be that Herakonides of Ephesos, Herakleitos, the philosopher?

—And you? the master replied. For I am Herakleitos.

—Knaps, the stranger said, from Arkadia. I am nobody.

—Is that not the same word as *dalos,* your name?

—There was a comet in the sky at my birth and it pleased my parents to commemorate the event in my name.

Selena laid out the bread on a white cloth and put on the tripod at which they sat a dish of figs stuffed with walnut meat and a bowl of goat's cheese.

—*Dzagreuoi!* the master said, tipping his wine.

—Your continued health, the stranger named Knaps said politely.

Selena stood at a distance which she considered honorable, knit her fingers like the laces of a boot, and tilted her chin.

Yes? the master asked with his eyes.

She tilted her chin the higher.

—But of course! Herakleitos said. Our guest would be ill served if we altered the discipline of our house to suit what we suppose is his pleasure. He does not want to go away thinking he has visited Herakleitos when he has not visited Herakleitos.

——Selena means, he explained to Knaps, whose mouth was full of figs and spiced wine, that she assumed we would pass over our morning exercises because of your presence. Were I to visit you in your rocky Arkadia, I should not expect you to discompose your day. So we shall have our music.

Knaps, a fig halfway to his mouth, nodded gravely. He was a young man, long of face, his long hair neatly bound at his nape in a manner which, Herakleitos noted wryly, the Ephesians would consider barbaric. His eyes were large and gray, and his ears stuck out like the handles of an amphora. His beard was a red fuzz remarkably like the down on one of Selena's Mongolian chicks.

——My day begins with a hearty breakfast, Herakleitos said. For years I used to think when I arose, taking only a sip of wine, but as I've got older, I defer to the flesh and fill my stomach. Then my family, such as it is, my housekeeper Selena, the slave Tmolos, and I, have a little music, for one must feed the foolishness of the heart. Tmolos is mute, born with no gift at all for speech. His hearing, however, is acute, though it is questionable if he understands all that he hears.

Selena came from the house bearing a lyre. It had an ancient look about it, as if it had been for most of its existence in the tomb of some Theban from the time of Orpheus.

Tmolos followed her with a more modern barbitos which he handed Herakleitos. He opened wide his eyes and jerked his head forward, as if to ask what next he must do.

——*The Dance of the Kourites*, Herakleitos said, and Selena sat on a bench, the old lyre upright on her knees. She kept her chin high, her back straight, her faded blue dress and black shawl hanging in fluted folds. Herakleitos placed his barbitos across his lap, and Tmolos poised two sticks crisscross over his head. Quietly he began to tap the sticks together, *tok, tok*, and his feet broke into a little dance. The metre of the sticks became more busy, with sudden silences, a swiftly delicate pattern of flat dry sound.

At a passage of wonderful intricacy, Selena joined the chittering of the sticks with a majestic arpeggio on her antique lyre, a march that might be the signal for the Lakedaimonian infantry to break into quick time. Her face kept its solemn indifference, though at the da capo she lowered and tossed her head to fetch the melody back around again.

Herakleitos held his hand over the strings of his barbitos, waiting his entry. Unlike Selena and Tmolos, he wore a broad grin.

When Selena raised a leg and pointed him in with her toe, a breach of what Knaps had taken to be her rather wooden bearing, Herakleitos brought the sweet treble of his strings into the harmony. Selena had begun a sonorous, rolling rhythm to which the barbitos danced a happy descant, and Tmolos was in an ecstasy with his sticks, leaping.

Knaps sat with his mouth open, his hands on his knees, looking from the smiling Herakleitos to the royal pose of Selena to the wild heels of Tmolos.

Another chorus, grand in its finale, and they were done.

Herakleitos stood to hand over his barbitos, bowing to Selena and Tmolos a courteous nod each. Tmolos acknowledged his nod by switching his hands on his knees so trickily that his legs seemed to go into each other, and Selena tossed her head as slightly as if she were twitching in her sleep.

—*Ah!* Herakleitos said. And now, O Knaps, shall we talk philosophy? I am fond of sitting under that old fig tree, where you see the stone table and the plaited straw chairs.

Herakleitos crumbled a leaf of sage and rubbed it between his hands. He closed his eyes and smelled his fingers.

—What honor do you pay in Arkadia to the Lady Artemis? Is her image of silver?

—There are country people who shout at the full of the moon, and she is the old darling of the midwives.

—Is she then principally the comfort of women and the simple?

—In some sense, I suppose, yes.

Knaps sat with his hands on his knees, uncomfortable in a comfortable chair.

—*Ah*, said Herakleitos, as if to drop the subject.

He took from the jar at his side a book on its sticks and unrolled it to the first column. Knaps sucked in his breath at the beauty of the writing. It was the Spartan infantry, a line of cranes across an inlet, Macedonian embroidery around the hem of a shepherd's coat.

—Let us begin by noting that understanding is common to all men.

—In degrees, Knaps said. Some men understand better than others.

—Obviously. But that isn't what I said. Understanding is common. All men understand that water is water, that a thorn is sharp, and that feet are for walking.

—I see, Knaps said, hesitating a minim.

—Understanding is common to all, yet each man acts as if his intelligence were private and all his own.

On the red tile floor of the *kella* in which they sat next day there stood against the one windowless wall a copious urn the color of marl. It was painted in the geometric style with handsome bands of the labyrinthine meander, draughtboard tessellation, crossed zigzags the open angles of which were filled with dots, and tendrils curled and countercurled. Between the bands was a frieze of wasp-waisted warriors, myrmidons, broken by a space in which an archon or basileus lay dead on a bier. His hunting dogs reclined beside him, and a priest of Apollo held a wand over his head.

On a lower frieze noble horses pulled chariots in which men fully armored stood like the gods of ants and hornets.

—It is, as you can see, Herakleitos said to Knaps the Arkadian, funerary. We keep our best flour in it. It would seem to come from up around Mykinai on the Argive plain, where the old border bandits in Homer's poems came from. I like the antiquity of it. The drawing is wonderfully barbaric, don't you think?

—Indeed, Knaps said.

After a day with Herakleitos he was learning to listen and agree. He had not come to a sophist who encouraged argument.

—Feeling probably precedes thought, Herakleitos said, carefully sipping his hot morning wine. It is clear from Homer and Hesiod that we Greeks couldn't *think* in the time of our barbarity, but note how the painter who decorated this urn could feel the truth of the world. He has given the figures the regularity of insects, of trees in an orchard. He knows how an image in a mirror answers the object mirrored. He sees how the world is a system of force and resistance, as when we bite or as we pattern a rope into a knot. We step, and the earth pushes back.

Knaps took out his folded papyros sheets. Herakleitos smiled.

The music this morning had been sweeter, some lilting song that differed radically from the martial piece of yesterday. It was music, Herakleitos explained, from the islands.

—The Lydian songs are quite lovely. They have charm. I find them a trifle sentimental, for all their obvious beauty. Selena likes to sing them at night, though the words are not always what you would call decent.

Knaps dipped his quill, not knowing whether he was to hear about music or the barbaric intuition of the Greeks.

—One of the straightest of lines, Herakleitos said, is a thread drawn tight, and yet not a fiber in it is any less curled and wavy as when it was on the sheep. Do you not find that remarkable?

Spun wool, Knaps wrote, *straight thread.*

—Let us, Herakleitos continued, look at the whole and its parts, of which the thread is an example. Look at the body, which works because of its joints. But what is a joint? A joint, an elbow or knee, both is and isn't. It is the point at which a force cooperates with its opposite.

Yesterday's discourse had been working toward some such concreteness, for it had been about seeing, discerning, grasping the hidden principle of things.

—Men who wish to know about the world, the philosopher had said, must learn about it in its particulars. Our knowledge will never be complete, just as our understanding will never be complete.

Knowledge is not intelligence. And yet both were the logos, the speech, the convivial signals of the world. Knaps had tried to follow the matter of the logos. It is eternal and yet men have not heard it speak. Men have heard it and not understood. What was it?

— That which is *said,* Herakleitos began. Into your ears flows the speech of the world: the wind, which you can usually interpret once you have a knowledge of wind. The speech of the animals, the dialects of rain, the jargon of the birds. Do you not pay as much attention to the creaking of a wagon wheel as to gossip in the agora?

— Step on the earth. The earth steps back. Push against the oak and the oak pushes back. That's one of the great verbs in the speech of the world, force and resistance. Resistance, you see, cooperates with force, so that there can be such things as the bow, the sailing ship, the lyre.

Pythagoras was a great walker, Herakleitos said one brilliant morning when they were striding beside the river. A flock of storks boomed up from the cattails, red cows stood in the shallows.

— He confused the dry and the hard, supposing that a stout calf and flexible knee were integral to his proving that the subtender of a right triangle squared is the same area as the joined areas of the gnomon squared and the base squared. His apprentices had to remain silent for the first three years of their training. Intellectual racehorses. And they go about still with a glazed look. Tell them a joke and they stare at you.

— Do you then refute Pythagoras?

— That would be refuting nature. But nature loves to hide, and what one man sees of her is but a harmony among harmonies. He found lovely harmonies, dazzling harmonies of number, ratios, intervals, rhymes. The most beautiful order of the world is still a random gathering of things insignificant in themselves.

They walked through goats.

—You have a friend? Herakleitos asked.

—I have a friend.

—Can you say why?

Knaps smelled the philosophy in the question.

—Because there is friendship. Because he is he and I am I. Because he is beautiful.

Herakleitos walked the faster.

—All beasts are driven to pasture, he said.

Was he talking about the shepherd ahead with hair like a torch in the wind, or about friends? The air was so sweet and the sky so deliberate a blue that he ventured a reply.

—Men do not know their own good?

—In part.

Dolphins in the rivermouth tore the water silver.

—Men are drawn by forces they do not understand?

—Your heartbeat, Herakleitos said, your digestion, your sneeze, your disgust, your dreams, your appetite, are these matters of the will, of the intelligence?

—They are not.

They were now climbing the rocky rise of wildflowers toward Herakleitos's white house.

—Well?

—These things are nature, are they not?

—Nature. The world. We are lived: the world breathes for us, hears for us, pulses through us heartbeat, eyesight, chill of wonder and fear, sleep and waking. The body is a grave with machinery for keeping us alive. And yet we live, too, in will and desire, in transparent intellect. It was the genius of the Greeks to sort out the two halves of things, to see that our bodies are of the earth, kin to seeds and the animals, made of ocean, rain, wind, and rock, while our minds are alive in a different way. The eye's response to light is probably analogous to the stomach's response to wine and barley, but of so subtler a fineness as to count as a different process, no?

——The body, then, is a beast which we drive to pasture?

——The mind is a beast which we drive to pasture. Consciousness, dear Knaps, is omnidirectional. It can regard itself regarding itself. No matter how you try, you can find no boundary to consciousness. It is a sea within, and has no shores. It has a bottom, I think, but one so deep in the body that we can never know it. *Listen.*

They stood stockstill.

A voluptuous, spry music charmed through the olives. Finger on lips, Herakleitos stole forward, drawing Knaps by the wrist. In the stoa Selena was playing the barbitos. Tmolos danced before her, his eyes closed, his fingers wiggling over his head.

Knaps at the palestra with his northlander bones, straw hair, wide chest, and honest gray eyes stood out among the pinguid Ephesians and sumptuous Persians. He wrestled lucidly, pinning his man with a nonchalant skill free of haste or fluster.

He moved in like a spider, all arms and legs, pounced like a cracked whip, and threw his agonist to the ground with a whomp. He broke neckholds with a jab of his heel.

He had his own strigil in his haversack, of ancient bone and twibill lines, which Herakleitos admired while pouring into his cupped hands from his olpe the spiced oil Selena cooked in the Cretan manner, of olive, terebinth, citron, rose, opopanax, dill.

Herakleitos smelled with delight the seaware odor of dusty Knaps whose nudity smeared with oil and talc shone like mountain copper, his pubic and axial tussocks flat with sweat, his hair wheaten and puzzled.

——Sword or spear? Herakleitos asked of a white scar like a gamma under the carapace of his knee.

——A snake, Knaps said. He had come to tell me that my father had been killed by reivers from the mountains and I stepped on him. I began to see the labyrinth before Mikkos sucked the venom out. I sacrificed a mouse to Apollo, honor for the snake.

—Mikkos is your friend?

—My other self.

He took the capon stone from his mouth and dropped it in his sack.

—How old were you?

—Twelve.

This morning, Herakleitos said, we dance the gryllus. It is an ancient step which we do when the summer gets on into itself, when there are moths on the walls, a spider in every corner, and leeches as thick in the river as grasshoppers in the timothy.

Selena held the antediluvian lyre as if it were the infant Linos and she his nurse. She had tied fillets of red and yellow wool to the horns. Tmolos wore a chiton of such faded blue that only an aftertaste of indigo lingered a dingy white. He stretched his mouth with his fingers and batted his eyes.

—*Kalos, Tmole emou, gorgonidzete!*

Knaps had begun to dance in the morning musics: a wild Arkadian partridge dance that made Selena laugh, and a handsome prancing step done with high knees and folded forearms.

—*Gikkos!* Tmolos cawed.

—It is indeed, Herakleitos said, the address of a warhorse on parade.

Tmolos whinnied, and switched his hands on his knees.

They all learned to dance The Arkadian Horse and marched around the house behind Selena and the archaic lyre, its fillets streaming in the first autumn gusts.

—Madder nor a hare with the Thargelian wind in his ears, Farmer Kossymbos said from his mule to his wife Thetis at the halter. Always have been.

And a Persian colonial official stopped his litter to watch. He remembered the day the Ephesians reorganized their assembly before the Satrapeia. This man Herakleitos had been called as one of the local magicians or wise men or grammarians. He had come to the rostrum with a cup into which he poured wine from a skin. He then broke

in herbs, stirred the mixture, and drank it. Smacking his lips with
satisfaction, he scanned the faces of the assembly and stepped down.
—What did *that* mean? the Satrap had whispered to his secretary.

There had been broad smiles among the Ephesians, all of whom
protested that they had no idea what the philosopher could have
meant by so enigmatic a gesture. He speaks in riddles, when, of
course, he speaks at all. A taciturn Greek!

One has heard, on the other hand, that he understands the divini-
ty of fire and has expressed approval that the Persian army moves into
battle with the sacred smith before.

Knaps wrote:

Time is a child building a sand-castle by the sea.

War is the father of us all, disclosing what gifts we have from the
gods, showing which of us are free and which are slaves.

Justice is contention, through which all things come to be. War is
therefore the natural state of man.

Everything becomes fire, and from fire everything is born, as in the
eternal exchange of merchandise and coin.

This world, which is always the same for all men, neither god nor
man made: it has always been, it is, and ever shall be: an everlasting
fire rhythmically dying and flaring up again.

Not enough and too much.

The first change of fire is the sea.

Selena was grating an African marrow into a collander of parsley
by a strait window through which Knaps could see past the pharaon-
ic cat sitting like a Demeter a red-sailed Tyrian merchantman crossing the mouth of the Cayster with flashing oars.

Tmolos was marching around the well to a Dorian jig on the harp,
four strutting steps, a skip, and a kick coinciding with a sprightly rest
in the melody. Then he stuck out his tongue, hitched his eyebrows,
caught the tune, and swung into the strut, scattering hens.

The first change of fire is the sea.

Stone is alive, wood is alive. For stone moves, the particles of which it is compacted trembling with a quiver that is beyond our senses. To be is to move.

—What a thing does under one condition, Knaps, it does under all. Rock flows as lava, and it flows, though it be marble, on a winter day. The one we see, the other we are forced to admit if we think about it.

The wine jug was of speckled stone and sat in a dazzle of shadow.

—Thus things partake of each other, Herakleitos said, a spray of one within the integrity of the other, atoms dancing among atoms. It is the body receives the nutriment of spiced wine, Cyprian honey on hot bread, with a slice of onion for the sting of contrast, but it is the psyche which has chosen these things for their music, their beauty. The psyche takes its share of the finer atoms, those that drift off as smoke: this is what we call aroma, bouquet. Unsalted beans cooked in ditch water would be as filling and no doubt as hardy.

They had eaten prawns dashed with mustard and garlic.

A day they spoke of trees jostling trees to drink light, the battles of owls and sparrows, the war between the sea and the shore, wind and rock.

—War is the father of all that is, Herakleitos said, and our king. Combat sorts freeman from slave, god from man. Is it not clear that war is the natural state of man?

—Justice is contention. Being is contention.

—But peace? Knaps asked.

—When Homer said that he wished war might disappear from the lives of gods and men, he forgot that without opposition all things would cease to exist.

—Cease to exist?

——Exactly so. Everything becomes fire, in time. The world rusts. But this is an exchange, as in the eternal swapping of money and things sold. What becomes of a dead mole? Have you ever watched?

Knaps looked upward, a finger on his chin.

——It is eaten or it rots.

——Eaten, it becomes muscle and fat for the eater, with manure left over to become grass and oak. And if not?

——It feeds maggots.

——Which are the young of flies.

——Ants and beetles come, and carrion crows.

——That is, then, the slow fire of rot or the quicker fire of digestion. But no minim of the mole goes away. It is melted back into the sum of things. Listen: this world is always the same for all men, but no man made it, nor any god. It always has been, it is, and always shall be: an everlasting fire, dying and flaring up again.

The psyche, Herakleitos explained, is a smokelike substance of finest particles, the same which joined in different ways make up all other things. They are of the least mass, these particles, and they are forever in motion.

——Only movement can know movement. The alertness of the mind is the swiftest movement. Light is next swiftest, sound next.

Knaps wrote on his papyros:

The psyche rises as a mist from things that are wet.

The psyche grows according to its own law.

A dry psyche is most skilled in intelligence and is brightest in virtue.

The psyche lusts to be wet.

The psyche is wet in drunkenness, in longing, in excitement, in rage. See how the drunkard must be led home by his little son.

Water is death to the psyche, as earth is death to water. Yet water is born of earth, the psyche from water.

The heart gets its way at the psyche's expense.

If every man had what he wanted, he would be no better than he is now.

Hide our ignorance as we will, an evening of wine reveals it.

The untrained mind shivers with excitement at everything it hears.

Herakleitos and Knaps stood in wild wheat above the olive groves, the royal blue of thistles beside the fluting of their cloaks.

—Demeter, Tykhe, Koré: what lovely metaphors! Religion is the highest music, no need to insist otherwise, yet every ear is now going deaf to its harmonies.

—But real? Knaps asked. A metaphor can be a real thing standing for a real thing.

—O realer than real! The world in its richness is a gaudy woman whose smell will not get out of my nose. She is wet and dry in just proportions, as our worship ought to be. But fear has gotten into it, and fear is wet. Its opposite, courage, is dry. The great truths are religious and must be defined by dry minds. Bigotry is wet, and bigotry is the disease of the religious alone.

Knaps was following and not following.

—Men are not intelligent, Herakleitos continued. The gods are intelligent. The mind of man exists in a logical universe but is not itself logical. The presence of the gods in the world goes unnoticed by men who do not believe in the gods. Man, who is an organic continuation of the Logos, thinks he can sever that continuity and exist apart from it.

—We are, and we are not alone. At night we extinguish the lamp and go to sleep, at death we extinguish the lamp and go to sleep.

—The gods live in our death, we die in their life. I cannot put it any plainer.

Knaps sat down to write.

The days grew shorter, the stars brighter, the mornings colder. Knaps had heard beautiful sentences since he came. *Character is fate. How*

*can you hide from what never goes away? Defend the law as you would
the city wall. Dogs bark at strangers. Good days and bad days, says
Hesiod, forgetting that all days are days.*

Ephesians, be rich! I cannot wish you worse.

*Life is bitter and fatal, yet men cherish it and beget children to suf-
fer the same fate.*

*Except for what things would we never have heard the word jus-
tice?*

Pigs wash in mud, chickens in dust.

The same road goes both up and down.

The beginning of a circle is also its end.

The river we stepped into is not the river in which we stand.

Everything is plotted in its course by all other things.

*To know God you must see that night is day, winter is summer, war
is peace, enough is too little: for these are all masks.*

All things come in seasons.

Even sleeping men are doing the world's business.

All is one.

Herakleitos with a saffron crocus tebenna bordered in lilies and
ramshorn crikelasia over his gown, in thirled tzangas and cartwheel
hat, entered the temple square from the street of the silversmiths.

Behind him under a parasol held by Tmolos, a parasol of Ugaritic
red, fringed, tasselled, and faded, walked Selena in shawls and stoles.
Her eyelids were rouged, a horned moon was written in ashes on her
forehead, and she carried the household snake and a silver mouse.

Knaps walked solemnly behind her bearing the scrolls.

When they were buying the cult animals, a smith had called Selena *priestess*, and the world was now a dream.

They passed the long tables of the moneylenders, the dove mer-
chants, the sellers of votive lamps and little bronze bees and horses.

They went through the great curtains of the outer door into a darkness lit by hundreds of small lamps. The air was oily and rich with in-

cense. As their eyes got used to the dimness they could see the rows of terracotta bears, the pewter deer, the shields in ranks upon the walls with their emblems, red looped snakes, blue hawks, black bulls.

Priests parted the inner curtain and they walked down the twilit nave to the goddess's image on its dais. Her golden hands were open in solicitude and blessing. A citadel crowned her neatly bound hair. Her many breasts hung like a cluster of titan udders in pomegranate profusion. Bears stuck like treefrogs to the bronze halo behind her head, lions climbed her sleeves, bears, cows, bees, and flowers ringed her long skirts in tiers, and among them they could see slim virgins with small hard breasts and bows.

Herakleitos led Selena forward to touch the snake's flicking tongue to a toe of the goddess and to place her silver mouse. Tmolos had a clay cat of his own modelling and baking to offer, an archaic figure with lemur eyes, bat ears, and smug mouth. Knaps set a whittled wooden horse beside the cat.

—And here, just as I promised, Herakleitos said in a firm, loud voice, is my book, O Mother of Lions, laying the scrolls before her black basalt feet.

1830

On the first night of the century Piazzi found the planet Ceres. It was in Saint Petersburg one bright morning when I was taking chocolate with the younger Prince Potyomkin of Tavris that I appreciated the flawless beauty of a Sicilian eye fulfilling the prognostications of Titius and Bode, whose mathematics indicated that there must be a planet whose orbit lies between that of Mars and Jupiter.

That it should be Giuseppi Piazzi! A monk, an astronomer, a follower of Caraffa the archbishop of Chieti who later became the fourth Paolo.

— It is like a page of the *Georgics*, I said, and the prince took out his monocle, breathed on it, and polished it with a large red handkerchief.

— So much comes to culmination, so much is carried forward. Here is a Christian still gazing at Arabian starlight, just as if the streets of Babylon were yet crowded with oxen, camels, and cages of blinded finches. But it is a telescope built by Herschel through which he looks, and his star maps are published by the academies. It is his privilege as discoverer to name the new planet. *Cerere*, he says. Ceres, the ancient Sicilian mother of the barley.

— *Komilfo*, Prince Potyomkin said, sipping his chocolate.

— Precisely. Yet there is the Virgilian pathos in his giving that antique name to the shattered fragment of a planet. Ceres is, I believe, only some five hundred kilometres in diameter. When in the next three years Pallas, Juno, and Vesta were discovered, it was plain that they together with Ceres were the exploded remnants of a whole planet. The good Piazzi must have felt that he was looking at the natural symbol of the disintegration of that golden world which the religion he professed had hesitatingly broken into tragic ruins. The tongue of a poet named that wandering star. The day is coming, my dear prince, when the astronomers will name a new star Jackson, or append to it a number.

— There are men abroad in Saint Petersburg even now, the prince remarked, who would name a star for a French actress, or a racehorse.

— We are, I think, entering the century of fire.

I said those words without thinking. They were off my tongue and I heard them with the same astonishment as the prince, who opened his mouth like a fish.

— Wars? he asked.

I nodded.

— You are, I recall, a poet?

— A poet, I replied.

He looked relieved. Your Russian gentry at this time took all Englishmen to be political scientists, just as all Germans were mathematicians and all Italians sculptors. But an Amerikansky, he was a cotton merchant, a Methodist, or a novelist who wrote about Wyandottes and Sioux. And here was an American poet who talked of stars with classical names found by Sicilian priests, and who babbled of fiery wars. I could see him dismiss my martial rumor as the product of an uninformed and ebullient mind.

There had been awful rains of stars in North America throughout my childhood and youth. For whole nights a fireworks of meteorites had hissed and sighed down the sky before I wrote my poem about the *nova* which flared before the eyes of Tycho Brahe, and I wrote my first story about the ghost of a horse leaping from a cascade of flame just after the leonids had been more torrential than men had remembered them for centuries. Fire, falling fire. St. Lawrence's Night was like a Washington Fourth of July, and all of a November the silver and red aerolites that stream from the Lion dropped like hail. I have seen a fire of rockets as thick as snow for two hours in the Virginia sky.

My first story, I have said. My only story would cleave more particularly to the truth. It comes from that Germany of the mind whose stately ministers are Baron von Hardenberg (he lay dying while Piazzi first saw Ceres the wanderer) and that double man who created (or was created by) the Tom Cat Murr as Ernst Theodor Wilhelm Hoffmann and composed *Undine* as Ernst Theodor Amadeus Hoffmann. Ah God! and we have Andrew Jackson!

But my poems I have taken from the star world. The fire of Germany is the phosphorescence of smoking tarns, moonlight through mist, the ambiguous spirituality of their philosophy. The German mind lives in the deeps, like Undine, and has claws, like Murr. It is at home in the night, dreaming its life and living its dreams.

But the fire of the Arabian stars is cold and remote, and exists in untold labyrinthine designs, in monsters picked out with points of light, in nebulae, in lost universes of glowing stardust, dead moons.

When I said that the century would be of fire, I meant I think both the German fire of spirit raging in matter and the Arabian fire of far subtler flame, not to be noticed by all. Was it not von Hardenberg who first went into the true nature of light when he chose to move in the night? The night is not only the penumbra of the earth falling outward into space like a cone of shadow. It is also the inward and downward of the earth and of man. He found his night in the caves of the sea, and his goddess, for all his piety, was the mermaid. The cold fire of her scales will be the sign of this century.

Could I have said that to Prince Potyomkin?

In our first exchanges after my arrival in Saint Petersburg he had talked of electricity and locomotives, of steam and clocks. Would not electricity give birth to social justice?

— Your slaves in Virginia, our serfs here in Muscovy, he said, will they not be freed from their labor by machines?

We found the broken Ceres the minute the century began. In the first three years of the century we found the shattered Pallas, ruined Juno, and the brightest of the four lost wanderers, the torn Vesta.

Pallas. Athene, the intelligent. She has survived in us overshadowed as if by some terrible rapacious bird, the hunnish crow or standard raven of the Goths. And Juno and Vesta, mother and bride, we have found their signs. Signs, signs.

What an augury they make, I wanted to say to the prince, but kept my thoughts to myself. Ceres and Pallas, body and mind, the earth's soul and our own. Juno, the soul pure, fruitful, full grown. Vesta, the soul still all potential, knowing itself only, pristine, springlike.

And all my life the stars have fallen like rain.

I smile to remember my mission at that time. For we smile at those overreaching ideals of our youth which in age we know to have been splendid follies. I was on my way to the Ionian island Zante, the sloped pastures of which in spring are purple with hyacinths. It lies with its six sisters in the violet sea—Corfu, Santa Maura, Cephalonia, Ithaca, Cythera, Paxos.

I to whose eyes the forsythia in Virginia has brought tears was going to see the lily fields of Leucadia. I who have lain sick with love for women of junoesque majesty in crinolines, Scotch shawls, and bonnets, was going to see Greeks whose cereal hair was bound in Turkish cloth, whose naked feet had trod the grape. *Isola d'oro!*

Had he not donned his armor there? It was on Zante that Byron was dressed by his admiring English servant and awed sergeants of the Suliotes in greaves, breast-plate, fringed epaulettes, the *zoné*, and the horse-tailed helmet. No one said *Achilles* when they bound the lame heel in the thonged sandal, but no other thought could have been in their minds.

And it was on Zante that they sealed the young laird in his leaden coffin.

Does not fire dominate all the imagery of the *Iliad?* Fire and wheat, fury and Ceres.

—*Mais?* Prince Potyomkin expressed his surprise. The French objection came to his mustached lips like the bleat of a sheep.

—You have come all the way to our Russian capital to seek military aid for the miserable Greeks in their war of independence? *To fight the Turks!*

——To fight for liberty, I said. *Elevtheria.*

Odysseus Elytis! Mavrocordato! Tersitza! Photos Zavellas! The prince was sensible of the heroic war which the Greeks were fighting in mountain redoubts and on plains the names of which recalled many pages of classical history. Russia, too, had engaged the Turk in battles of incredible intensity. The very name Potyomkin was a misery to the Turkish high command.

He spoke with deference and a certain *hauteur,* fiddling with the lace folds of his shirt.

In this room my fellow Virginian John Randolph of Roanoke, the descendant of Pocahontas, had sat, possibly in the Louis Quinze chair, the alpaca of his black trousers strange against the rosewood and watered silk. Joel Barlow had been here. I could see him in all his American awkwardness, wearing no doubt a raspberry waistcoat and yellow cravat.

Beneath an engraving of Franklin stood a copy of Houdon's bust of Voltaire. My eye took in the *Encyclopedia* of Diderot, who, the prince assured me, had punctuated his Gallic wit at the Muscovite court by slapping Her Imperial Majesty Katherine on her thigh; the *Aphorisms* of Bacon; the *Ricordi* of Guicciardini; Scheffer's *Lapponia;* Linnaeus's curious *Praeludia Sponsalia Plantarum.*

A Chinese vase tall as an adolescent girl took the best of the blue Russian light which the prince's generous windows allowed into the room where we were spending our morning.

It is elective affinities that knit the discrete particulars of our world into that artificial fabric whose essence we perceive as beauty. That tall Chinese vase, is it not rich in correspondences? Mr. Keats has seen the just resemblance of a graceful Grecian urn and a maiden in the chill integrity of her chastity. Was not Pallas's bosom, as fable has it, the mold for the first Attic vase?

My first awakening to the adhesive state came as a fragrance of honeysuckle when I was pondering Sappho's perception of correspondences between a girl of ravishing beauty and the splendid grace of a ship. Are not ships bosomed with sails and painted with those wide rich bold eyes which the Egyptians assigned to Isis and the Hellenes to Diana? And beside those magic eyes on the prows of their haughty ships the Greeks painted an arched dolphin, Apollo's fish which they associated with the water life of the womb.

Affinities, affinities. Listening to the Princess Potyomkin playing arias from Wolfgang Mozart's *Zauberflöte* on the harpsichord, I have heard how the Gothic soul can marry into the daughters of the south, joining the mathematics of the German with the lucidity of Italian song.

I first saw the Princess Potyomkin walking a brace of greyhounds against a frieze of birches. She was as lissome as those white trees, as slender as her noble dogs.

Fable and romance had told me amply of the ladies of Spain and Italy, and I knew with my own eyes the bright-eyed English women, the petulant, languid girls of Virginia. But of Russian princesses I knew no more than the daughters of Tartary or the dusky queens of Abyssinia.

Like Byron's austere and proud daughter, Anna Potyomkin was a mathematician. She had found curious and unaccountable patterns among the prime numbers at the age when the virgins of Richmond and Baltimore knew little more than the steps of a waltz, some crewel work, and the difference between the insignia of a major and a colonel. One misty evening I learned how beautifully she played the harp, a tall silver harp made in Ravenna at which she sat with the poise of Penelope at the loom.

If her hands at the harpsichord made a dance of numbers and pranced gaily through a progression of exact resolutions, her fingers on the strings of the harp were mastered by another spirit. Here she improvised, leaving some *andante* strain that had suggested Arabia to dream through a pause into a hot *arpeggio* of Gypsy strangeness.

It pleased the princess to recognize my admiration by inquiring into my position in this world. I was, I think, scarcely a gentleman to her; indeed, the name of gentleman is unknown in Russia. I was a nobody with a semblance of polite manners.

But one of the abilities of genius is to make a little go a long way. I mentioned the Marquis de Lafayette and she nodded gravely, impressed.

——The General, you know, is a citizen of the United States by act of our Congress. I had the honor of commanding the militia when he visited Virginia.

She looked a bit as if she hoped she hadn't started something she couldn't stop.

I mentioned Thomas Jefferson.

——Ah! *Jefferson!* Can you convey in words what he is like, *effectivement?*

——He looked something like Houdon's Voltaire, I ventured. He was very old when I dined with him. His eyes were kind and severe. He had a habit of touching the corners of his eyes with a large handkerchief.

——You were very young when you were presented?

——It was during my first year at the university which he founded. He liked to have the students to dinner, always a few at a time, so that he could talk with us.

I described my visits while I was in the Army to Sullivan's Island near Fort Moultrie. This interested her more than statesmen. I told her of Dr. Ravenel and his passion for marine zoology. I drew sand dollars for her in an album which she had fetched, turtles, crabs, many kinds of shells.

I drew her the gold bug, *Callichroma splendidum.*

Had I studied the mathematics at the university? No more, I had to admit, than appears in the curriculum of an engineer. She talked of Fourier and Maria Gaetana Agnesi.

Unlike the prince her brother, she was in astronomy an enthusiast. In the round stone seat in the garden, leaves falling into our laps, we talked of the stars, the sun and the moon, the eccentric orbits of the planets.

Athena, she told me, in the most powerful of telescopes is but an asterisk of gold.

She had read Volney, and we speculated on the peculiar correspondences of ruins in the vast aether of space and at Persepolis and Petra, Ceres broken in the sky and in the wastes of Turkey. I recited for her the *Ozymandias* of Shelley, and translated it into a rough French.

She thought it odd that an American should be so moved, so passionate, about the ruins of antiquity.

—Your new world must look like so many doll's houses just taken from their Christmas boxes, every brick as new as from the kiln, every stone as white as snow.

—*Mais non, ma princesse,* I said. It is your Saint Petersburg that is new. It is like Venice in the fifteenth century. Nothing here is worn or dilapidated or touched by the tooth of time.

Account for it as you will, it is America that is old. Washington Irving is not romancing when he draws a New York as seasoned and mellow as Amsterdam. The land itself is old, you see, and the first Americans, like the Muscovites and Finns, built in wood. These early buildings are brothers of the ark. We did not bring with us that talent for keeping things up, so that a village in the Carolinas looks a thousand years older than a French village which in fact was built in the time of Montaigne.

An ignorant observer would judge that Richmond is older than Edinburgh.

Once, on a thundery November afternoon, I had occasion while visiting my native Boston, to ride in a friend's carriage to the township of Medford. It was that kind of day when the light, leaden and dull, can still glow in the hectic yellows and melancholy reds of fallen leaves, and turn the upper windows of houses into bronze mirrors of western light.

I was particularly struck by one such house, a massive old box of a mansion in three or four stories, as symmetrical as a moth, and its stone as mottled gray as a cliff looking onto the sea. It was deep in elms, that noble American tree, and I would have credited the assertion that this house was old in the childhood of Shakespeare, and indeed it was built in the years when Milton was a young man, before there was a Saint Petersburg at all.

It is generally known as the Royall House, after the two Isaac Royalls, father and son, who occupied it in the last century, though I find more antiquity of tone in the name by which it was originally known, the name still used by the older generation. They call it the House of Usher.

Our sense of the old is always modern. Starlight is hundreds of years old. We live in the phoenix time of antiquity.

A Greek peasant digging in his garden discovered on the island of Melos when I was eleven that statue of Aphrodite which the Marquis de Rivière, ambassador to the Sublime Porte, and his resourceful secretary M. de Marcellus, purchased for the Palais du Louvre, and which connoisseurs and enthusiasts call the Venus de Milo. It is not so exquisitely mother-naked as the Aphrodite of Kyrene, that miracle of womanly beauty, nor so lissome as the marble torso from Cnidus.

Old as it is, it belongs now to our age which found it more than to its own, which we cannot imagine, much less inhabit.

—These shattered Venuses are like the crumbling bits and pieces of the lady planet strewn in the orbit between Mars and Jupiter.

—You are a man of sentiment, M. Perry, the princess said to me one afternoon, as well as a man of no little mystery, even accounting for the fact that my alien eyes cannot interpret accurately the outward signs of an American. For all I know, your president may do his own shopping and wear carpet slippers on the street.

—Our Neva is the Potomac, I said, and I can assure you that of a morning one may see venerable senators bathing naked in its waters.

—I quite believe it, she said. What I meant, however, is that I as a woman notice the frayed cuffs of your funereal coat, the shine of the elbows and knees of your rather French *confection*. Nor can you deny that you would welcome owning a new shirt. You have no gloves, and the footman tells me that you always arrive without an outer coat.

—*Madame!* I protested.

—Hear me through. My brother and I have found in you a congenial soul, our actions will have made that clear. But we have also found you to be a mystery.

She smiled with graciousness.

—Won't you tell us who you are?

—I am, *ma chère princesse*, Edgar A. Perry, of Virginia. I am taken in my own country and in England for a gentleman. I scarcely know what you mean when you demand to know who I am.

—Well, then, she said, giving up her smile, my brother is waiting to see you in the greenhouse. We discussed this matter and agreed that I was to face the mystery. If you refused to be candid with me, as I believe you have refused, then I must give you over to my brother.

I was shaken, stung. I made a deep, most courtly bow. I left.

And this was all the work of my angel, who is a master of the odd. Could this sudden rent in our friendliness be simply the end of their patience? My very first visit to the Potyomkin house I tracked dog shit on the rug. They paid not the least attention, though I was in an ecstasy of confusion when I noticed it.

And the second beautiful walk I took with the princess and her greyhounds, I trod on her skirt and tore it. She did not mention the matter, and asked me not to trouble my thoughts over a trifle when I offered a stuttered apology.

And when I drank my tea from my saucer, in the American manner, there was only a polite curiosity in their well-bred glances.

I had since my introduction to the prince been sensitive to the fact that he must think an obviously indigent soldier of fortune will sooner or later open the subject of a subscription to the Greek Cause. I know the look from Allan's eyes, and from my classmates and fellow officers.

Perhaps my not asking him had put him on tenterhooks.

I made my way to the greenhouse down the stately avenue of elms, European elms, which have not the Greek loveliness of the American elm.

Might I not live out my life and never know the elm enough? Every leaf of that Dorian tree is the outline of a handsome eye, whether of a Callisto with naked feet and dressed in the pelt of an elk, girdled with a snake's skin diamonded silver and brown, or of an Apollo with the

loins of a lion, a nose plumb, straight, and with the planes of a toma-
hawk.

The laurels and the rhododendrons are too Celtic, and the oak too
druid and barbaric for my lyre. There is a girlish frivolity in the apples
and plums, though the pear, a Roman tree, has its lady's grace and fine
Virgilian russet bounty in the fall.

But the elm, the elm, that noble, stately tree. It is invariably upright, like the pine and cypress, but it does not grow to their giant's
height, and tempers with a Spartan measure and seemliness their
deuteronomic grandeur.

The elm is modest in its union of strength and grace. It grows as
slow as the cedar, branching with military, with Gallic clarity of design, each limb like a few arrows leaning their fortuitous ways in a
quiver, but this disarray is the repose of discipline and not the sprawl
of carelessness.

Did the prince wish to see me because just last week I had knelt in
the wet rot of autumn leaves and kissed the princess's hand?

There was an ambiguity surpassing conjecture in her eyes, and the
wind rose up around us in that half barbaric Russian garden with its
alien Diana blackened by snows and fierce ponent winds, its English
flower beds, its Italian stone benches unmellowed by the pale north-
ern sun, and rose up in my soul as cold and fretful as a winter storm.

Another such wind sprang up as I walked to the greenhouse. Flare
and die, flare and die is the pulse of the world. Tycho's star blazed and
disappeared.

Urbs antiqua fuit.

In Karazkhan, the prince told me, they have caught and given to
peasants what may be the last herd of wild horses in Europe.

Time is but the bringing and the taking away of sudden beauty as
brief as the day of the moth. It is in the autumn, *per amica silentia lunae,* that she returns, when country churches are as quiet as un-
manned ships drifting toward the poles. The pure flame of the lamp
trembles and goes blue. The mirrors are strange with moonlight from

the stairwell, the log is white, and shoals of wind wash about the house, the tides of time.

In the lid of my dispatch case I had pasted a map of Greece, its broken coasts and fragile islands all green and yellow on the hyacinth of its seas.

Here sailed the white-bosomed barks so long ago, ribbed and prowed as beautifully as the tall Helen of Sparta, their long keels laid in the shipyards at Nicaea, their course blue, the wind that drove them flowery with the fragrance of the world, spiced oil and wine, fields of dill and borage, rhododendron and poppy.

The agate lamp within her hand!

The colonnade from the garden path to the greenhouse was a shimmer of leaffall down its Ionic perspective. I could see the prince in his Persian smoking-jacket pacing the gravel walks.

—Sir, I could hear his noble voice, you are registered, I see, at the Evropa as one Henri de Rennet. There can be no mistake. And yet the United States Minister, Mr. Henry Middleton, knows you by yet a third name. Will you be so kind as to explain this charade?

—Delighted to, your Majesty, I would have said. My name is André Marie de Chénier. I was guillotined thirty-six years ago, *le septième de Thermidor, l'an 1.* I am a ghost.

Fall back, he would, one hand on his forehead, the other on his heart. *Canaille!* more likely, and boot me out the door.

I walked to the tall wrought-iron gates that led to the box-hedge avenue that gave onto the Prospekt at a door in the wall.

The mighty bells in the churches were chiming. It had begun to snow.

The Bowmen of Shu

Here we are picking the first fern shoots and saying when shall we get back to our country, away from *das Trommelfeuer*, the gunners spent like winded dogs, white smoke and drizzle of sparks blowing across barbed wire in coils, the stink of cordite. 27 December 1914. Avalanches of shrapnel from field guns firing point-blank with fuses set at zero spray down in gusts, an iron windy rain. Here we are because we have the huns for our foemen. It's with pleasure, dear Cournos, that I've received news from you. We have no comfort because of these Mongols. You must have heard of my whereabouts from Ezra to whom I wrote some time ago. Since then nothing new except that the weather has had a change for the better. We grub the soft fern shoots, the rain has stopped for several days and with it keeping the watch in a foot deep of liquid mud, the crazy duckwalks, hack and spit of point guns.

HOOGE RICHEBOURG GIVENCHY

The smell of the dead out on the wire is all of barbarity in one essence. Also sleeping on sodden ground. The frost having set it, we have the pleasure of a firm if not warm bed, and when you have turned to a warrior you become hardened to many evils. When anyone says *return* the others are full of sorrow. Anyway we leave the marshes on the fifth January for a rest behind the lines, and we cannot but look forward to the long forgotten luxury of a bundle of straw in a warm barn or loft,

also to that of hot food, for we are so near the enemy and they behave
so badly with their guns that we dare not light kitchen fire within two
or three miles, so that when we get the daily meal at one in the morning it is necessarily cold, but alike the chinese bowmen in Ezra's poem
we had rather eat fern shoots than go back now, and whatever the suffering may be it is soon forgotten and we want the victory.

SCULPTURAL ENERGY IS THE MOUNTAIN

Sculptural feeling is the appreciation of masses in relation. Sculptural ability is the defining of these masses by planes. The Paleolithic
Vortex resulted in the decoration of the Dordogne caverns. Early
stone-age man disputed the earth with animals.

LES FALLACIEUX DÉTOURS DU LABYRINTHE

The rifles, *crack! thuck!* whip at the bob of helmets of the *boches* in the
trenches across the desolation of an orchard. If they stir too busily at
a point, our *mitrailleuses* rattle at them, their tracers bright as bees in
a garden even in this dead light. With my knife I have carved the stock
of a German rifle into a woman with her arms as interlocked rounded
triangles over her head, her breasts are triangles, her sex, her thighs.
Like the Africans I am constrained by the volume of my material, the
figure to be found wholly within a section of trunk. De Launay handles the piece with understanding eyes and hands. He is an anthropologist working on labyrinths, and has a major paper prepared for
the *Revue Archéologique*. I am, I tell him, a sculptor, descended from
the masons who built Chartres. We have seen a cathedral burn, its
lead roof melting in on its ruin. De Launay sees a pattern in this hell.
We are the generation to understand the world, the accelerations of
the turn of vortices, how their energy spent itself, all the way back to
the Paleolithic (he tells me about Cartailhac and Teilhard and Breuil).
But our knowledge, which must come from contemplation and careful inspection, has collided with a storm, a vortex of stupidity and id-
iocy. His tracing of the labyrinth from prehistory forward has put him
in a real labyrinth of trenches, its Minotaur the Germans, that

cretinous monster of pedantic dullness. Yet, Henri, he says, we are learning the Paleolithic in a way that was closed to us as *savant* and *sculpteur*. His smile is deliciously ironic in a face freckled with mud spatter, his eyes lively under the brim of his helmet.

MAÇON

How veddy interesting, Miss Mansfield said, sipping tea, when I told her I was descended from the craftsmen who carved Chartres. *I could have died of shame,* Sophie screeched at me as soon as we were outside. These people, she said, will have no respect for you. I am of the Polish gentry, which is hard enough to get them to understand. Very much the *pusinka.*

SMOKING RIVERS OF MUD

We say will we be let to go back in October. There is no ease in royal affairs. We have no comfort. Our sorrow is bitter. But we would not return to our country. What flower has come into blossom. We have time to busy ourselves with art, reading poems, so that intellectually we are not yet dead nor degenerate. Whose chariot, the General's horses, his horses even, are tired. They were strong. We have no rest. Three battles a month. By heaven, his horses are tired. The generals are on them, the soldiers are by them. If you can write me all about the Kensington colony, the neo-greeks and neo-chinese. Does the *Egoist* still appear? What does it contain? My best wishes for a prosperous and happy 1915. Yours Sincerely Henri Gaudierbrzeska.

THE NORTH BORDER. BLUE MOUNTAINS. BARBARIANS.

The horses are well trained. The generals have ivory arrows and quivers ornamented with fishskin. The enemy is swift. We must be careful. When we set out, the willows were drooping with spring. We come back in the snow. We are hungry and thirsty, our mind is full of sorrow. Who will know of our grief? The newspapers say that our trench labyrinths are comfortable, that the British throw grenades with the ease of men accustomed to games of sport from their infancy. Tiger in the bamboo. Thunder from beyond the mountain. How and when we shall survive who knows? Stink of cordite. Rain of ash.

THE IMP

Stands in mischief, knees flexed to scoot.

DAS LABYRINTH

Between Neuville-St.-Vaast to the north and Arras to the south, and Mt. St.-Eloi and Vimy east and west, lay the underground maze of tunnels, mines, fortresses in slant caves, some as deep as fifty feet, which the Germans called The Labyrinth, as insane a nest of armaments and men as military strategy ever conceived. Its approaches were seeded with deathtraps and mine fields. It was invisible to aerial observation. Even its designers had forgotten all the corridors, an *Irrgarten* lit with pale battery-powered lights. Foch himself came to oversee its siege. The British hacked their way toward Lille, the French toward Lens, past The Labyrinth. The offensive began 9 May 1915. Out from Arras, past Ste.-Catherine, 7ᵉ Compagnie, 129ᵉ Infanterie, IIIᵉ Corps, Capitaine Ménager the Commandant, marched on the road to Vimy Ridge, Corporal Henri Gaudier at the head of his squad. Except for mad wildflowers in sudden patches, their tricolor was the only alleviation in the gray desert of craters, burnt farms, a blistered sky.

THE SOLDAT'S REMARK TO GENERAL APPLAUSE

Fuck all starters of wars up the arse with a handspike dipped in tetanus.

BRANCUSI TO GAUDIER

Les hommes nus dans la plastique ne sont pas si beaux que les crapauds.

THE WOLF

Is my brother, the tiger my sister. They think *eat*, they think grass, bamboo, forest, plain, river. Their regal indifference to my drawing them, on my knees outside their cages, is the indifference of the stars. I feel abased, ashamed, worthless in their presence. But I close, a little, the gap between me and them, in catching some of their grace. And afterwards, they will say, *He drew the wolf, the deer, the cat. His sculpture was of stag and birds, of men and women in whom there was animal grace.*

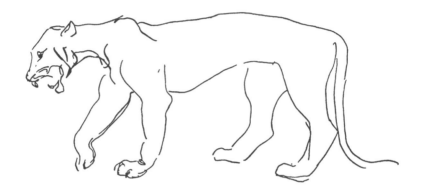

THE CATHEDRAL BURNT IN FRONT OF MY EYES

Rheims. My lieutenant sent me to repair some barbed wire between our trenches and the enemy's. I went through the mist with two fellows. I was on my back under the wire when *zut!* out comes the moon. The *boches* could see me *et alors! pan pan pan!* Their fire cut through the tangle above me, which came down and snared me. I sawed it with my knife in a dozen places. The detail got back to the trench, said I was done for, and with the lieutenant's concurrence they blasted away at the *boches,* who returned the volleys, and then the artillery joined in, with me smack between them. I crawled flat on my stomach back to our trench, and brought the repair coil of barbed wire and my piece with me. The lieutenant could not believe his eyes. When the ruckus quieted down, I went back out, finished the job, and got back at 5 a.m. I have a gash, from the wire, in my right leg, and a bullet nick in my right heel.

LA ROSALIE

The bayonet, so called because we draw it red from the round guts of pig-eyed Germans.

FONT DE GAUME

A hundred and fifty meters of blind cave drilled a million years ago by a river underground into the soft green hills at Les Eyzies de Tayac in the Val Dordogne, in which, some forty thousand years ago, hunters of Magdalenian times painted and engraved the immediate reaches with a grammar of horses and bison, and deeper up the bore, mammoths, reindeer, cougars, human fetuses, human hands, a red rhinoceros, palings of lines recording the recurrence of some event, masks or faces, perhaps of the wind god, the rain god, the god of the wolves, and at the utmost back depth, horse and mountain cat.

NIGHT ATTACK

We crept through a wood as dark as pitch, fixed bayonets, and pushed some 500 yards amid fields until we came to a wood. There we opened fire and in a bound we were along the bank of the road where the Prussians stood. We shot at each other some quarter of an hour at a distance of 12 to 15 yards and the work was deadly. I brought down two great giants who stood against a burning heap of straw.

SOLDAT

I have been fighting for two months and I can now gauge the intensity of life.

DOGFIGHT

Enid Bagnold, horse-necked, square-jawed, nymph-eyed, finally came to sit, after weeks of postponing, Sophie sniffy with jealousy, suspicion, fright. The day was damp and cold. Gaudier lumped the clay on its armature and set to, nimble-fingered, eyes from the Bagnold to the clay. His nose began to bleed. He worked on. The Bagnold

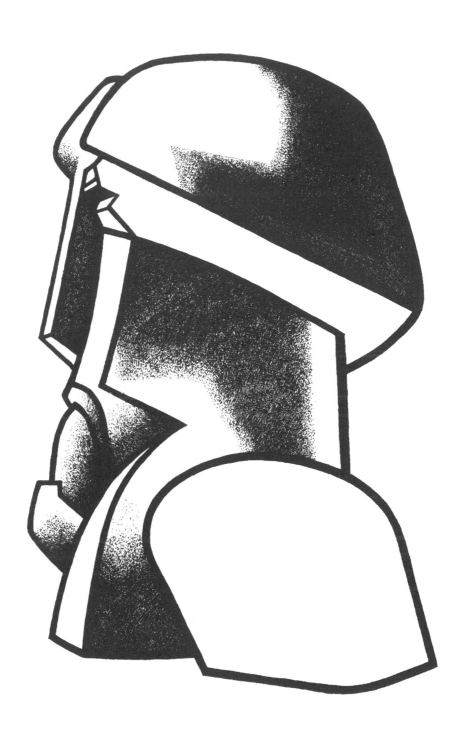

said, Your nose is bleeding. I know, said Gaudier. In that sack on the wall behind you there's something to stop it. She looked in the bag: clothes. Some male and dirty, some female and dirty. Rancid shirts, mildewed stockings. She chose a pair of Sophie's drawers and tied them around Gaudier's face, to soak up, at least, some of the blood, which had reddened his neck and smock. Lower, he said, I can't see. Take your pose again, quickly, quickly. She dared not look at him, wild hair, bright black eyes ajiggle above a ruin of bloody rags. The light was going swiftly, the room dark and cold. He worked on, as if by touch. And then a barrage of roars pierced the air. A dogfight outside. My God, she said. Tilt your chin, he said. Keep your neck tall. She tried the pose, wondering how he could see her in the dark. The dogfight raged the louder. Gaudier went to the window. The streetlamp at that moment came on, and she watched him with the fascination of horror, masked as he was in bloody cloth, staring out at the dogfight. He watched it with dark, interested eyes, his hands white with clay against the dirty window. Monsieur Gaudier! she said, are you quite in command of yourself? You may go, he said.

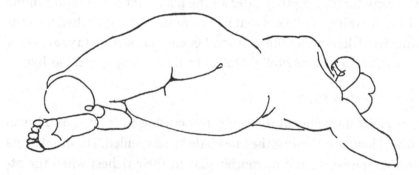

PARTRIDGES

Horses are worn out in three weeks, die by the roadside. Dogs wander, are destroyed, and others come along. With all the destruction that works around us, nothing is changed, even superficially. Life is the same strength, the moving agent that permits the small individual to assert himself. The bursting shells, the volleys, wire entanglements, projectors, motors, the chaos of battle do not alter in the least the outlines of the hill we are besieging. A company of partridges scuttles along before our very trench.

FRITH STREET

Sat on the floor at Hulme's widow's while he talked bolt upright in his North Country farmer's body and stuttered through his admiration and phlegmatic defense of Epstein's flenite pieces, so African as to be more Soninke made than Soninke derived, *feck undity in all its so to speak milky bovinity* (and Marsh clasping his hands, as if in prayer, and giving responses, *teddibly vital isn't it I mean to say* and *the phallic note,* with Ezra cutting his wicked eye at me from his Villon face). Sat with the godlike poet Brooke and the catatonically serious Middleton Murray, and the devout, Tancred, Flint, FitzGerald, and the fair-minded skeptics, Wadsworth and Nevinson. The ale was good and Hulme chose his words with booming precision and attack.

RODIN

Conceive form in depth. Under all the planes there is a center in the stone. All things alive swell out from a center. Observe relief, not outline: relief determines the contour. Let emotion stream to your center as water up a root, as sunlight into a leaf. Love, hope, tremble, live.

PARIS 1910

The chisel does not cut the stone, but crushes it. It bites. You brush away, blow away the dust the fine blade has crumbled. The mind drifts free as you work, and memories play at their richest when the attention is engaged with the stone. There was Paris, there was the decision, there was Zosik. England and Germany have nothing like the Parisian café where of a spring evening you sit outside making a glass of red wine last and last. It was at the Café Cujas that he met another stranger to the city, a poet, a Czech poet—Hlaváček? Svobodová? Bezruč? Dyk?—who, talking of Neruda, of Rimbaud, sorted out

Gaudier's array of ambitions and focused them upon sculpture. Rodin! Phidias! Michelangelo! It was the one art that involved the heroic, the bringing of a talent to its fullest maturity to do anything at all. It was an art that demanded the flawless hand, a sense of perfection in the whole, a pitiless and totally demanding art. But it had not been to the Czech that he had announced his commitment, but to the woman Sophie, not as an intention or experiment but as a road he was upon, boldly striding out. *Moi? Je suis sculpteur.* She, for her part, was a writer, a novelist. She had never shown anyone her work, it was too personal, too vulnerable before an unfeeling and uncomprehending world. Night after night he heard her story, not really listening, as it was her face, her eyes, her spirit that he loved, envying her her maturity— she was thirty-nine, he a green and raw seventeen—and her story was a kind of badly constructed Russian novel. She was a Pole, from near Cracow. Her father threw away a considerable inheritance on gaming and shameless girls. She was the only daughter of nine children, and she was made to feel the disgrace of it, as she was useless as a worker, would have to be provided with a dowry in time. Her brothers called her names, and reproached her with her inferior gender. At sixteen she was put out to work, as her family was tired of supporting her as a burden. They found an old man, a Jew, and offered her to him as a wife. But he, like any other, demanded a dowry with her. This threw Papa Brzesky into a fit. A Jew want a dowry! There were three other attempts to marry her off. Two were likely business for the undertaker. The other was a sensitive young man of broken health whom she loved, the apple of his mother's eye. He came courting and played cards with Mama Brzeska, who one day accused him of cheating and chased him out of the house. Then her father went bankrupt. Sophie made her way to Cracow, hoping to study at the university, but she was neither qualified to enter it nor able to pay the tuition it asked. She came to Paris, took a nursemaid's job, and was driven away by the snide remarks of the other servants, who were ill-bred. She went from menial job to menial job until her health, never robust, gave way. Then she was taken on as a nurse to a rich American family about to return to Philadelphia. She was to look after a ten-year-old boy and his sister. The boy died soon after. The sister begged to hear dirty stories, and when Sophie refused to tell her any, complained to her parents that the nurse bored her to tears. Entertain the child, commanded the parents, so Sophie told her dirty stories, and was promptly fired for moral turpitude and kicked out without a reference. She found refuge in an orphanage in New York run by nuns. They farmed her out as a nanny. Fathers made advances to her, which she could have accepted and gotten rich. But all this time she kept her body pure and virgin. What money she could manage to save she sent to her youngest brother in Poland, enabling him to emigrate to America. He came, was disappointed, worked as a garbage boy for a hotel, accused Sophie of having tricked him, and would not speak to her ever afterward. A nursing job came along that took her to Paris again. Here she was destitute, and returned to Poland, where she was taken in by a rich uncle. This uncle was a widower and lived in sin with her cousin, whom he had enticed into his bed by telling her that Sophie had often done so. The shock of this lie unstrung her nerves and made a wreck of her composure for the rest of her life. Her brothers taunted her with having gone to America and failed to come back rich. She took up a life of dissipation. If no one believed in her virtue, why keep it? But dissipation undermined her constitution, and she had to recuperate at Baden, little as she could afford it. She then fell in love with a wealthy manufacturer aged fifty-three. He was witty, bright, kind, and in possession of a keen appreciation of the beauties of Nature. He courted her for a year without asking for her hand. When she tried to bring matters to a head, they had a fight that nearly sent them both to the hospital and thence to their graves. In this fracas he disclosed to her that he loved another, by whom he already had a son, and wished to remain free in case the other ever agreed to be his wife. She felt that her sanity was going. Her rich lover paid for her recuperation at a home in the country. She wrote him daily; he answered none of her letters. She would contemplate for hours the most painless means of doing away with herself. She returned to her family in Poland, where they taunted her with her

failure, her age, her pretensions, her ugliness. She made her way to Paris again, and began to observe with fascination the faun-like young man who came every evening to the Bibliothèque Ste.-Geneviève to read books of anatomy. They met on the steps one evening at closing time, and walked along the Seine. She could scarcely believe it when he said he was in love with her.

THE BRITISH MUSEUM

Out of the past, out of Assyria, China, Egypt, the new.

EPSTEIN, BRANCUSI, MODIGLIANI, ZADKINE

Out of the new, a past.

VORTEX

From Rodin, passion. From John Cournos, courage. From Alfred Wolmark, spontaneity of execution. From Epstein, the stone, direct cutting. From Brancusi, purity of form. From Modigliani, the irony of grace. From Africa, the compression of form into minimal volume. From Lewis, the geometric. From Horace Brodsky, *camaraderie de la caserne*. From Ezra Pound, archaic China, the medieval, Dante, recognition. From Sophie, love, abrasion, doubt, the sweetness of an hour.

THE BRONZES OF BENIN

The Calf Bearer, T'ang sacrificial vessels, the shields of New South Wales, Soninke masks, the Egypt of *The Scribe* and *The Pharaoh Hunting Duck in the Papyrus Marsh*, Hokusai, Font de Gaume, Les Combarelles.

JE REVIENS D'UN ENFER

The young anthropologist Robert de Launay, the student of mazes whose paper on labyrinths has been accepted for publication, has been shot through the neck outside the Labyrinth at Neuville-St.-Vaast, drowned in his own blood before the medics could see to the wound. *Je t'écris, cher Ezra, du fond d'une tranchée que nous avons*

*creusée hier pour se protéger des obus qui nous arrivent sur la tête reg-
ulièrement toutes les cinq minutes, je suis ici depuis une semaine et
nous couchons en plein air, les nuits sont humides et froides et nous en
souffrons beaucoup plus que du feu de l'ennemi nous avons de repos
aujourd'hui et ça fait bien plaisir.*

ST.-JEAN DE BRAYE

In the dry, brown October of 1891 there was born to Joseph Gaudier
of St.-Jean de Braye, maker of fine doors and cabinets, descendant of
one of the sculptors of Chartres, a son whom he baptized Henri.

CHARLEVILLE

Far to the south the one-legged Rimbaud lay dying in Marseilles,
which he imagined to be Abyssinia. He was anxious that his caravan
of camels laden with rifles and ammo should get off to a start before
dawn, for the march was to Aden. *Armed with the fierceness of our patience,* he once wrote, *we shall reach the spendid cities at daybreak.*

TARGU JIU

In Craiova the fourteen-year-old Constantin Brancusi was learning to
carve wood with chisel and maul. He was a peasant from Pestisani
Gori across a larch forest from Targu Jiu, which he left when he was
eleven, in the manner of the Rumanians, to master a trade. He would
enter the national school for sculptors, and then walk from Rumania
to Paris.

L'ENFANT DIFFICILE

He did not spank well, the child Henri. He doubled his fists, held his
breath, and arched his back in an agony of stubbornness, until at an
early age his parents began to reason with him before whacking his
behind. He reasoned back. As he grew older, he kicked them when he
was punished, and they reasoned the harder. *A very philosopher,* his
father said, and his mother put her head to one side, crossed her hands
over her apron, and looked at her son with complacent disappoint-

ment. *The rogue,* she said, *the darling little rogue.* He drew, like all children. His mother taught him to draw rabbits, and to surround them with grass and flowers. With his father's marking pencil, carefully sharpened for him with a penknife, he drew ships, igloos, medieval trees, the cathedral at Orléans, and American Indians in their eagle-feather bonnets. At six he turned to insects. At first he drew gay fritillaries and gaudy moths. Only flowers had their absolute design and economy of form, which he thought of as *sitting right.* A roseleaf hopper was tucked into its abrupt parabola as if it were a creature all hat, and yet if you looked it had feet and eyes and chest and belly just like the great dragonflies and damsels of the Loiret, or the mason wasps that built their combs under the eaves of the shed. But it was the grasshoppers and crickets that he drew most. From the forelegs of the grasshopper he learned the stark clarity of a bold design one half of which was mirror image of the other half. The wings of moths were like that, but the principle was different. Wings worked together, the grasshopper's forelegs worked in opposition to the hindlegs, and yet the effort of the one complemented the effort of the other, like two beings jumping into each other, both going straight up. Earwigs, ants: nothing could be added, nothing subtracted. Who could draw a mos-

quito? In profile it was an elegance of lines, each at a perfect angle to the others. *Bugs*, his sisters said. Uncle Pierre gave him a box of colored pencils, and he drew pages of ladybirds and shieldbugs and speckled moths.

ARTILLERY BARRAGE. THE LABYRINTH. JUNE 1915.

Smoke boiling black, white underbelly, blooming sulphur, falling dirt and splinters. The daytime moon. Larks.

HENRI LE PETIT

The first day of school, his new oilcloth satchel in his lap, his new pencil box in his hands, he breathed the strange new smell of floor polish and washed slate blackboards in numb expectation. The upper half of the classroom door was glass, through which a bald gentleman in a celluloid collar came and peered from time to time. The teacher was a woman who handled books as he had never seen them handled before, with professional delicacy, grace, smart deliberateness. Down the front of her polka-dot dress she wore a necktie, like a man on Sunday, and a purple ribbon ran from her glasses to her bosom, anchored there by a brooch. The letter A was a moth, B was a butterfly, C was a caterpillar, D was a beetle, E an ant, F a mantis. G and H he knew: he had learned them the other way round, with a dot after each, to indicate who drew his drawings.

RAILWAY ARCH 25

His Font de Gaume. Planes, the surfaces of mass, meet at lines, each tilted at a different angle to light. The mass is energy. The harmony of its surfaces the emotion forever contained and forever released. Here he drank and roared with Brodsky, here he sculpted the phallus, the menhir, the totem called *Hieratic Bust of Ezra Pound. It will not look like you, you know*. It will look like your energy.

SOPHIE

All night by her bed, imploring her. It is revolting, unspiritual, she said.

PIK AND ZOSIK

Brother and sister. Even Mr. Pound believed it. Pikus and Zosiulik. The neurotic Pole and her sly fawn of a lover.

MON BON DZIECKO UKOCHANY

According to the little book which I am reading about Dante, the devil lived on very good terms with very few people, because of his terrible tendency to invective and reproach, and his extraordinary gift for irony and irresistible sarcasm—just like my own funny little Sisik. To be quite honest, Sisik, I love you passionately, from the depth of all my being, and I feel instinctively bound to you; what may often make me seem nasty to you is a kind of disagreeable horror that you don't love me nearly so much as I love you, and that you are always on the point of leaving me.

CAPITAINE MÉNAGER

Nous admirions tous Gaudier, non seulement pour sa bravoure, qui était légendaire, mais aussi et surtout pour sa vive intelligence et la haute idée qu'il avait de ses devoirs. A ma compagnie il était aimé de tous, et je le tenais en particulière estime car à cette époque de guerre de tranchées j'étais certain que—grâce à l'exemple qu'il donnerait à ses camarades—là où était Gaudier les Boches ne passeraient pas.

THE OLD WOMAN TO PASSERSBY

J'ai perdu mon fils. L'avez-vous trouvé? Il s'appelle Henri.

CHARGEZ !

One after another in those weeks of May and early June of 1915, the sugar refinery at Souchez, the cemetery of Ablain, the White Road, and the Labyrinth yielded to the fierce, unremitting blows of the French. The Labyrinth, all but impregnable, was a fortification contrived with tortuous, complicated tunnels, sometimes as deep as fifty feet below the surface, with mines and fortresses, deathtraps, caves and shelters, from which unexpected foes could attack with liquid fire or gas or knives. In the darkness and dampness and foulness of those Stygian vaults where in some places the only guiding gleams were from electric flashlights, men battled for days, for weeks, until June was half spent. What wonder that the Germans could scarcely believe the enemy had made it their own?

CORPORAL HENRI GAUDIER

Mort pour la Patrie. 4 Octobre 1891—5 Juin 1915.

THE RED STONE DANCER

Nos fesses ne sont pas les leurs. Il faut être absolument moderne.

The Chair

The Rebbe from Belz is taking his evening walk at Marienbad. Behind him, at a respectful distance, walks a courtier carrying a chair by its hind legs. This is for the Rebbe to sit on, should he want to sit.

The square seat of this upraised chair, its oval back upholstered with a sturdy cloth embroidered in a rich design of flowers and leaves, its carved, chastely bowed legs, and the tasteful scrollwork of its walnut frame, give it a French air. Like all furniture out of context it seems distressed in its displacement. It belongs in the company of capacious Russian teacups and deep saucers, string quartets by Schumann, polite conversations, and books with gilt leather bindings.

One of the Rebbe's disciples, a lanky young man with long sidelocks beautifully curled and oiled, hastens from the Hotel National. He has a bottle cradled in his arms. He is taking it to a mineral spring to have it filled. The Rebbe wants soda water. He hums as he walks, this disciple, the lively tune *Uforatzto*, a happy march that expresses his joy in being sent for a bottle of soda water for the Rebbe.

The Rebbe's carriage with its tasseled red velvet window curtains comes for him at half past seven every evening, when the shadows have gone blue. He drives to the forest. His court walks behind. One of them carries his silver cane, another an open umbrella, out to his side. It is not for him, but for the Rebbe, should it rain. Another carries a shawl folded on a cushion, in case the Rebbe feels a chill. And one carries the wellbred chair.

It is, by the common reckoning, the year 1916. The armies of the gentiles are slaughtering each other all over the world.

Somewhere along the leafy road the Rebbe will stop the carriage and get out. His court will assemble behind him. He is going to observe, and meditate upon, the beauty of nature, which, created by the Master of the Universe and Lord of All, is full of instruction.

On this particular July evening a fellow guest at the Hotel National has asked and been given permission to walk in the Rebbe's following. He is a young lawyer in the insurance business in Prague, Herr Doktor Franz Kafka. Like all the rest, he must keep his distance, and always be behind the Rebbe. Should the Rebbe suddenly turn and face them, they must quickly run around so as to be behind him. And back around again should he turn again.

The Rebbe, a man of great learning, is neither short nor tall, neither fat nor thin. Wide in the hips, he yet moves with a liquid grace, like a seal in water. He will overflow the slender chair if with a vague ripple of fingers he commands it to be placed so that he can sit on it. Then his followers will range themselves behind him, the secretary leaning a little to catch his every word, the shawl bearer at the ready, should the Rebbe raise his hands toward his shoulders. The secretary takes down what he says in a ledger. These remarks will be studied, later. They will question him about them. The Rebbe means great things by remarks which seem at first to be casual. He asks questions which are traps for their ignorance. The entourage does not always read his gestures correctly. If he has to put into words what he means by an open hand, or raised eyes, or an abrupt halt, he will add a reprimand. *Hasidim is it you call yourselves?* he will say. *Or is it oafs maybe? For brains I'm thinking it's noodles you have.*

If he asks for the soda water, they've had it. The one chosen to fetch it had gone to the Rudolph Spring. It was the opinion of everyone he asked that it was further along this road, that road, another road. And it never was. He'd passed it, or it was another three minutes just around to the left. Around to the right. The Rudolph Spring, the Rudolph Spring, could that be its name? Some answers as to its whereabouts were in foreign languages and a waste of time. Some, sad to say, paid no attention at all to the frantic disciple of the Rebbe from Belz, hard to believe, but true. Moreover, it began to rain. Finally, a man told the disciple that all the mineral springs close at seven. How could a spring be closed? he asked, running off in the direction pointed out. The Rudolph Spring was indeed closed, as he could see long before he got there. The green latticed doors were shut, and a sign reading CLOSED hung on them. *Oi veh!* He rattled the doors, and knocked, and shouted that the Rebbe from Belz had sent him for soda water. All they had to do was fill his bottle and take his money, the work of a moment. All of life, it occurred to him, is one disappointment after another, and he was about to weep when a stroller suggested that he make haste and run to the Ambrosius Spring, which closed a little later than the others. This he did. The Ambrosius was open, by the mercy of God. There were women inside washing glasses. But when he asked them to fill his bottle, the women said that they were through with their work for the day. They should stay open for everybody who can't remember the long hours they were there filling bottles yet? Is the Rebbe from Belz different already? He should learn better how business is conducted in Marienbad.

Who will write the history of despair?

Dr Kafka waits at the steps of the Hotel National for the Rebbe and his following. In Prague Dr Kafka was famous among his friends for the oxlike patience with which he waited. Once, waiting in the street outside a small Parisian theatre Dr Kafka and a donkey had made friends. He was waiting to buy a ticket to *Carmen*, the donkey was waiting to go on in Act II. They both had big ears, Dr Kafka and the donkey. They were both patient by nature, both shy. Waiting is an act of great purity. Something is being accomplished, in a regular and steady way, by doing nothing at all.

First the Rebbe arrived, and then the carriage. So the Rebbe had to wait a little, too. He had a long beard, beautifully white, and very long sidelocks. These are symbols of sound doctrine and piety. The longer your locks, it is said, the greater the respect you get from the Rebbe.

All boys with long sidelocks he called handsome and smart. One of his eyes, blind, was as blank as if it had been of glass. One side of his mouth was paralyzed, so that at his most solemn he seemed to be smiling ironically, with a witty and forgiving understanding of the world. His silk kaftan was worn open, held in place by a broad oriental belt. His hat was tall, and of fur. His stockings and knee britches were white, like his beard.

The Rebbe, walking at a plump pace, savors nature in the woods. So Chinese dukes must walk of an evening, stopping to smell a hibiscus, casually reciting a couplet that sounds like notes on a zither, about another hibiscus centuries before, a hibiscus in a classical poem which had made the poet think of a noble woman, a jade owl, and a warrior's ghost on the frontiers maintained against the barbarian hordes.

One of the Rebbe's legs is gimp, perhaps only sore from sitting all day at the Torah. When he gets down from his carriage he has a good cough. Then he sets out, looking. When he stops, the entourage stops, and Dr Kafka behind them. If he turns, they swing with him, like a school of fish behind their pilot. He points out things, such as details of buildings in the woods, which they all strain to see. Is that a tile roof? he asks. They consult. Yes, one says, we think you are right, O Rebbe. It is a tile roof. Where does that path go? No one knows. What kind of tree is that? One thinks that it is a pine, another a fir, another a spruce.

They come to the Zander Institute high on a stone embankment and with a garden in front of it, and an iron fence around it. The Rebbe is interested in the Institute, and in its garden. What kind of garden, he asks, is it? One of the entourage, whose name Dr Kafka catches as Schlesinger, runs up to the fence, elbows out, head thrown back. He really does not look at the garden, but turns as soon as he has reached its gate, and runs down again, knees high, feet plopping. It is, he says breathlessly, the garden of the Zander Institute. Just so, says the Rebbe. Is it a private garden? They consult in whispers. Yes, says their spokesman, it is a private garden. The Rebbe stares at the garden, rocking on his heels. It is, he says, an attractive garden, and the secretary takes this remark down in his ledger.

Their walk brings them to the New Bath House. The Rebbe has someone read the name of it. He strolls behind it, and finds a ditch into which the water from the bathhouse drains. He traces the pipes with his silver cane. The water must come from there, he says, pointing high, and run down to here, and then into here. They all follow his gestures, nodding. They try to make sense of pipes which connect with other pipes. The New Bath House is in a modern style of architecture, and obviously looks strange to the Rebbe. He notices that the ground floor has its windows in the arches of an arcade. At the top of each arch is an animal's head in painted porcelain. What, he asks, is the meaning of that? No one knows. It is, one ventures, a custom. Why? asks the Rebbe. It is the opinion that the animal heads are a whim of the designer, and have no meaning. Mere ornament. This makes the Rebbe say, *Ah!* He walks from window to window along the arcade, giving each his full attention. He comes around to the front of the building. Looking up at the golden lettering in an Art Nouveau alphabet, he reads again *New Bath House*. Why, he asks, is it so named? Because, someone says, it is a new bathhouse. The Rebbe pays no attention to this remark. It is, he says instead, a handsome, a fine, an admirable building. Good lines it has, and well-pondered proportions. The secretary writes this down. Look! he cries. When the rain falls on the roof, it flows into the gutter along the edge there, do you see, and then into the pipes that come down the corners of the building, and then into this stone gutter all around, from which it goes to the same ditch in back where all the pipes are from the baths. They walk around the building, discovering the complete system of the drainpipes. The Rebbe is delighted, he rubs his hands together. He makes one of the entourage repeat the plan of the pipes, as if he were examining him. He gets it right, with some correction along the way, and the Rebbe gives him a kind of blessing with his hands. Wonderful! he says. These pipes are wonderful.

Who will write the history of affection?

They come to an apple orchard, which the Rebbe admires, and to a pear orchard, which he also admires. O the goodness of the Master of the Universe, he says, to have created apples and pears.

The chair held aloft by its bearer, Dr Kafka notices, has now defined what art is as distinct from nature, for its pattern of flowers and leaves looks tawdry and artificial and seriously out of place against the green and rustling leaves of apple and pear trees. He is tempted to put this into words, as a casual remark which one of the entourage just might pass on to the Rebbe, but he reconsiders how whimsical and perhaps mad it would sound. Besides, no word must be spoken except at the command of the Rebbe.

Instead, he prays. Have mercy on me, O God. I am sinful in every corner of my being. The gifts thou has given me are not contemptible. My talent is a small one, and even that I have wasted. It is precisely when a work is about to mature, to fulfill its promise, that we mortals realize that we have thrown our time away, have squandered our energies. It is absurd, I know, for one insignificant creature to cry that it is alive, and does not want to be hurled into the dark along with the lost. It is the life in me that speaks, not me, though I speak with it, selfishly, in its ridiculous longing to stay alive, and partake of its presumptuous joy in being.

Fifty-Seven Views
of Fujiyama

Months, days, eternity's sojourners. Years that unfold from the cherry in flower to rice thick in the flat fields to the gingko suddenly gold the first day of frost to the red fox across the snow. The sampan pilot from Shiogama to Ishinomaki, the postman galloping from Kyoto to Ogaki, what do they travel but time? Our great journey is through the years, even when we doze by the brazier. Clouds move on the winds. We long to travel with them. For I, Bashō, am a traveler. No sooner, last autumn, did I get home from a fine journey along the coast, take the broom to the cobwebs in my neglected house on the Sumida River, see the New Year in, watch the wolves slinking down from the hills shoulder-deep in white drifts, look in wonder all over again, as every spring, at the mist on the marshes, than I was ready to set out through the gates at Shirakawa. I stitched up the slits and rips in my trousers, hitched a new chinstrap to my hat, rubbed my legs with burnt wormwood leaves (which puts vigor into the muscles), and thought all the while of the moon rising full over Matsushima, what a sight that would be when I got there and could gaze on it.

• • •

We set out, she and I, a fine late summer day, happy in the heft and chink of our gear. We had provender for a fortnight in the wilderness along the Vermont Trail, which we took up on a path through an orchard abandoned years ago, where in generous morning light busy with cabbage butterflies and the green blink of grasshoppers an old

165

pear tree still as frisky and crisp as a girl stood with authority among dark unpruned winesaps gone wild, and prodigal sprawling zinnias, sweetpeas, and hollyhocks that had once been some honest farmwife's flowers and garden grown from seeds that came in Shaker packets from upstate New York or even Ohio, now blooming tall and profuse in sedge and thistle all the way to the tamaracks of the forest edge, all in that elective concert by which the lion's fellowship makes the mimosa spread. This trail was blazed back in the century's teens by a knickerbockered and tweed-capped comitatus from Yale, carrying on a tradition from Raphael Pumpelly and Percy Wallace and Steele MacKaye, from Thoreau and Burroughs: a journey with no purpose but to be in the wilderness, to be in its silence, to be together deep among its trees and valleys and heights.

• • •

Having, with great luck, sold my house by the river, thereby casting myself adrift, so to speak, from obligations and responsibilities, I moved in for a while with my friend and patron, the merchant Sampu, himself a poet. *Bright flash makes me blink: spring field, farmer's spade.* But before I went I brushed a poem for my old doorpost. *Others now will sing high in peach blossom time behind this door wild grass blocks.* And at dawn I set out, more of night still in the sky than day, as much by moonlight fading as by sunlight arriving, the twenty-seventh of March. I could just make out the dim outline of Fuji and the thin white cherry blossoms of Ueno and Yanaka. Farewell, Fuji! Farewell, cherry blossoms! Friends had got up early to see me off, indeed to go with me for the first leg of the journey by boat, as far as Senju. It was not until they left me that I felt, with a jump of my heart, the three hundred miles I was proposing to go. Water stood in my eyes. I looked at my friends and the neat clusters of houses at Senju as if through rain. *Fish and bird regret that springtime is so brief.* This was my parting poem. My friends took copies, and watched till I was out of sight.

• • •

On the beach at Sounion. Tar and seaweed shift in the spent collapse and slide of shirred green water just beyond our toes. We had been to see Byron's name carved with a penknife on a column of Poseidon's temple. Homer mentions this cape in the *Iliad*, perhaps all of Attika that he knew. It was here that the redstone *kouros* was excavated who stands in Athens by the javelin-hurling Zeus. We lie in Greek light. The silence is musical: the restlessness of the Ionian, the click of pebbles pushed by the seawash. There is no other sound. *I am Hermes. I stand by the gray sea-shingle and wait in the windy wood where three roads meet.* A poem? From the *Anthology*. Wet eyelashes, lens of water in navel. Another. *To Priapos, god of gardens and friend to travelers, Damon the farmer laid on this altar, with a prayer that his trees and body be hale of limb for yet a while, a pomegranate glossy bright, a skippet of figs dried in the sun, a cluster of grapes, half red, half green, a mellow quince, a walnut splitting from its husk, a cucumber wrapped in flowers and leaves, and a jar of olives golden ripe.*

• • •

All that March day I walked with a wondering sadness. I would see the north, but would I, at my age, ever return? My hair would grow whiter on the long journey. It was already Genroku, the second year thereof, and I would turn forty-five on the way. My shoulders were sore with my pack when I came to Soka, a village, at the end of the day. Travel light! I have always intended to, and my pack with its paper overcoat, cotton bathrobe (neither of which was much in a heavy rain), my notebook, inkblock, and brushes, would have been light enough except for gifts my friends loaded me with at parting, and my own unessential one thing and another which I cannot throw away because my heart is silly. We went, Sora and I, to see the sacred place of Muro-no-Yashima, Ko-no-Hana Sakuya Hime, the goddess of flowering trees. There is another shrine to her on the lower slopes of Fuji. When she was with child, Ninigi-no-Mikoto, her husband, would not believe that she was pregnant by a god. She locked herself into a room, set fire to it, and in the flames gave birth to Hohodemi-no-Mikoto, the fire-born noble. Here poets write of the smoke, and the peasants do not eat a speckled fish called *konoshiro*.

• • •

We set out, she and I, like Bashō on the narrow road to the deep north from his house on the Sumida where he could not stay for thinking of the road, of the red gate at Shirakawa, of the full moon over the islands of Matsushima, he and Kawai Sogoro in their paper coats, journey proud in *wabi zumai,* thinking of wasps in the cedar close of an inn, chrysanthemums touched by the first mountain frost. A few years before Minoru Hara and I had climbed Chocorua to find a single lady slipper on a carpet of pine needles, to which he bowed, Chocorua that Ezra Pound remembered in the concentration camp at Pisa, fusing it with Tai Shan in his imagination, Chocorua where Jessie Whitehead lived with her pet porcupines and bear, Chocorua where William James died, Thoreau's Chocorua that he strolled up laughing that people used the word *climb* of its easy slopes. We set out into the deuteronomical mountains Charles Ives rings against *The Rock-strewn Hills Join in the People's Outdoor Meeting* with the chime of iron on iron, sabre, bell, and hammer, bugle and messkit, ramrod and spur, remembering how congenial and incantatory music led the caissons over the Potomac to Shiloh.

· · ·

I spent the night of March thirtieth at Gozaemon the Honest's Inn at Nikko Mountain. Such was my landlord's name, which he made much of, assuring me that I would sleep out of harm's way on his grass pillows. When a stranger so advertises his honesty, you take more care than ever, but this innkeeper was as good as his name. There was no more guile in him than in Buddha the merciful, and Confucius would have approved of his scrupulousness and manners. Next day, April first, we climbed Nikko, Mountain of the Sun's Brilliance. The sainted Kobo Daishi named it and built the temple on it a thousand years ago. Its holiness is beyond words. You can see its benevolence in every field round about. In it I wrote: *New leaves, with what holy wonder do I watch the sunlight on your green.* Through the mist we could just make out Mount Kurokami from the temple on Nikko. The snow on its slopes belies its name, Black-Haired Mountain. Sora wrote: *I arrived at Kurokami with my hair shorn, in new clean summer clothes.*

Sora, whose name is Kawai Sogoro, used to chop wood and draw water for me. We were neighbors. I aroused his curiosity and made him a student of scenery. He too wanted to travel to see Matsushima in its beauty, and serene Kisagata.

• • •

Crickets creaking trills so loud we had to raise our voices, even on the beach down from the cycladic wall under the yellow spongy dry scrub with spiky stars of flowers. It is, he said, as if the light were noisy, all of it Herakleitos's little fine particles cheeping away, madly counting each other. *Thotheka! entheka! thekaksi! ikosieksi! khilioi! Ena thio tris tessera!* Hair of the family of hay, torso of the family of dog, testicles of the family of Ionian pebbles, glans of the family of plum. Give us another poem, here by the fountain-pen-blue-ink sea. *To Apollo of the Lykoreans Evnomos of Lokris gives this cricket of bronze. Know that, matched against Parthis in the finals for the harp, his strings rang keen under the pick until one of them snapped. But the prancing melody missed never a beat: a cricket sprang onto the harp and sounded the missing note in a perfection of harmony. For this sweet miracle, O godly son of Leto, Evnomos places this little singer on your altar.* From the *Anthology*. So it's Apollo and not Herakleitos running these nattering hoppergrasses and their katydid aunts and crickcrack uncles? And salty-kneed old Poseidon singing along from the sea.

• • •

So Sora, to be worthy of the beauty of the world, shaved his head the day we departed, and donned a wandering priest's black robe, and took yet a third name, Sogo, which means Enlightened, for the road. When he wrote his haiku for Mount Kurokami, he was not merely describing his visit but dedicating himself to the sacredness of perception. We climbed higher above the shrine. We found the waterfall. It is a hundred feet high, splashing into a pool of darkest green. Uramino-Taki is its name, See from Inside, for you can climb among the rocks and get in behind it. I wrote: *From a silent cave I saw the waterfall, summer's first grand sight for me.* I had a friend at Kurobane in Nasu County. To get there you cross a wide grassy moor for many's the mile, following a path. We kept our eyes on a village in the distance as a landmark, but night came on and rain began to pelt down before we could get there. We spent the night at a farmer's hut along the way. Next day we saw a farmer with a horse, which we asked the loan of. The paths over the moor, he said, are like a great net. You will soon get lost at the crossroads. But the horse will know the way. Let him decide which path to take.

• • •

These were the hills whose elegiac autumns Ives summons with bronze Brahms as a ground for Lee standing in his stirrups as he crossed the Mason and Dixon Line while a band of Moravian cornets alto, tenor, and baritone, an E-flat helicon bass horn, drums battle and snare, strutted out the cakewalk dash of *Dixie*. The rebels danced in rank and gave a loud *huzzah!* These are the everlasting hills that stand from dawn time to red men to French hunter to Calvinist boot to rumors from farm to village that the bands played waltzes and polkas under the guns at Gettysburg when the cannonade was at its fiercest. We trod these hills because we loved them and because we loved each other, and because in them we might feel that consonance of hazard and intent which was the way Ives heard and Cézanne saw, the *moiré* of sound in the studio at West Redding where a Yale baseball cap sat on a bust of Wagner, the *moiré* of light in the quarries and pines at Bibémus. What tone of things might we not involve ourselves in the gathering of in these hills? With each step we left one world and walked into another.

• • •

I mounted the farmer's horse. Sora walked beside us. Two little children ran behind us. One was a girl named Kasane. Sora was delighted with her name, which means *many petalled*. He wrote: *Your name fits you, O Kasane, and fits the double carnation in its richness of petals!* When we reached the village, we sent the horse back by itself, with a tip knotted into the saddle sash. My friend the samurai Joboji Takakatsu, the steward of a lord, was surprised to see me, and we renewed our friendship and we could not have enough of each other's talk. Our happy conversations saw the sun across the country sky and wore the lantern dim way past moonrise. We walked in the outskirts of the town, saw an old academy for dog hunters—that cruel and unseemly sport was of short duration in ancient times—and paid our respects to the tomb of the lady Tamamo, a fox who took human shape. It was on this grave that the samurai archer Yoichi prayed before he shot a fan, at a great distance, from the mast of a drifting boat. Her grave is far out on the moor of grass, and is as lonely a place as you can imagine. The wind traveling through the grass! The silence! It was dark when we returned.

• • •

Leaves not opposite on a stem arrange themselves in two, five, eight, or thirteen rows. If the leaves in order of height up the stem be connected by a thread wound round the stem, then between any two successive leaves in a row the thread winds round the stem once if the leaves are in two or three rows, twice if in five rows, thrice if in eight, five if in thirteen. That is, two successive leaves on the stem will be at such a distance that if there are two rows, the second leaf will be halfway round the stem, if three rows, the second leaf will be one-third of the way around, if five, the second will be two-fifths of the way around; if eight, three-eighths; if thirteen, five-thirteenths. These are Fibonacci progressions in phyllotaxic arrangement. The organic law of vegetable growth is the surd towards which the series one-half, one-third, two-fifths, three-eighths, and so on, approximates. Professor T. C. Hilgard sought for the germ of phyllotaxis in the numerical genesis of cells, the computation of which demonstrates Fibonacci progressions in time.

• • •

The tomb of En-no-Gyoja, founder of the Shugen sect, who nine hundred years ago used to preach everywhere in humble clogs, is in Komyoji Temple. My friend Joboji took me to visit it. In full summer, in the mountains, I bowed before the clog-shod saint's tall image to be blessed in my travels. Unganji the Zen temple is nearby. Here the hermit Buccho, my old Zen master at Edo, lived out his life in solitude. I remember that he once wrote a poem in pine charcoal on a rock in front of his hut. *I would leave this little place, with its five foot of grass this way, five foot of grass that way, except that it keeps me dry when it rains.* We were joined by some young worshipers on the way. Their bright chatter made the climb seem no time at all. The temple is in a wood of cedars and pine, and the way there is narrow, mossy, and wet. There is a gate and a bridge. Though it was April, the air was very cold. Buccho's hut is behind the temple, a small box of a house under a big rock. I sensed the holiness of the place. I might have been at Yuan-miao's cave or Fa-yun's cliff. I made up this poem and left it there on a post: *Even the woodpeckers have not dared touch this little house.*

· · ·

The first thing to go when you walk into the wilderness is time. You eat when you are hungry, rest when you are tired. You fill a moment to its brim. At a ford shoaling over rocks we doffed our packs, took off our boots and jeans, and waded in our shirttails for the childishness of it. Creek-washed feet, she said, as God intended. We dried in the sun on a boulder as warm as a dying stove, and fribbled and monkeyed with each other, priming for later. Jim Dandy! she said, and purred, but we geared up and pushed on, through Winslow Homer glades and dapple and tones that rose as if horn-heralded across sunny fields and greendark woods and tonalities now lost except for the stubborn masks of their autochthony, Ives imitating a trumpet on the piano for Nikolai Slonimsky and hearing at Waterbury gavottes his father had played during the artillery barrage at Chancellorsville, Apollinaire hanging a N'tomo mask of the Bambara on his wall beside Picassos and Laurencins, Gaudier drawing Siberian wolves in the London Zoo, tonalities with lost coordinates, for essences survive by chance allegiances and griefs: the harness chains on the caissons moving toward Seven Pines, dissonance and valence.

· · ·

We ended our visit at Kurobane. I had asked of my host that he show me the way to Sessho-seki, the famous killing stone which slew birds and bugs that lit on it. He lent me a horse and guide. The guide shyly asked me, once we were out on the road, to compose a poem for him, and so delighted was I with the surprise of his request, that I wrote: *Let us leave the road and go across the moors, the better to hear that cuckoo.* The killing stone was no mystery. It is beside a hot spring that gives off a deadly gas. Around it the ground was covered with dead butterflies and bees. Then I found the very willow about which Saigyo wrote in his *Shin Kokin Shu*: *In the shade of this willow lying kindly on the grass and on the stream as clear as glass, we rest awhile on the way to the far north.* The willow is near the village Ashino, where I had been told I would find it, and we too, like Saigyo, rested in its shade. *Only when the girls nearby had finished planting rice in a square of their paddy did I leave the famous willow's shade.* Then, after many days of walking without seeing a soul, we reached the Shirakawa boundary gate, the true beginning of the road north. I felt a peace come over me, felt anxiety drop away. I remembered the sweet excitement of travelers before me.

• • •

All of that again, he said, I long to see all of that again, the villages of the Pyrenees, Pau, the roads. O Lord, to smell French coffee again all mixed in with the smell of the earth, brandy, hay. Some of it will have changed, not all. The French peasant goes on forever. I asked if indeed there was any chance, any likelihood, that he could go. His smile was a resigned irony. Who knows, he said, that Saint Anthony didn't take the streetcar into Alexandria? There hasn't been a desert father in centuries and centuries, and there's considerable confusion as to the rules of the game. He indicated a field to our left, beyond the wood of white oak and sweet gum where we were walking, a field of wheat stubble. That's where I asked Joan Baez to take off her shoes and stockings so that I could see a woman's feet again. She was so lovely against the spring wheat. Back in the hermitage we ate goat's cheese and salted peanuts, and sipped whiskey from jelly glasses. On his table lay letters from Nicanor Parrá and Marguerite Yourcenar. He held the whiskey bottle up to the cold bright Kentucky sunlight blazing through the window. And then out to the privy, where he kicked the door with his hobnail boot, to shoo off the black snake who was usually inside. *Out! Out! You old son of a bitch! You can come back later.*

• • •

The great gate at Shirakawa, where the North begins, is one of the three largest checkpoints in all the kingdom. All poets who have passed through it have made a poem of the event. I approached it along a road overhung with dark trees. It was already autumn here, and winds troubled the branches above me. The unohana were still in bloom beside the road, and their profuse white blossoms met those of the blackberry brambles in the ditch. You would think an early snow had speckled all the underwood. Kiyosuke tells us in the *Fukuro Zoshi* that in ancient times no one went through this gate except in his finest clothes. Because of this Sora wrote: *A garland of white unohana flowers around my head, I passed through Shirakawa Gate, the only finery I could command.* We crossed the Abukuma River and walked north with the Aizu cliffs on our right, and villages on our left, Iwaki, Soma, Miharu. Over the mountains beyond them, we knew, were the counties Hitachi and Shimotsuke. We found the Shadow Pond, where all shadows cast on it are exact of outline. The day was overcast, however, and we saw only the gray sky mirrored in it. At Sukagawa I visited the poet Tokyu, who holds a government post there.

• • •

Dissonance chiming with order, strict physical law in its dance with hazard, valences as weightless as light bonding an *aperitif à la gentiane* Suze, a newspaper, carafe, ace of clubs, stummel. And in a shatter and jig of scialytic prismfall quiet women, Hortense Cézanne among her geraniums, Gertrude Stein resting her elbows on her knees like a washerwoman, Madame Ginoux, of Arles, reader of novels, sitting in a black dress against a yellow wall, a portrait painted by Vincent in three quarters of an hour, quiet women at the centers of houses, and by the pipe, carafe, and newspaper on the tabletop men with a new inwardness of mind, an inwardness for listening to green silence, to watch tones and brilliances and subtleties of light, dawn, noon, and dusk, Etienne Louis Malus walking at sunset in the gardens of the Palais du Luxembourg, seeing how twice refracted level light was polarized by the palace windows, alert to remember what we would see and hold and share. From fields of yellow sedge to undergrowth of wild ferns tall as our shoulders, from slippery paths Indian file through trees to bear walks along black beaver ponds we set out to see the great rocks rolled into Vermont by glaciers ten thousand years ago.

• • •

Tokyu, once we were at the tea bowl, asked with what emotion I had passed through the great gate at Shirakawa. So taken had I been by the landscape, I admitted, and with memories of former poets and their emotions, that I composed few *haiku* of my own. The only one I would keep was: *The first poetry I found in the far north was the work-songs of the rice farmers.* We made three books of linked *haiku* beginning with this poem. Outside this provincial town on the post road there was a venerable chestnut tree under which a priest lived. In the presence of that tree I could feel that I was in the mountain forests where the poet Saigyo gathered nuts. I wrote these words then and there: *O holy chestnut tree, the Chinese write your name with the character for* tree *below that of* west, *the direction of all things holy.* Gyoki the priest of the common people in the Nara period had a chestnut walking stick, and the ridgepole of his house was chestnut. And I wrote this *haiku: Worldly men pass by the chestnut in bloom by the roof.* We ended our visit with Tokyu. We came to the renowned Asaka Hills and their many lakes. The *katsumi* iris, I knew, would be in bloom, and we left the high road to go see them.

• • •

Sequoia Langsdorfii is found in the Cretaceous of both British Columbia and Greenland, and *Gingko polymorpha* in the former of these localities. *Cinnamomum Scheuchzeri* occurs in the Dakota group of Western Kansas as well as at Fort Ellis. Sir William Dawson detects in strata regarded as Laramie by Professor G. M. Dawson, of the Geological Survey of Canada, a form which he considers to be allied to *Quercus antiqua*, Newby., from Rio Dolores, Utah, in strata positively declared to be the equivalent of the Dakota group. Besides these cases there are several in which the same species occurs in the Eocene and the Cretaceous, though wanting in the Laramie. *Cinnamomum Sezannense*, of the Paleocene of Sézanne and Gelinden, was found by Heer, not only in the upper Cretaceous of Patoot, but in the Cenomanian of Atane, in Greenland. *Myrtophyllum cryptoneuron* is common to the Paleocene of Gelinden and the Senonian of Westphalia, and the same is true of *Dewalquea Gelindensis*. *Sterculia variabilis* is another case of a Sézanne species occurring in the upper Cretaceous of Greenland, and Heer rediscovers in this same Senonian bed the Eocene plant *Sapotacites reticulatus*, which he described in the Sachs-Thüringen lignite beds.

• • •

But not a single *katsumi* iris could we find. No one we asked, moreover, had ever heard of them. Night was coming on, and we made haste to have a quick look at the urozuka cave by taking a shortcut at Nihonmatsu. We spent the night at Fukushima. Next day I stopped at Shinobu village to see the stone where *shinobu-zuri* cloth used to be dyed. It is a composite stone with an amazing facet smooth as glass of many different minerals and quartz. The stone used to be far up the mountain, I was told by a child, but the many tourists who came to see it trampled the crops on the way, so the villagers brought it down to the square. I wrote: *Now only the nimble hands of girls planting rice give us an idea of the ancient dyers at their work*. We crossed by ferry at Tsuki-no-wa—Ring around the Moon!—and came to Se-no-ue, a post town. There is a field nearby, with a hill named Maruyama in it: on this hill are the ruins of the warrior Sato's house. I wept to see the broken gate at the foot of the hill. A temple stands in the neighborhood with the graves of the Sato family in its grounds. I felt that I was in China at the tombstone of Yang Hu, which no person of cultivation has ever visited without weeping.

• • •

Through forests of sweet gum and hickory rising to larch, meadows of fern and thistle, we came toward the end of a day to an old mill of the kind I had known at Price's Shoals in South Carolina, wagons and mules under its elms, dogs asleep in the shade beneath the wagons, chickens and ducks maundering about. This New England country mill was, however, of brick, with tall windows, but with the same wide doors and ample loading platforms. It was a day in which we had lost time. I interrupted our singing along a logging road to say that my watch had stopped. So had hers, she said, or the map was cockeyed, or night comes earlier in this part of New Hampshire than anywhere else in the Republic. Clouds and a long rain had kept most of the day in twilight. A new rain was setting in for the night. But there was the mill, and we were saved from another night of wet such as we had endured the second night out. Tentless, we had slept in our bedrolls zipped together into one on a slope of deep ferns and waked to find ourselves as wet as if we had slept in a creek. The map showed shelter ahead, which we had expected to reach. But there had been the strange advancement of the day in defiance of my watch, which had stopped hours ago and started up again. What luck, to chance on this old mill.

• • •

In the temple I saw, after tea with the priests, the sword of Yoshitsune and the haversack of his loyal servant Benkei. It was the Feast Day of Boys and the Iris. *Show with pride,* I wrote of the arms in the temple, *the warrior's sword, his companion's pack on the first of May.* We went on and spent the night at Iisuka, having had a bath in a hot spring beforehand. Our inn was dirty, lampless, and the beds were pallets of straw on an earthen floor. There were fleas in the pallets, mosquitoes in the room. A fierce storm came up in the night. The roof leaked. All of this brought on an attack of fever and chills, and I was miserable and afraid of dying next day. I rode awhile and walked awhile, weak and in pain. We got as far as the gate into County Okido. I passed the castles at Abumizuri and Shiroishi. I'd wanted to see the tomb of Sanekata, one of the Fujiwara, a poet and exile, but the road there was all mud after the rains, and the tomb was overgrown with grass, I was told, and hard to find. We spent the night at Iwanuma. *How far to Kasajima and is this river of mud the road to take?*

• • •

Our packs off, the sleeping bags laid out and zipped together, supper in the pan, we could listen to the rain in that windy old mill, hugging our luck and each other. Packrats in little white pants, and spiders, and lizards, no doubt, I said, and we will make friends with them all. Her hair had lost the spring of its curls and stuck rakishly to her forehead and cheeks, the way I had first seen it as she climbed from a swimming pool in the Poconos. What are you talking about? she asked. She searched my eyes with a smiling and questioning look. I thought by such comic inquisitiveness that our luck was hard to believe. The mill there, Sweetheart, I repeated, pointing. A grand old New England water mill, dry as a chip and as substantial as Calvin's *Institutes.* She looked at the mill, at me again, and her mouth fell open. The stone steps to the door rose from a thicket of bramble we would have to climb across with care. There was something of the Florentine in all these old brick mills. Their Tuscan flavor came from architectural manuals issued by Scotch engineering firms that had listened to Ruskin and believed him when he said there was truth in Italian proportions and justice in Italian windows.

• • •

With what joy I found the Takekuma pine, double-trunked, just as the olden poets said. When Noin made his second visit to this tree, it had been cut down for bridge pilings by some upstart of a government official. It has been replanted over the years, it always grows back the same, always the most beautiful of pines. I was seeing it in its thousandth year. When I set out on my journey the poet Kyohaku had written: *Do not neglect to see the pine at Takekuma amid late spring cherry blossoms in the far north.* And for him, as an answer, I wrote: *We saw cherry blossoms together, you and I, three months ago. Now I have come to the double pine in all its grandeur.* On the fourth of May we arrived at Sendai across the Natori River, the day one throws iris leaves on the roof for good health. We put up at an inn. I sought out the painter Kaemon, who showed me the clover fields of Miyagino, the hills of Tamada, Yokono, and Tsutsuji-ga-oka, all white with rhododendron in bloom, the pine wood of Konoshita, where at noon it seems to be night, and where it is so damp you feel the need of an umbrella. He also showed me the shrines of Yakushido and Tenjin. A painter is the best of guides.

• • •

The Bay of Spezia, mulberry groves, sheds where the silkworms fatten, but here, the sun in golden sheets and slats on the floor, young Revely's study was all Archimedes and Sicily, or a tabletop by Holbein with instruments in brass and walnut, calipers, rules, maps, calculations in silverpoint and red ink. Under a map in French colors, slate blues and provincial yellows, poppy reds, cabbage greens, a sepia line from Genua across the Lunae Portus to Pisa, there sat in harmonic disarray a wooden bowl of quicksilver (a cup of Tuscan moonlight, a dish for gnomes to sip down in the iron roots of mountains where the earthquake demons swill lava and munch gold), cogged wheels, a screw propeller, drawings of frigates, steamboats, a machinery of gears and levers colored blue and yellow, lighthouses with cyclopean lamps, plans of harbors and moorings, a heap of rosin, a china cup full of ink, a half-burnt match, a box of watercolors, a block of ivory, a volume of Laplace, a book of conic sections, spherics, logarithms, Saunderson's *Algebra*, Simms's *Trigonometry*, and most beautiful of all this Archimagian gear, the newly unpacked theodolite, tilted in its fine calibrations, gleaming index and glass.

• • •

When we parted, the painter Kaemon gave me drawings of Matsushima and Shiogama and two pairs of sandals of straw with iris-purple straps. *I walk in iris blossoms, it seems, so rich the blue of my sandal laces.* He also gave me drawings to guide my way along the Narrow Road to the Deep North. At Ichikawa I found the tall inscribed stone of Tsubo-no-ishibumi. The characters were legible through lichen and moss. Taga Castle was built on this site the first year of Jinki by order of General Ono-no-Azumabito, Governor of the Far North by de-

cree of the Emperor, rebuilt in the sixth year of Tempyohoji by Emi-
no-Asakari, Governor General of the Provinces East and North. This
stone is 965 years old. Mountains break and fall, rivers shift their
beds, highways grow up in grass, rocks sink into the earth, trees with-
er with age, and yet this stone has stood from ancient times. I wept to
see it, and knelt before its presence, very happy and very sad. We went
on across the Noda-no-tamagawa River to the pine forest of Sue-no-
matsuyama, where there is a temple and graveyard that gave me
melancholy thoughts of the death that must end all our lives, whatever be our love of the world.

                    • • •

I could imagine the inside: spiderwebs and dog droppings, the in-
evitable Mason jar and flattened crump of overalls that one always
found in abandoned buildings, a newspaper gone brown and some
enigma of a utensil that turned out to be the handle of a meat grinder
or meal sifter or mangle gearing. I anticipated rills of ancient flour in
the seams of sills, the flat smell of mildewed wheat, the quick smell of
wet brick. Mill? she said. Her smile was strangely goofy. She took me
by the sleeve. What mill? Then I stood dumb and cold. There was no
mill. Ahead of us was the edge of a wood, nothing more. The dusk
thickened as we looked at each other in the rain. We went on, stub-
bornly. We knew better than to follow a blazed trail by dark. We
hoped that the campsite with shelter marked on the map was just on
the other side of the wood before us. It was not yet wholly dark. Were
it not a rainy day, we might plausibly have an hour's half-light yet:
plenty of time to nip through the wood, get to the shelter, and be dry
for the night. You say you saw an old mill? Underfoot there were
rocks and roots again. We longed for the easy tread of the logging
road.

                    • • •

We came to Shiogama just as the curfew bell was tolling, the darken-
ing sky completely cloudless, the island of Magaki-gashima already
but a shadow in a sea that was white with moonlight. We could hear
the fishermen counting their take. How lonely it is to enter a town at

dusk! We heard a blind singer chanting the rustic folksongs of the north. Next day, we worshiped at the Myojin Shrine of Shiogama, a handsome building. The way to it is paved, the fence around it is painted vermilion. It pleased me that the powers of the gods are so honored here in the Deep North, and I made a sincere obeisance at the altar. An ancient lantern burns near the altar to keep alive the memory of Izumi-no-Saburo, that gallant warrior of five hundred years ago. In the afternoon we took a boat to Matsushima, two miles out. Everyone knows that these are the most beautiful islands in all Japan. I would add that they rival Tungting Hu in Hunan and Si Hu in Chekiang. These islands are our China. Every pine branch is perfect. They have the grace of women walking, and so perfectly are the islands placed that Heaven's serenity is apparent everywhere.

• • •

Ezra Pound came down the *salita* through the olive grove, white mane jouncing as he stepped his cane with precision stride by long stride. He wore a cream sports jacket, a blue shirt with open collar, pleated white slacks, brown socks and espadrilles. The speckled bony fingers of his left hand pinched a panama by the brim. The way was strewn with hard green olives torn from their branches by a storm the week before. *Shocking waste,* Miss Rudge said, *and yet it seems to happen year after year, and somehow there's always an olive crop, isn't there, Ezra?* Then, over her shoulder, she asked me if I knew the Spanish for *romance. Ezra wants to know, and can't remember. As in* medieval romance? I ask, startled. *Romanthé, I think.* Novela *would be a later word.* Relato, *perhaps. Ezra,* she called ahead, *would that be right? No!* he said, a quiver of doubt in his voice. Romancero, I said, *is a word Mr. Pound himself has used of Spanish balladry.* Romancero, *Ezra?* Miss Rudge said cheerfully. Single file was the rule on the *salita.* He always went first, up or down, steep and rough as it was. *Not the word,* he said, without looking back.

• • •

Ojima, though called an island, is a narrow strip of land. Ungo, the Shinto priest, lived here in his retirement. We were shown the rock where he liked to sit for hours. We saw small houses among the pines, blue smoke from their chimneys, the red moon rising beyond them. My room at the inn overlooked the bay and the islands. A great wind howled, and clouds scudded at a gallop across the moon; nevertheless, I kept my windows open, for I had that wonderful feeling that only travelers know: that this was a different world from any I had known before. Different winds, a different moon, an alien sea. Sora, too, felt the peculiarity of the place and the moment, and wrote: *Flute-tongued cuckoo, you must long for the heron's wings of silver to fly from island to island at Matsushima.* So fine was my emotion that I could not sleep. I got out my notebook and read again the poems my friends gave me when I set out, about these islands: a poem by Sodo in Chinese, a *waka* by Dr. Hara Anteki, *haiku* by the samurai Dakushi and Sampu. Being at Matsushima made the poems much richer, and the poems made Matsushima a finer experience.

• • •

We juggled in debate whether we should doss down then and there in leafmuck and boulder rubble, or, heartened by the thin light we found in clearings, suppose that the failure of the day was more rain-dusk than the beginning of night, and push on. We found at least an arm of the lake on the map in a quarter of an hour. It was a spillway which we had to cross on a footlog. Rabbitfoot, I said, and don't look down. We got across more in dismay at the unfairness of a footlog to deal with in failing light and drizzle than with any skill with footlogs. What a miserable mean thing to do, she said, putting a blithering log to balance across with both of us winded and wet and you seeing hotels. The rain had settled in to stay. We had fair going for a while and then we came upon swamp. There was no question of camping in water that came over our shoe tops. I broke out a flashlight, she held onto my pack so as not to get lost from me, and we nosed our way through ferns and huckleberries, sinking up to our shins in mud. I think I'm scared, she said. Of what? Nothing in particular. Of everything. I'm scared, I said, if for no other reason than that I don't know where we are.

• • •

We set out for Hiraizumi on the twelfth, our immediate plans being to visit the Aneha Pine and Odae Bridge. Our way was along a woodcutter's path in the mountains, as lonely and quiet a trail as I have ever trod. By some inattention to my instructions I lost my way and came instead to Ishinomaki, a port in a bay where we saw a hundred ships. The air was thick with smoke from chimneys. What a busy place! They seemed to know nothing of putting up foot travelers, or of the art of looking at scenery. So we had to make do with shoddy quarters for the night. We left next day by a road that went I knew not whither. It took us past a ford on the Sode, the meadows of Obuchi, and the grasslands of Mano. We followed the river and came at last to Hiraizumi, having wandered a good twenty miles out of our way. We looked with melancholy on the ruins of the Fujiwara estate, now so many rice paddies. We found Yasuhira's abandoned house to the north of the Koromo-ga-seki Gate. Though the grandeur of the Fujiwara lasted three generations only, their achievements will be remembered forever, and looking on the ruins of their castles and lands I wept that such glory has come to nothing, and covered my face with my hat.

• • •

In July I saw several cuckoos skimming over a large pond; and found, after some observation, that they were feeding on the *libellulae,* or dragonflies, some of which they caught as they settled on the weeds, and some as they were on the wing. Notwithstanding what Linnaeus says, I cannot be induced to believe that they are birds of prey. A countryman told me that he had found a young fern-owl in the nest of a small bird on the ground; and that it was fed by the little bird. I went to see this extraordinary phenomenon, and found that it was a young cuckoo hatched in the nest of a titlark; it was become vastly too big for its nest. The dupe of a dam appeared at a distance, hovering about with meat in its mouth, and expressing the greatest solicitude. Ray remarks, that birds of the *gallinae* order, as cocks and hens, partridges and pheasants, are *pulveratrices*, such as dust themselves, using that method of cleansing their feathers, and ridding themselves of their vermin. As far as I can observe, many birds that wash themselves would never dust; but here I find myself mistaken; for common house sparrows are great *pulveratrices,* being frequently seen groveling and wallowing in dusk roads; and yet they are great washers. Does not the skylark dust?

• • •

Tall grass grows over the dreams of an ancient aristocracy. Look there! Did I not see Yoshitsune's servant Kanefusa in the white blur of the un-ohana flowers? But not all was gone. The temples remain, with their statues and tombs and sutras. *Dry in the rains of May, the Hikari Do keeps its gold and gloom for a thousand years.* We reached Cape Ogoru next day, and the little island of Mizu in the river. Onward, we came to the Dewa border, where the guards questioned us so long and so suspiciously (they rarely see foot travelers even in the best of weather) that we got a late start. Dusk caught us on the mountain road and we had to stay the night with a tollkeeper, and were lucky to find even this hut in so desolate a place. *Fleas and lice bit us, and all night a horse pissed beside my mat.* The tollkeeper said that many mountains lay between us and Dewa. I was most surely apt to get lost and perish. He knew a stout young man who would consent to be our guide, a strapping fellow with a sword and oak staff. He was indeed necessary: the way was an overgrown wilderness. Black clouds just above our heads darkened the thick underwood of bamboo.

• • •

Where we are, she said, is slogging our way by flashlight through a New England swamp up to our butts in goo and I'm so tired I could give up and howl. The important thing to understand, I said, is that we aren't on the trail. We were, I think, she said, when we got off into this. We couldn't be far off it. Off the trail, she said in something of a snit, is off the trail. And there's something wrong with my knees. They're shaking. We're probably walking into the lake that stupid log back there went over an outlet of. I turned and gave her as thorough an inspection as I could under the circumstances. She was dead tired, she was wet, and her knees did indeed shake. Lovely knees, but they were cold and splashed with mud. I slipped her pack off and fitted it across my chest, accoutred front and back like a paratrooper. We went on, the flashlight beam finding nothing ahead but bushes in water, a swamp of ferns. There was a rudimentary trail, it seemed. At least someone had put down logs in the more succulent places. It is the trail, I insisted. A yelp from behind, a disgusted and slowly articulated *Jiminy!* and while I was helping her up, sobs. Don't cry, Sweetheart! It rolled. The motherless log rolled when I stepped on it.

• • •

In Obanazawa I visited the merchant poet Seifu, who had often stopped on business trips to see me in Edo. He was full of sympathy for our hard way across the mountains, and made up for it with splendid hospitality. Sora was entranced by the silkworm nurseries, and wrote: *Come out, toad, and let me see you: I hear your got-a-duck got-a-duck under the silkworm house.* And: *The silkworm workers are dressed like ancient gods.* We climbed to the quiet temple of Ryushakuji, famous for being in so remote and peaceful a site. The late afternoon sun was still on it, and on the great rocks around it, when we arrived, and shone golden in the oaks and pines that have stood there for hundreds of years. The very ground seemed to be eternity, a velvet of moss. I felt the holiness of the place in my bones; my spirit partook of it with each bow that I made to the shrines in the silent rocks. *Silence as whole as time. The only sound is crickets.* Our next plan was to go down the Mogami River by boat, and while we were waiting for one to take us, the local poets at Oishida sought me out and asked me to show them how to make linked verses, of which they had heard but did not know the technique. With great pleasure I made a whole book for them.

• • •

Could she stand? She thought so. It hurt, but she could stand. I shone the flashlight as far as I could ahead. Treetops! Treetops ahead, Samwise. Higher ground, don't you think that means? She limped frighteningly. We sloshed on. I could tell how miserable she was from her silence. We were slowly getting onto firmer ground. I studied her again by flashlight. She was a very tired girl with a sprained ankle or the nearest thing to it. I was getting my second wind, and put it to good use by heaving her onto my hip. She held to my neck, kissing my ear in gratitude. By coupling my hands under her behind, I could carry her to high ground if it was near enough. We reached forest, with roots to slip on and rocks to stumble over. The flashlight found a reasonably level place. I cleared trash from it while she held the light. We spread our tarpaulin, unrolled and zipped together the sleeping bags. It was our pride that we were hiking without a tent, though at that moment we longed for one. We undressed in the rain, stuffing our damp clothes into our packs. At least they wouldn't get any wetter. We slipped naked into the sleeping bag. Too tired to shiver, she said. She got dried peaches and apples from her pack, and we chewed them, lying on our elbows, looking out into the dark.

　　　• • •

The Mogami River flows down from the mountains through Yamagata Province, with many treacherous rapids along the way, and enters the sea at Sakata. We went down the river in a farmer's old-timey rice boat, our hearts in our mouths. We saw Shiraito-no-take, the Silver-Stringed Waterfall, half-hidden by thick bamboo, and the temple of Sennindo. Because the river was high and rough, I wrote: *On all the ruins of May in one river, I tossed along down the swift Mogami.* I was glad to get ashore. On the third of June we climbed Haguro Mountain and were granted an audience with Egaku the high priest, who treated us with civility and put us up in a cabin. Next day, in the Great Hall with the high priest, I wrote: *This valley is sacred. The sweet wind smells of snow.* On the fifth we saw the Gongen Shrine, of uncertain date. It may be the shrine Fujiwara-no-Tokihira in the *Rites and Ceremonies* says is on Mount Sato in Dewa, confusing the Chinese for *Sato* and *Kuro, Haguro* being a variant of *Kuro.* Here they teach Total Meditation as the Tendai sect understands it, and the Freedom of the Spirit and Enlightenment, teaching as pure as moonlight and as sweet as a single lantern in pitch dark.

　　　• • •

He and Bruni, the watercolor painter, you know, they were the closest of friends, used to argue God something terrible. He was an atheist, Tatlin, and Bruni was a very Russian believer. It terrified me as a child. Tatlin would take us to swim in the river in the spring, and he wore no icon around his neck and didn't cross himself before diving in. He was wonderful with children, a grown-up who knew how to play with us without condescending, but with other people he was self-centered, vain about his singing voice. Pasternak, now, had no way with children at all. He didn't even see them. Tatlin made his own lute, a replica of a traditional Slavic lute such as blind singers had, strolling from village to village. Especially in the south. What did Tatlin look like? O, he was lanky, as you say, skinny. He had slate-gray eyes, very jolly eyes that had a way of going dead and silvery when he fell into a brown study. His hair was, how shall I put it, a gray blond. When he sang the blind singers' songs he made his eyes look blind, rolled back, unseeing. The voice was between baritone and bass. He was not educated, you know. He lived in the bell tower of a monastery.

• • •

On Haguro Mountain there are hundreds of small houses where priests meditate in strictest discipline, and will meditate, to keep this place holy, as long as there are people on the earth. On the eighth we climbed Mount Gassan. I had a paper rope around my shoulders, and a shawl of white cotton on my head. For eight miles we strove upward, through the clouds, which were like a fog around us, over rocks slick with ice, through snow. When we came to the top, in full sunlight, I was out of breath and frozen. How glorious the sight! We spent the night there, on beds of leaves. On the way down next day we came to the smithy where Gassan used to make his famous swords, tempering them in the cold mountain stream. His swords were made of his devotion to his craft and of the divine power latent in the mountain. Near here I saw a late-blooming cherry in the snow. I cannot speak of all I saw, but this cherry will stand for all, determined as it was, however late, however unseasonable, to bring its beauty into the world. Egaku, when I returned, asked me to make poems of my pilgrimage to this sacred mountain.

• • •

Bedded down in dark and rain, we felt both a wonderful security, warm and dry in our bed, and a sharp awareness that we didn't know where in the world we were. That swamp grew there since they print-

ed the map, she said. I feel, I said, as if we were all alone in the middle of a wood as big as Vermont. We could be six feet from the lake, or
on the merest island of trees in the world's biggest swamp. I don't
care where we are, she said. We're here, we're dry, we're not in that
swamp. We hugged awhile, and then lay on our backs to distribute
the rock weight of our exhaustion, a hand on each other's tummy for
sympathy and fellowship. You saw a mill? she said. A fine old water
mill, of red brick, about a hundred years old, I suppose. As plain as
day. I said that I was both glad and a bit frightened to have seen it, a
superimposition of desire on reality. The first ghost I'd ever seen, if a
mill can be a ghost. If it had been real, we would have had a hot supper, with coffee, and could have set up house, and got laid, twice running, after a wonderful long time of toning things up beforehand,
with porcupines standing on their hind legs and looking through the
windows. But she was asleep.

· · ·

*How cold the white sickle moon above the dark valleys of Mount
Haguro.* How many clouds had gathered and broken apart before we
could see the silent moon above Mount Gassan. Because I could not
speak of Mount Yudono, I wet my sleeves with tears. *Tears stood in
my eyes,* Sora wrote, *as I walked over the coins at Yudono, along the sacred way.* Next day we came to Tsuru-ga-oka Castle, where the warrior Nagayama Shigeyuki welcomed me and Zushi Sakichi, who had
accompanied us from Haguro. We wrote a book of linked verse together. We returned to our boat and went down the river Sakata. Here
we were the guests of Dr. Fugyoku. I wrote: *Cool of the evening in the
winds crisscrossing the beach at Fukuura, and twilight: but the tip of
Mount Atsumi was still bright with the sun. Deep into the estuary of
Mogami River the summer sun has quenched its fire.* By now my fund
of natural beauty was bountiful, yet I could not rest until I had seen
Lake Kisagata. To get there I walked ten miles along a path, over rocky
hills, down to sandy beaches and up again. The sun was touching the
horizon when I arrived. Mount Chokai was hidden in fog.

· · ·

We woke next morning to find that we were no more than twenty yards from the campsite we were trying to reach. Golly, she said, looking out of the sleeping bag. A black lake lay in a cedar wood whose greenish dark made its shores seem noonbright in early morning. We rose naked and put our clothes on bushes in the sun. She spied blueberries for our mush. I managed to get wood ash in our coffee, and we had to eat with the one spoon, as mine had got lost. The lake was too brackish to swim in, so we stood in the shallows and soaped each other, dancing from the chill of the water. I was rinsing her back with handsful of water poured over her shoulders when I saw a pop-eyed man gaping at us from beyond our breakfast fire. His face was scholarly and bespectacled and he wore a Boy Scout uniform. The staff in his hand gave him a biblical air. He was warning away his troop with a backward hand. Hi! she hailed him. We're just getting off some grime from the trail. We got lost in the rain last night and came here through the swamp. We'll give you time, he said with a grin. Oh for Pete's sake, said she, proceeding to soap up my back. We're just people. They've seen people, haven't they?

• • •

If the half-light and the rain were so beautiful at Kisagata, how lovely the lake would be in good weather. Next day was indeed brilliant, I sailed across the lake, stopping at the mere rock of an island where the monk Noin once meditated. On the far shore we found the ancient cherry tree of Saigyo's poem, in which he compares its blossoms to the froth on waves. From the large hall of the temple Kanmanjuji you can see the whole lake, and beyond it Mount Chokai like a pillar supporting Heaven, and the gate of Muyamuya faintly in the west, the highway to Akita in the east, and Shiogoshi in the north, where the lake meets the breakers of the ocean. Only two lakes are so beautiful: Matsushima is the other. But whereas Matsushima is gay and joyful, Kisagata is grave and religious, as if some sorrow underlay its charm. *Silk tree blossoming in the monotonous rain at Kisagata, you are like the Lady Seishi in her sorrow. On the wet beach at Shiogoshi the herons strut in the sea's edge. Some sweetmeat not known elsewhere is proba-*

bly sold at Kisagata on the feast days. Teiji has a poem about Kisagata: *In the evening the fishermen sit and rest in their doorways.* Sora
wrote of the ospreys: *Does God tell them how to build their nests higher than the tide?*

• • •

I loved her for her brashness. Her seventeen-year-old body, in all the
larger and speculative senses aesthetic and biological, was something
to see. It was Spartan, it was Corinthian: hale of limb, firmnesses con-
tinuing into softnesses, softnesses into firmnesses. There was a little
boy's stance in the clean porpoise curve of calf, a tummy flat and
grooved. Corinth asserted itself in hips and breasts, in the denim blue
of her eyes, the ruck of her upper lip, in the pert girlishness of her
nose. We aren't proud, she said. I can't recommend the pond here, as
it's full of leaf trash from several geological epochs back. The blueberries over there on that spit are delicious. By this time there were Boy
Scout eyes over the scoutmaster's shoulders. We went back to our
stretch of the beach, dried in the sun while making more coffee, and
fished shirts from our packs in deference to our neighbors. It was further along the trail that day that we found in a lean-to a pair of Jock-
ey shorts, size small, stuck full of porcupine quills. One of our Boy
Scouts', she said. Do you suppose he was in or out of them when
Brother Porky took a rolling dive?

• • •

Leaving Sakata, we set out on the hundred-and-thirty-mile road to
the county seat of Kaga Province. Clouds gathered over the mountains on the Hokuriku Road, down which we had to go, and clouds
gathered in my heart at the thought of the distance. We walked
through the Nezu Gate into Echigo, we walked through the Ichiburi
Gate into Ecchu. We were nine days on the road. The weather was wet
and hot all the way, and my malaria acted up and made the going
harder. *The sixth of July, the nights are changing, and tomorrow the
Weaver Star and the Shepherd Star cross the Milky Way together.* At
Ichiburi I was kept awake by two Geisha in the next room. They had
been visiting the Ise Shrine with an old man, who was going home the

next day, and they were plying him with silly things to say to all their friends. How frivolous and empty their lives! And next day they tried to attach themselves to us, pleading that they were pilgrims. I was stern with them, for they were making a mock of religion, but as soon as I had shooed them away my heart welled with pity. Beyond the forty-eight shoals of the Kurobe, we came to the village of Nago and asked to see the famous wisteria of Tako.

• • •

Hephaistiskos, our Renault bought in Paris, who had slept in a stable in Villefranche, kicked a spring outside Tarbes, and spent the night under the great chestnut tree in the square at Montignac, under palms at Menton, and under pines at Ravenna, was hoisted onto the foredeck of the *Kriti* at Venice for a voyage down the Adriatic to Athens. We had no such firm arrangements for a berth. Along with two Parisian typists of witty comeliness; two German cyclists blond, brown, and obsequious; a trio of English consisting of a psychiatrist and her two lovers, the one an Oxford undergraduate, the other the Liberal Member from Bath; and a seasoned traveler from Alton, Illinois, a Mrs. Brown, we were billeted on the aft deck, in the open air, with cots to sleep on. All the cabins were taken by Aztecs. *Mexican Rotary and their wives*, explained the lady psychiatrist, who had Greek and who had interviewed the Captain, leaving a flea in his ear. The sporting bartender had shouted to us over the Greek band, in a kind of English, that it was ever the way of the pirate who owned this ship to sell all the tickets he could, let the passengers survive by their wits. *It's only a week. No say drachma, say thrakmé.*

• • •

The wisteria of Tako, I was told, was five lonely miles up the coast, with no house of any sort nearby or along the way. Discouraged, I went on into Kaga Province. *Mist over the rice fields, below me the mutinous waves.* I crossed the Unohanayama Mountains, the Kurikaradani Valley, and came on the fifteenth of July to Kanazawa. Here the merchant Kasho from Osaka asked me to stay with him at his inn. There used to live in Kanazawa a poet named Issho, whose verse was known over all Japan. He had died the year before. I went to his grave with his brother, and wrote there: *Give some sign, O silent tomb of my friend, it you can hear my lament and the gusts of autumn wind joining my grief.* At a hermit's house: *This autumn day is cold, let us slice cucumbers and mad-apples and call them dinner.* On the road: *The sun is red and heedless of time, but the wind knows how cold it is, O red is the sun!* At Komtasu, Dwarf Pine: *The right name for this place, Dwarf Pine, wind combs the clover and makes waves in the grass.* At the shrine at Tada I saw the samurai Sanemori's helmet and the embroidered shirt he wore under his armor.

   • • •

The Liberal Member from Bath, the Oxford undergraduate name of Gerald, and the lady British psychiatrist demonstrated the Greek folk dances played by the band. *A Crimean Field Hospital,* I said of our cots and thin blankets set up as our dormitory on the fantail of the *Kriti. Exactly!* said the Liberal Member from Bath, accepting us thereby. *Rather jolly, don't you think?* The Parisian typists chittered and giggled. *Pas de la retraite! Que nous soyons en famille.* Mrs. Brown of Alton tucked a blanket under her chin and undressed with her back to the Adriatic. The Parisian typists came to her aid, and they became a trio, with their cots together, like the English. They stripped to lace bras and panties, causing the Liberal Member from Bath to say, O *well, there's nothing else for it, is there?* The German boys undressed pedantically to pissburnt briefs of ultracontemporary conciseness. We followed suit, nothing daunted, and the Liberal Member from Bath did everybody one better, and took off every stitch, a magnified infant, chubby of knee, paunchy, with random swirls and tufts of ginger hair. The Parisian typists squealed. The Germans looked at him with keen slit eyes. He was surely overstepping a bound.

   • • •

Sanemori's helmet was decorated with swirls of chrysanthemums across the visor and earflaps; a vermilion dragon formed the crest, between two great horns. When Sanemori died and the helmet was enshrined, Kiso Yoshinaka wrote a poem and sent it by Higuchi-no-Jiro:

With what wonder do I hear a cricket chirping inside an empty helmet. The snowy summit of Shirane Mountain was visible all the way to the Nata Shrine, which the Emperor Kazan built to Kannon, the Goddess of Mercy. The garden here was of rocks and pines. *The rocks are white at the Rock Temple, but the autumn wind is whiter.* At the hot spring nearby, where I bathed: *Washed in the steaming waters at Yamanaka, do I need also to pick chrysanthemums?* I was told by the innkeeper that it was here that Teishitsu realized his humiliating deficiencies as a poet, and began to study under Teitoku when he returned to Kyoto. Alas, while we were here, my companion Sora began to have a pain in his stomach, and left to go to his kinpeople in Nagashima. He wrote a farewell poem: *No matter if I fall on the road, I will fall among flowers.*

• • •

The Liberal Member from Bath had indeed overstepped a bound in taking off all his clothes on the fantail of the *Kriti.* Just as the lady psychiatrist was urging her other lover, the Oxford undergraduate, to join him in cheeking these outrageous foreigners for booking us passages and then deploying us out here under the sky in what the American archaeologists so aptly dub The Crimean Field Hospital, the Captain of the ship, together with the Steward, made their way through a tumult of pointing Mexican Rotarians and arrived in our midst whirling their arms. The Liberal Member stared at them pop-eyed. *What's the Pirate King saying? Who can understand the blighter?* He says you must put on your clothes, I offered. He says you are an affront to morals and an insult to decency. *He does, does he?* said the lady psychiatrist. *Gerald dear! Off with your undershorts.* She then, with help from Gerald dear and the Liberal Member, set out on a speech in Greek which we realized with an exchange of glances was a patchwork of Homeric phrases, more or less syntactical on the psychiatrist's part, but formulaic from her chorus, so that her *what an overweening hatefulness has crossed the barrier of thy teeth* was seconded by Gerald dear's *when that rosyfingered dawn had shed her beams over mortals and immortals together.*

• • •

When Sora left me, because of his illness, I felt both his sadness and mine, and wrote: *Let the dew fade the words on my hat, Two Pilgrims Traveling Together.* When I stayed at the Zenshoji Temple, they gave me a poem of Sora's that he had left there for me: *All night I heard the autumn wind in the hills above the shrine.* I too listened to the wind that night, grieving for my companion. Next morning I attended services, ate with the priests, and was leaving when a young monk ran after me with inkblock, brush, and paper, begging for a poem. I wrote: *For your kindness I should have swept the willow leaves from the garden.* Such was my sweet confusion at being asked for a poem that I left with my sandals untied. I rented a boat at Yoshizaki and rowed out to see the pine of Shiogoshi. The beauty of its setting is best caught in Saigyo's poem: *Urging the wind against the salt sea, the Shiogoshi pine sheds moonlight from its branches.* At Kanazawa I had been joined by the poet Hokushi, who walked with me as far as the Tenryu-ji Temple in Matsuoka, far further than he had meant to go.

• • •

We notice the ugliness of the Hellenistic and Roman style of Greek lettering as compared to the Archaic. Small columns of marble lying about that look as if they might have been grave markers. The Tower of the Winds with its curious figures that look Baroque: a few columns left standing, forming a corner of the street. This sort of ruin is actually what is most prevalent, especially at the theatres and at Eleusis, dismantled Roman ruins built on top of the Greek. An excavation trench near the church with a large urn only half dug out, under an olive tree. More piles of marble, looking very unorderly and as if the archaeologist had never been there: no attempt to order, classify, straighten. Little indication of street levels, except around the standing columns, these being straight shafts of marble, rather than sections fitted together. The Greek snails. We photographed a snailshell in your hand held beside a piece of marble ornament. What a motif. The pattern on the snails much more closely resembling the Geometric and Cycladic jars. The snails are caught by the sun as they climb a column and cooked there in their shells, which cling to the stone.

Their spiral design is a chestnut brown band separated from a charcoal band by a thin white line.

• • •

It was only three miles to Fukui. The way, however, was dark, as I had started thither after supper. The poet Tosai lived there, whom I had known in Edo ten years before. As soon as I arrived I asked for him. A citizen directed me, and as soon as I found a house charmingly neglected, fenced around by a profusion of gourd vines, moonflowers, wild cockscomb kneedeep, and goosefoot blocking the way to the front door, I knew this was Tosai's home and no other's. I knocked. A woman answered, saying that Tosai was downtown somewhere. I was delighted that he had taken a wife, and told him so with glee when I routed him out of a wineshop later. I stayed with him for three days. When I departed, saying that I wanted to see the full moon over Tsuruga, he decided to come with me, tucking up his house kimono as his only concession to the road. The peak of Shirane gave way to that of Hina. At Asamuzu Bridge we saw the reeds of Tamae in bloom. With the first migrating geese in the sky above me. I entered Tsuruga on the fourteenth. The moon was to be full the next night. We went to the Myojin Shrine of Kei, which honors the soul of the Emperor Chuai, bringing, as is the custom, a handful of white sand for the courtyard.

• • •

Most of them are plants that are abundantly represented in nearly all the more recent deposits, such as *Taxodium Europaeum,* found all the way from the Middle Bagshot of Bournemouth to the Pliocene of Meximieux, *Ficus liliaefolia, Laurus primigenia,* and *Cinnamomum lanceolatum,* abundant in nearly all the Oligocene and Miocene beds of Europe. *Quercus chlorophylla* occurs in the Mississippi Tertiary as well as at Skopau in Sachs-Thüringen, and is also abundant in the Miocene, and *Ficus tiliaefolia* is found in the Green River formation at Florissant, Colorado. The two species of hazel, and also the sensitive fern from the Fort Union deposits regarded by Dr. Newberry as identical with the living forms, must be specifically so referred until fruits or other parts are found to show the contrary. Forms of the

Gingko tree occur not only in the Fort Union beds, but in the lower Laramie beds at Point of Rocks, Wyoming Territory, which differ inappreciably except in size of leaf from the living species. A few Laramie forms occur in Cretaceous strata.

• • •

This was a custom begun by the priest Yugyo, so that at the full of the moon the area before the shrine would be as white as frost. *The pure full moon shone on Yugyo the Bishop's sand.* But on the night of the fifteenth it rained. *But for the fickle weather of the north I would have seen the full moon in autumn.* The sixteenth, however, was fine, and I went shell-gathering on the beach. A man named Tenya came with me, and his servants with a picnic. We savored the loneliness of the long beaches. *Autumn comes to the sea, and the beach is more desolate than that at Suma. Clover petals blown into the sea roll up with fine pink shells in the waves.* I asked Tosai to write an account of our day's excursion and to deposit it at the temple for other pilgrims. My friend Rotsu met me when I returned, and went with me to Mino Province. We rode into Ogaki on horseback, and we were met by Sora. At Joko's house we were welcomed by Zensen, Keiko, and many other friends who acted as if I had returned from the dead. On the sixth of September I left for the shrine at Ise, though I was still tired from my journey to the far north. *Tight clam shells fall open in the autumn, just as I, no sooner made comfortable than I feel the call of the road.* Friends, goodbye!

Colin Maillard

Down the slope of the knoll by the river six boys herded a seventh. Their school, partly brick turrets, partly modern slabs of rectilinear glass, was far behind them, inserted into a line of cedars across the horizon. There were puffs of white clouds in the bright blue sky. Down on the river a farmer was burning off a field. Further up the slope a woman in long skirts was collecting butterflies in a net. Her straw gardening hat was kept in place by a red scarf tied under her chin.

Every attempt of the seventh, smaller boy to break and run for it was thwarted by blocking shoulders and quick footwork.

Up from the meadow where six Holsteins grazed stood a post that had once held a salt lick, or been part of a gate, or of some structure the rest of which had long since been carried away. Wind and rain had made it smooth and gray.

Aage, Bo, Martin, and Peder wore white kneepants and blue sweatshirts. Ib was in American jeans, and Bent wore short pants, like the little boy Tristan.

—Stand, Aage said to Tristan, still and easy. I'll do the rest.

—Martin and Peder, Bo said, are going to fight.

—Not till after, Martin said.

—And not here, Peder said. Back of the hill, and in our underpants, so's not to get blood on our clothes.

—Crazy, Ib said.

Tristan stood, worried and submissive, while Aage unbuttoned his blouse and took it off with a flourish.

——Hang it on the post, he instructed Martin.

Aage worked Tristan's undershirt up. His voice was calm and menacing. A few more unfastenings and pulls, and Tristan stood mothernaked, cheeks and ears the color of a radish.

——Here in the sack, Peder said.

He shook out a dress, blue with white dots, a frilled hem, and a pink ribbon through the lace at the collar.

——Sexy, Bent said.

——Looks more like a nightgown, said Bo.

——You're going to make me wear a dress? Tristan asked.

——We told you not to talk, Aage said. Stick your arms through the sleeves.

——It's only a game, Martin said. Isn't it, Ib? Ib doesn't tell lies.

——Not only a game, Ib said, but a game with the rules backward. You're It, we decided last night, and instead of you having the blindfold, we are the blindfoldeds.

——Except for the haircut, he looks like a girl.

——What for? Tristan asked.

——The more you talk, Aage said, the worse it's going to be for you, squirt.

——Pigeon to the Master, Bo said, and you'll wish you were dead.

——This is the drill, Bent said. We're blindfolded, you're not. If you were to get clean away, slim chance, you can't go back, not in a dress.

——What happens when you catch me?

——We told you not to talk.

Aage looked at Bo, merry with a secret, and Bo flipped his fingers against his blue sweatshirt. Bent zipped down the fly of his short pants and crossed his eyes. Ib guffawed. Martin glared at Peder, Peder at Martin.

A skipper on flixweed opened its wings twice before darting off, with a dip, zigzag and fluttery.

——*Sylvestris Poda*, Tristan said. I don't care. Give me the sniffles, this dress.

Aage bound Bo's eyes with a scout kerchief, Bent Ib, and on around until they were all blindfolded, except Tristan, who stood miserable and confused in his dress. Bo's white quiff stuck up like a grebe's tail from the scarf belting his eyes, and they all moved like windup toys.

In every direction there were green and brown fields, and a silver sliver of sea to the west.

—You're there, somewhere, Aage said. If you talk, or holler, we'll know where you are, and get you.

They began to mill, with stiff arms and open hands.

—It's me, you've got, smugger, Bo said. Feel for a dress.

—There was an owl, a Great Gray, *Strix nebulosa,* on a limb, Bent said, on the fir.

Tristan ducked Ib's flailing grope.

—Outside my window.

—We could all be frigging each other, Peder said, in brotherly bliss.

Nipped under Aage's reach, changing course like a rabbit.

—Not Peder and Martin: they're going to fight.

—Same thing, Bo said.

It was not bright to think of green graph paper and algebra when who knew what was about to happen to him, but Tristan did.

—Everybody stand still. Blind people can feel what's around them.

Or of the yellow willow by the river and the heron that stood on one leg downstream from it.

—Wind.

—Arms out.

—Turn slow, all of us in close.

—We could hold hands, in a circle, and move in.

—If he's inside.

—He's inside. Aren't you, Tristan?

Silence.

He could see. They couldn't. No reason why they should ever catch him.

—The owl was looking in at our window.

—Which blinded him.

Thing was, to make no noise and to account for every direction at once. Stay on your toes, stay down, keep turning.

—Who groped my crotch? Martin asked.

——Peder, probably, Bo said.

Bent, squirming away from Ib, made a wide opening in the circle, through which Tristan nipped, and walked backward, on his toes. Then he turned and ran as fast as he could. From the dip on the other side of the knoll he could see the woman with her butterfly net, the farmer burning off his field. The shine had gone off the sea. He minded being barefoot more than the dress. The dress was like a dream, and no fault of his, but to have let his shoes be taken away from him was lack of character.

——Bullies, he said out loud. And unfair.

But he'd fooled them, there was that. And he would never know what they would have done to him if they'd caught him.

——Don't think like that! he said, stomping his foot.

If he made a big circle, he could get back to the school without being caught, provided it was a good while before they realized he'd given them the slip.

If he were in Iceland, or on Fyn, there would be ponies he could commandeer and ride. If he were on the other side of the school, there would be a road, with cars. It would be grand if a helicopter choppered down, with police or soldiers, to rescue him, deliver him in glory to the school, having kindly given him a flight jacket to wear over this miserable dress. And the woman netting butterflies was too far inside the long way around he had to circle. If his luck held, he could be a long way ahead of them before the pack was on his heels.

He kept to the sides of knolls. His breathing was wet and sharp, as when you're taking a cold.

Heather and bracken and gorse and knotgrass, and all as fast in rubble as a cat's tail in a cat. All people with socks and sneakers were rich, didn't they know? And pants. And did his balls feel good because he was free? If he was: they might be tearing after him, with longer legs, and with shoes, and here he was crying, like a baby.

Where you are is how you feel. Back there, dipping under their trawling arms, pivoting on his heel, ducking and dashing, there was no time: everything happened at once. And then time turned on again.

He didn't dare look back. For one thing, every direction now looked the same. For another, he didn't want to know if they were behind him in a pack, or worse, fanning out, to come at him on all sides.

A stitch in your ribs goes away, he knew, if you keep running, and there was second wind, good old second wind. And luck, there was luck.

Had the sky ever been emptier or everywhere so far away?

Luck, he felt in his bones, had a warrant for his safe passage over these scrub meadows. The wood's edge would be just beyond the next rise, or the next. Then he could go along the wood, even disappear into it, if need be. There was a longish stretch of open fields after that, before the next wood, but that one had paths in it, and through it he could get back to the school.

But he had to go around hills, not over them, where they could see him.

What was all this about, anyway? Playing Colin Maillard with the rules reversed, and him in a dress? Aage he'd suspect anything of, always ready for a jape as he was, especially if it was a way of sucking up to Bo. Bent was a mean little rat to be in on this. How did Ib get mixed up in it?

His nose stung inside, and the back of his mouth.

He'd cut the underside of two toes, the little one on his left foot, the long one beside the big toe on his right. His knees hurt. His shins hurt.

He stumbled and fell sprawling.

I will not cry, he heard himself saying. I will fucking not fucking cry.

When he got up, he couldn't believe that the use of his left ankle was not his anymore. The pain would go away. Luck wouldn't do something like this to him. It absolutely wouldn't. He needed all the luck he could get.

Worse, he heard voices.

The voices made him angry. It was wonderfully easy now not to blubber, not to even think of defeat. He was going to get away. A whonky ankle wasn't going to stop him.

The voices were to his left. They weren't a hue and cry. They were mingled in with each other. Ib's he recognized, and Aage's. He heard *all this crap about a fair fight* and *we won't stop you.*

He forgot that his ankle wouldn't work, and fell again. Where *were* they?

On the other side of the knoll to his left. He remembered: Martin and Peder were to fight. He hated fights. They were more senseless, even, than making him wear a dress to play *blindebuk* backward.

The whole stupid world was crazy. Plus it didn't seem to notice.

He gave up hopping, and crawled toward the top of the knoll. There was a big rock he could lie flat behind, and look. Their minds, at least, weren't on him anymore. There was sweet relief in that. And they wouldn't pick on him when he had a hurt ankle.

Aage and Bo were with Martin, who was stripped down to his undershorts. Peder was undressing, throwing his clothes to Ib and Bent. He had smaller undershorts than Martin, blue with a white waistband. They'd left on their socks and sneakers, as the ground in the hollow where they were was as rocky and scrubby as the fields he'd run so fast over.

The late afternoon was filling the hollow with shadow. Aage was whispering in Martin's ear. Bo sat, Martin's clothes in his lap.

Peder walked over and stood nose to nose with Martin, talking very low between clenched teeth. His hands tightened into fists. Martin was breathing fast, his chest jumping as if he'd run farther and harder than Tristan.

But they hadn't run at all. He saw that he'd apparently been making a steady turn to the left, when all the while he thought he was running in a straight line. The post where they'd played Colin Maillard was the next knoll over. Talk about unlucky.

He was scared. He hated what he was seeing, and didn't want to see. Martin and Peder almost touching, breathing into each other's mouths, looking into each other's eyes as if trying to look into each other's heads. Aage stood eerily still, waiting, with a strange expression on his face. Bo's knees were quivering. Ib had his hands on his hips, legs wide apart. Bent was licking his lips.

Peder hit first, a jab into Martin's midriff that sounded like a melon splitting and doubled Martin over. Before he could straighten up, Peder kicked him in the chest, a fierce football punt of a kick that made him fall backward.

Tristan closed his eyes and pushed his face against the ground. He heard grunts, ugly words, scuffling.

Aage, Bo, Ib, and Bent were saying nothing at all.

When he dared a look, Peder was on top of Martin, pummeling his face with both fists, which were bloody. Martin's legs were flailing against the ground.

Tristan was halfway down the slope, running with a dipping limp, before he realized that he had moved at all.

—Make him quit! he was shouting.

Bo looked up at him in surprise. Aage grinned.

—Keep back, he said. A fight's a fight.

With a porpoise heave and flop, Martin twisted from under Peder, jabbed his knee into his crotch, and pulled free. Peder's face was white with pain, his mouth making the shape of a scream. Martin was bleeding from the nose in spurts, and he was sobbing in convulsions, his shoulders jolting. He wiped the blood from his mouth, and fell on Peder with both fists hammering on his terrified face.

Tristan locked his arms around Martin's waist and pulled.

—Help me get him off, you assholes! he shouted. You fucking stupid shits!

—Stay out of this, Aage shouted. It's none of your fucking business.

—Where'd he come from, anyway? Ib asked.

By tightening his armlock and pushing as hard as he could, Tristan rolled Martin off Peder, who got up with a paralytic jerk, gagging. Backing away on knees and elbows, he retched and puked.

Bo said quietly:

—I think they've fought enough.

—Me too, Bent said.

—Oh shit, Aage said. They haven't even begun. Shove Tristan baby there toward the school with a foot against his ass, so's we'll have boys only again, and let's get on with it.

—I think they've fought enough, Aage, Bo repeated. Something's wrong with Martin. There's too much blood.

—How can we get them to the infirmary, Bent asked with a scared voice, without all of us getting it in the neck?

—Cripes! Ib said. Peder's conked out.

—Fainted.

—Knocked out.

—Shake him.

—Get the puke out of his mouth.

—Let the bastard die, Martin said, spitting blood. Turn me loose, Tristan.

Bo and Ib lifted Peder by the shoulders, trying to get him to sit up.

—Don't like the way his head lolls, Bo said.

—He's coming around. Look at his eyes.

—They'll never get cleaned up and get back to school looking as if they haven't had a fight. It's a fucking war, here.

—Who says the fight's over? Aage asked.

—Oh shut up, you stinking sadist, Tristan said. You're mental, you know that?

Aage, pretending speechlessness, covered his mouth with both hands.

—Peder! Bo hollered. Are you all right?

—Look, Ib said, we've got Peder unconscious and maybe bleeding to death, huh, and we're acting like morons. Let's do something.

—Do what?

—Carry him to the infirmary, for starters.

—Let him die, Martin said.

—Wipe some of the blood off with Tristan's dress, Bo said. Take it off. Go get your clothes, on the post next hill over.

—Can't, Tristan said. Turned my ankle running from you pigs, and can't go that far.

—I'll get them, Bent said.

—So off with the dress. Let's rip it in two, half for Martin, half for Peder.

—Peder's opening his eyes.

—The whole point of the fight, Aage said, was for somebody to win it. You can't have a fight without a winner and a loser.

—Stuff it, Ib said.

—And fuck it, Martin said. I've had it. If Peder has too. He, by God, looks it.

—No way, Ib said, we can keep this from Master. Looks like a train hit both of you.

Tristan stood naked as an eft, on one leg. Ib kept spitting on the wad he'd made of the halved dress, wiping blood off Martin.

Peder waved Bo away, who was trying to do the same for him.

—Stand him up, Bent said. See if he can.

Peder gave him the finger, scrambled up, and pitched forward, to vomit again.

—What, Tristan asked, was the fight about, anyway?

—You don't want to know, Ib said. Can you walk on that leg?

—Sure, Tristan said, I think so.

—All we need right now, Bent said, is for somebody to come along to see two of us looking like a slaughterhouse and one naked cripple. Master would eat pills for the next two days.

—Turn anybody's stomach, Tristan said. Turns mine. Fighting's stupid, you know?

—If anybody asked your opinion, Aage said.

—Why did you make me play blindman's bluff in a dress? Look, I'm not afraid of any of you, huh? And I'm not taking any more bullying, OK?

—Would you fucking listen? Aage said.

Bo mopped Martin. Ib and Bent helped Peder up, whose knees were trembling.

—I'm all right, Peder said, his voice thick. Just let me alone a bit.

He pulled off his briefs to wipe his face. He felt his testicles with cautious fingers.

—Still there.

—Bo, Peder said, feel my balls and see if you think anything's wrong. One word out of anybody, and you get it in the mouth, I fucking promise.

—The rules were no rules, Aage said, so you can't bitch about kneed balls.

—Since when were you God? Tristan asked.

—Nobody's whining, Aage, Peder said. You get a knee in your balls and see if you don't puke.

—Let Martin feel, Bo said. He did it, and that's where it started, and you've got to make up. That's what a fight's for, yes?

—Up on the hill, Bent said, when I fetched Tristan's clothes, which you might put on after I went to the trouble, good deed and all, you know, the woman murdering butterflies seemed to be drifting this way. She's the one who glares at us on the way to the candy store.

—How did whichwhat start with Peder's balls? Tristan asked. All my togs are inside out.

—Do we let Tristan in? Bo asked. We've made him bust his ankle, and he did give us the slip.

—Ib and Bo and me, we vote yes, Bent said. Martin? Peder?

—He's too little, Martin said. Or is he?

—Feel my balls, Martin, Peder said. See if they're OK. I'm not mad anymore.

—Let me, Aage said. I'll give you a straight answer.

—No, Peder said. Martin. And there's a damned tooth loose.

—It was you that wanted to fight, Martin said.

—So let's have your opinion as to whether I'm ever going to be a father.

—What's *in*? Tristan asked. I have two toes about to come off, if anybody's interested, to go with my bum ankle.

—There's a poor imitation of a creek on the far side of the wood, you know, Ib said. We can get the blood off Martin and Peder.

—But not the bruises, fat lips, and shiners.

—My balls are going to look like a black grapefruit. What do you
think, Martin?

—If you come OK, next time you jack off, then they aren't busted,
right? Let's see the tooth.

—What am I in? Tristan asked.

—What's your vote, Aage?

Aage shrugged and quiddled his fingers.

—I'm already outvoted. I steal the dress, I solve Peder and Martin's
problem, I invent inside-out Colin Maillard, and all at once I'm a
clown.

—Life's like that, Peder said.

—Look, Bo said, it's getting cold out here. Let's head out, the shortest way back, and to every question we answer absofuckinglutely
nothing. Stare right over the top of the head of anybody asking any
question. OK?

All nodded, including Tristan.

They cast long, rippling shadows on the brown meadows, Bo carrying Tristan piggyback, Aage with his hands in his pockets, Martin
and Peder each with an arm around the other's shoulders, Ib and Bent
skipping along behind.

Juno of the Veii

Terra-cotta she was, and her hands were on her breasts, offering milk. Her big kindly eyes were painted white, with blue pupils. Long braided hair gilded, robe polychrome, Tuscan yellow stripes alternating with Sicilian green, silver sandals on her feet. Her expression was the way your mother looked at you in fun, playing that trick of love to cajole you into doing something you'd rather not.

She was the Juno of the Veii, and she was to be taken from her countrified temple to Rome.

Camillus had asked for pure youths to carry her on a litter, and the adjutant without a blink about-faced, looking wildly for a warrant officer. You rise in the ranks by obeying Camillus while the command is in the air between his beard and your ears.

—Clean, the adjutant said, scrubbed.

—Young, the sergeant said, means that they won't have had time to sin with any volume. Say recruits who aren't up to their eyes in debt, fresh of face, preferably with their milk teeth, calf's eyes, good stock, and washen hair.

—Take them to the flamen, the adjutant said, who'll get them into white tunics and clarify their minds for going into the *fanum* to bring the figure out, proper.

The first charge had been at dawn, and horrible. No trumpets.

—Use their roosters, the corporal said.

No guidons, no battle lines. Go in like creeping rats.

—Six *gregarii*, the sergeant said. We'll choose the best four. Wash them within an inch of their lives, dress their hair as if for a wedding.

We were all in a muck sweat from the siege. Some of us had burrowed under the wall, many of us were bloody, several had broken arms. The Falsicans had put up a fight, but with Camillus that has never got anybody anywhere.

The surrender was before noon.

—You are now Romans, Camillus said. Your enemies are our enemies.

There was fear in every face, and confusion. We tried to cheer them up with a parade around the walls.

Sistrum sistrum tympany horn.

And then Camillus had gone into their temple, being very religious, very correct. Meanwhile, we had the local wives filling tubs of water in the square. The sergeant kept lining up handsome privates with the straightest noses he could find, the broadest shoulders, trimmest waists, most soldierly legs. The priest was at them asking if they were virgins, if they were pious, what household gods they were devoted to, if they were distinguished enough to have participated in the cleansing of the trumpets on the Field of Mars, if they'd ever hunted without propitiating Diana afterward, if there was any incest, blasphemy, or habitual bad luck among them, and so on.

Though none admitted to virginity, the priest was not born yesterday, and came up with six tall striplings who washed in the tubs in the street, surrounded by a ring of staring children, pigs, and dogs. There were comments from the locals, which we understood by tone of voice alone. The priest went from tub to tub, casting spells on the water. The quartermaster brought a jug of oil and a jar of talcum.

—Do goats count?

—You mean sisters, don't you?

—What about with the sergeant?

—Boys, boys, the priest said. You are going to bear a *sacrum*. Suppress these scandalous, worldly *ioca*, out of reverence for Juno. Behind your ears, between your toes, under your foreskins. Scrub on those rusty knees.

We could see that the sergeant wanted to say *they have been in a battle, Your Grace*, but was restraining himself with his hands behind his back, keeping his dignity.

They dried with towels, oiled themselves, with jests saltier than in the tubs, strigiled down while being blessed by the priest, and repeated, with one degree of accuracy or another, a strange old prayer.

Camillus himself held inspection.

— Name, soldier?

— Lucius, sir.

— Are there impurities of mind or deed which would render you unclean for transporting the Mater of the Veii?

— No, sir.

— You realize the seriousness of your duty?

— Yes, sir.

— Name, soldier?

— Marcus, sir.

Same question, same answer, down the line. Burrus, the red down on whose cheeks made him look like a fox, and Caius, with rusty knees, were nominated supernumeraries.

Two rows of drummers lined the path to the temple, keeping back profane noises and such spirits of the air and the dead as might botch our enterprise.

Camillus, his way strewn with barley, went into the temple first.

No thunder sounded, only the tumbling warning of the drums.

The detail came behind him, looking more like altar boys than soldiers.

We heard later that he spoke in the old Latin, identifying himself as a child by adoption and favor of Mater Matuta, guardian of farmers and soldiers at dawn.

— I come worshipfully to beg your permission to take you to Rome, where you will have a house of honor among our great gods. I have clean young men of pure morals to carry you on their shoulders.

It was Marcus who was surest what then happened.

Roman generals do not bend for god or man. So Camillus stood at attention until she gave her sign.

Some of the detail said that the statue nodded, and spoke in darkest Etruscan, full of whistles and clicks, and this is what Camillus reported to the conscript fathers.

But Marcus said that she smiled.

A Gingham Dress

These butter peas are a dime the quart. Fifteen for the runners and a nickel the okra. Lattimer here picked the dewberries. He's a caution, ain't he? Going on nine and still won't wear nothing but a dress and bonnet. Says he's a girl, don't you, Lattimer? He's as cute as one. Everybody says that.

Say what, Leon? That's what I was telling Mrs. Fant. He'll grow out of it.

We'll be sure to bring watermelons when they're in. It's been so dry. Good for the corn but keeps the melons back. Our cantaloupes, I always say, are sweet as sugar. We stand good to have some next time down. The mushmelon, the honeydew, and the ice-box: we raise all three.

What, Lattimer? Of course Mrs. Fant has a ice-box. He likes to know what things people have in their houses. He was saying on the way down that he wished he could see ever bird in ever cage all over town.

We heard tell it was in the paper about the church up to Sandy Springs. Leon says it puts us on the map. Nothing to do with us. We go Baptist. These are the Pentecostals, church right at the turn off to Toccoa. The way I understand it is that their preacher went on vacation, to Florida, and he ast this Rev. Holroyd, from Seneca, to take his flock while he was away, you see. Well, first thing he saw was neckties on the men. And he said the Holy Bible is against any necktie. You ever hear such a thing? But they taken them off.

What, Leon? Leon says he thinks he'll join their church.

Our preacher, speaking of wearing and not wearing, don't know no better but what Lattimer is a girl. He comes to us on the Sunday only, from over to Piney Grove. Of course, you are, dear heart, if you say you are. On the Wednesday we get a lady preacher. Comes over from Saluda, regular as clockwork, and does a beautiful service. Sings, plays the piano, reads from Scripture just like a man. She knows that Lattimer is a boy. Knew it right off. She said first time she set eyes on him, *That's a boy in a dress.*

Leon says *Anybody would.* But this Mrs. Dillingham, Rev. Dillingham I ought to say, says she don't see why not. She says as long as he's not lewd, she sees no harm.

Anyway, here's Rev. Hunnicutt back from Florida and the first thing they ast him is do Christians wear neckties. What they wrote in the paper was that about half the church wanted Rev. Holroyd to stay on, as knowing Scripture better than Rev. Hunnicutt, and the other half was content with Hunnicutt, who says there's not a word in the Bible about any necktie.

It is funny, ain't it, Lattimer? He listens to every word you say, and remembers it. And sings along with the radio. He has a lovely voice, if I do say so. The Gospel Hour's his favorite. Holds his doll up and makes like it's singing, too. He helps in the kitchen, you know, as kindly as a daughter, and can wring a chicken's neck good as I can. Wants his hair long, but Leon draws the line there. So he's a girl with boy's hair.

You'll not regret them butter peas. They cook up best with salt pork, I always say. Let's see now, would you want some of Lattimer's dewberries, a pint?

This Roosevelt is something else, ain't he? They say he's a Jew. And his wife sits down and eats with niggers. I never seen the beat.

You'd think the boys would tease, but they don't. He's that dear. One of the MacAlister boys, Harper, calls him his sweetheart.

A thing I don't hold with is one person telling another how to lead their life, like with the neckties and the two preachers. They say the half the flock that holds with Holroyd are going to build another church right across the highway.

What, Leon? Of course we're mountain people. He says mountain people have always lived the way they want to. Leon *will* sit in the car and talk to the dashboard while I'm selling produce.

Lattimer, now, wants a gingham dress he saw in the window of Lesser's uptown. Why, I said, all I need is a yard and a half of gingham off the bolt at Woolworth's, some rickrack for the collar, a card of buttons, and I can sew one just like it. Pleats and all. I've used the pattern many's the time, for Sue Elizabeth's red dress she wears to school for one, Maddie Mae's pink dress for another.

What, Leon? Leon says it's cheaper than a pair of overalls. That's true. Well, I guess that's it. What say, Lattimer? It's not polite to whisper, I've always heard. What? Lattimer wants you to know he thinks your permanent wave is becoming.

Yes, Leon, we're through.

Badger

Into Scoresbysund seamed with frost and blue with hindered green, the brave sails of Erik Nordenskiöld; into the yellow hills and red villages of the Medes, Tobias, his dog, and the archangel Rafayel; into Nørreport, by train from Kongens Lyngby, Allen. Badger was waiting for him in the station lavatory, laughing at his cleverness in being there.

—What a bog, Badger said. My, you're handsome, as boys go, and you've come off without the cello and the Telemann sonata in four movements you've practiced all week. Thorvaldsen says that he gets lots of fife-and-drum stuff from the Lutheran Sodality Marching Band, and unseemly hornpipes and rock and roll from around on Nyhavn, but has never heard the kind of recital we give on Amagertorv. Very superior cat, you understand, is Thorvaldsen, and always has the church organ and string quartets to drop mention of when I brag about your street concerts on the cello.

Allen flicked off the blue ascot his mother made him wear to go with his eyes, and poked it into his haversack. Then he pulled his shirt over his head, replacing it with a gray sweatshirt from the haversack. Next he exchanged his short pants for exiguously shorter ones, the zipper of which did not go all the way up.

—Barepaw, too? Badger asked.

—No underwear, either, friend Badger.

—I assume, then, Badger said while offhandedly rooting at a flea,

215

that you being twelve years old and all, and the cello nowhere in sight, and Edna not along, we don't allude to this outing back home?

—I don't think so, no. We're only out to learn a thing or two, anyway. No big deal.

—No no, of course not. I see we're going to put the haversack into the locker, to be retrieved on the way back. You think of everything.

—Not exactly in diapers still, you know.

Badger laughed, as he loved a conspiracy. He loyally did not ask where they were going. He would find out.

WHITE PRAIRIE ASTER

I long ago lost a hound, a bay horse, and a turtledove, and am still on their trail. Many are the travelers I have spoken concerning them, describing their tracks and what calls they answered to. I have met one or two who have heard the hound, and the tramp of the horse, and even seen the dove disappear behind a cloud, and they seemed as anxious to recover them as if they had lost them themselves.

ENGLISH STONECROP

—If, Badger remarked on Gothersgade, we go into the Rosenborg Have we'll see naked girls sunbathing.

—*Ork jo!* Allen said. Later. First, we're going to the botanical garden.

—Because I'm home asleep on your bed, and dogs aren't allowed, as we chase the ducks and make the grebes nervous, and are cheeky to the swans?

—*Tetigisti acu.*

—Plautus. But why the botanical garden? Greenland wildflowers. You like those. Ghost of Hans Christian Andersen in the hothouse, upside-down over the begonias, legs opening and closing like scissors.

—To sweeten my dare with delay.

—Oh, that.

FISH

In Hendrik Goudt's engraving, Tobias, lugging the fish, steadied by

Rafayel, is crossing a stream on stepping stones. Nimrod, the dog, is gathering himself to jump to the next stone as soon as Rafayel's foot is out of the way. There are oxen on the far side of the stream. Two frogs, who must soon stretch themselves into elastic leaps or be trod on, to their way of thinking, by a twelve-year-old, an angel, and a dog, having no way of knowing that Rafayel is weightless and must move, step by step, as if he were a mass responding to gravity, get set to jump. The sky, above lush trees, has clouds and geese.

5

Peter Freuchen, brushing frost from his beard, brought the wall of ice between the black sea and a black sky close enough in his binoculars to see the long grooves of exact crystal that wrinkled its surface.

BALTIC SAILOR

The stranger facing Allen was blond and trim. His intense gaze made the blue discs of his eyes seem slightly crossed. His shirt sleeves were rolled above his elbows. His jeans were pleated with creases across the top of the thighs and at the knees. Twenty, friendly, made in Scandinavia.

RED-BEAKED GREBE

In 1653 or thereabouts Rembrandt bought a plate by Hercules Segers, of Tobias and the angel Rafayel and the dog Nimrod. He changed it to a Flight into Egypt. Tobias became Joseph, Rafayel Mary, and Nimrod the donkey.

—And, said Badger, in Moses van Uyttenbroeck's picture Nimrod is barking at ducks and scaring them off the lake.

—Tobias and Rafayel are both twelve in that, and Tobias is dragging the fish.

—Yes, but this is in the Bible. Why does Nimrod get to worry ducks, and in a civilized and most advanced country like Denmark dogs can't go near the duck pond without being shouted at by the constabulary?

—What you see, you know, Allen said, you own. You take it in. Everything's an essence. Papa, you remember, when I was explaining this to him, said that at twelve you understand everything. Afterward, you have to give it up and specialize.

—Ducks are not to be believed. Give up coherent light for articulate light. Puppies understand everything, too, and then have to get a job looking after twelve-year-olds in downtown København with no shoes or socks, smitch of pants with lazy zipper, and a pullover shirt as might be worn by the bucket boy on an eel trawler.

—The film of essences, one photon thick, is continuous. Everything apprehended is in the continuum of this film. So all correspondences, the relation of information to other information, are first of all differences. Colors, shapes, textures. Quit yawning. This is important.

—It rather tried your papa's patience, didn't it, until you said that the great thing is affability, not the kinship but the kindness of one thing to another.

—And Mama remarked what a sweet pagan she had for a son.

—Edna stuck out her tongue.

—*You* sighed and whuffed.

8

Because they, too, were his, the lilac arbor and beds of Greenland wildflowers blue and yellow, Allen walked with studied idleness along the dappled paths of the botanical garden, his dare to himself prospering with delay.

—Getting your courage up, aren't you? Badger asked while looking with slitted eyes at a swan. You could be on roller skates, in your spatter jeans. You could be eating pea pods in Gray Brothers. You could be into the second movement of the Telemann.

—I have things to learn.

—The caterpillar of the codling moth feeds on the kernels of apples and pears.

KIERKEGAARD IN THE TROLLWOOD

The stranger facing Allen was blond and trim. His intense gaze made the blue discs of his eyes seem slightly crossed. His shirt sleeves were rolled above his elbows. His jeans were pleated with creases across the top of the thighs and at the knees. Twenty, friendly, made in Scandinavia

CRICKETS IN FLIXWEED

An aristocracy of swans pushed haughtily through a commonality of ducks and a yokeldom of grebes.

—When a buck flea backs up, scrunched in, to jump, I snip the tickle, he jumps, I snap, he bites, I snick. Fuckering flea.

On a path that curved through deep lilies and high shrubbery, Allen, eyes hypothetically sneaky, lips puckered in supposition, unzipped, as if to pee, as might be. The school nurse, a good sort, had looked at it during his last physical, with an amused smile, and winked. Harald's had a callus on it, and looked bruised, like Papa's.

—With friendly numbers, Badger said, the divisors of the one add up to the other. The example given by Pythagoras is two hundred twenty and two hundred eighty-four.

—Cold nose, Allen said. Bugger off.

—The divisors of two hundred twenty are one two four five ten eleven twenty twenty-two forty-four fifty-five and one hundred ten, and they add up to two hundred eighty-four, which is the number friendly to two hundred twenty. Now you can't get it back in your pants, can you?

—A friend is another self, like the friendly numbers two hundred twenty and two hundred eighty-four. Didn't think I was listening, did you?

—And the divisors of two hundred eighty-four add up to two hundred twenty.

—So what does it mean, O Badger?

—That as many ways as one friend can be divided sum up to the other. Better stuff your dick back in, there's somebody coming. You smell as if you were with Harald eating chocolate and listening to a Bach partita.

—Looks like big business hard in my pants, wouldn't you say?

—Oh, absolutely. Hate fleas. You're a handsome boy.

—You're a handsome dog.

—The lion in the zoo is a cat who's a dog. Monkey is a dog who's a spider.

OHIO BEE, OHIO HONEY

I long ago lost a hound, a bay horse, and a turtledove, and am still on their trail. Many are the travelers I have spoken concerning them, describing their tracks and what calls they answered to. I have met one or two who have heard the hound, and the tramp of the horse, and even seen the dove disappear behind a cloud, and they seemed as anxious to recover them as if they had lost them themselves.

12

Mellow gold and muted silver, a bed of flowers. Harald's scoutmaster says that a disposition to fall in love makes everybody look good. The truly beautiful, like Harald, don't need rationalizing, but you can think of a hooked nose as kingly and a snub nose as cute and a rough complexion as masculine and a sallow face as sensitive.

—That's Plato, Badger said. Is it for Harald that we're here in the botanical garden wondering how the divisors of a friendly number add up to the components of its friend? What we have are differences containing samenesses. Differently distributed. That's nicely tricky, *jo*?

YELLOW WILLOWS ALONG A RIVER

To tune his ears to the hearing of Tobias, Rafayel discovered with cunning questions that human beings cannot hear the roaring fires of the stars or thunder on the wanderers or the hiss of winds across space. Nor could they hear the creak of trees growing, the tread of ants, or the rumble of seedlings breaking ground to stand in light.

14

—Thorvaldsen down on Sankt Annæ Plads likes to be called *Your Grace*, like his person the bishop.

—You're a funny dog, Badger, to like cats.

—Why not? He's fun to talk to. Cats don't like dogs because we smell butts and they resent it. They smell mouths, did you know? Anyway, I get along with His Grace Thorvaldsen the Holstein cat. They know things, cats. Their ear is more critical than a dog's. Good nose, too, but the whole race of them is so prudish and inhibited as to seem to have no nose at all. Did you know that the bishop's parish includes Greenland? I was telling him about you and Harald leapfrogging each other the whole length of the Købmagergade, and he began to brush his chest and inspect his paws.

—The boys we saw when we were coming from the station, Allen said, copperknob and towhead, who were sharing a Coke at a small table in that sandwich shop.

—Towhead's hair is very grebe chick, Badger said. We were supposed to take it for punk, wouldn't you say? You envy them their one Coke, age, and decisively creased jeans.

—Do I, now?

—Oh yes. You and Harald don't have to share a Coke. You each have your own.

—I'd rather share.

—Are you in love with Harald?

A duck belonging to the Rosenborg moat was crossing the Gothersgade, halting traffic.

—Probably, Allen said.

—Is that a good thing or a bad?

—Good, I'd say. Very good.

—Well, then.

—Precisely.

—Headed for the Rosenborg Have, are we?

—Why not, friend Badger?

—Why not, indeed.

TENT INTERIOR BY LANTERN LIGHT

A stout wind fell on them from the north. Their tent tried to fly away before they could peg it to the forest floor. The rain, fine and swiveling, began when the tent was almost trig and their gear was half un-packed. They were inside, Harald and Allen, snug and with the lantern lit, when the rain began to blow sideways.

— Nothing neater, Harald said. Off our clothes.

— We'll freeze.

— Into dry, I mean, until dossing down.

— Sardines, crackers, cheese, chocolate milk.

— Coffee in the thermos, as filled at Rungsted Kro. Socks.

— What about socks?

— To hang above the lantern. First, to sniff. Me, yours, Olaf does.

— Here. Jesu Kristus, you really are. Like Badger.

— Nice. Thing is, to know the person you like. Olaf talks about the se-cret and privileged smells. Shirt.

— Wouldn't get me anywhere to be embarrassed, would it?

— Everything smells like lilac.

— Jasmine. Body oil, after my bath. And sweat from hiking all day.

— Body oil.

— Keeps my skin from drying out and itching.

— What a baby you are, still. Briefs.

— Briefs. Soon as I get them off. Am I to copycat? What do I sniff for, if I sniff?

— Put me a sardine and a bite of cheese on that cracker. Olaf sniffs to drive himself crazy, he says. But he's lovely crazy to begin with. Makes his wizzle stand, all twenty centimeters.

— And then what?

— Listen to the rain.

16

Drum and fife! The Queen's Guards were marching from the barracks in ranks of three, files of ten, in busbies and blue, musettes on their butts, their sergeant-major strutting to *There Is a Tavern in the Town.*

SCHOLAR WITH LION AND POT OF BASIL

The stranger facing Allen was blond and trim. His intense gaze made the blue discs of his eyes seem slightly crossed. His shirt sleeves were rolled above his elbows. His jeans were pleated with creases across the top of the thighs and at the knees. Twenty, friendly, made in Scandinavia.

TIME SINKS IN ORION

A girl with pink nipples and high hard breasts was taking off her jeans in the Rosenborg, among as many sunbathers as seals on an Aleutian beach. A triangle of arcs, her *slip*, flag red, and her friend with a swimmer's back and saucery hollows in his solidly boxed buttocks was cupped into a gauze pouch and cingle. Their mouths were grazing each other's lips in slow circles, their jeans still around their ankles. Badger trotted over to smell.

— Kelp and olive, his, he said, laughing. Tuna and mayonnaise, hers.

— You're awful, you know, pal Badger. You belong to a different order of being.

— Dog, part lion, part wolf. When you and Harald swapped underpants, you sniffed his before putting them on.

— They smelled of clean laundry, with a whiff of hay-mow.

19

Hillside thick with meadow flowers, midges, butterflies, gnats, a wall of Norway pines on the other rim of the dip, an empty sky, a lonely place rich in silence, in remoteness, in stillness. He and Harald, piecemeal naked by the time they'd got to the middle of the slant field, shirts over their shoulders, sneakers untied, suddenly looked at each other, serious with surmise and then all monkey grins. Best of friends, Harald. He was naked first. They lay in dense grass, gazing up into the absolute August blue.

— There's snug, Harald said, hand straying, like our tent that rainy night in the forest.

— Slushy inside, too, like drenched, sperm from chin to knee.

— And there's open, like here, where you can see to the top of the sky, and in all directions. There's nowhere as private as the middle of a field.

DUTCH SKY PILED WITH CLOUDS

Tobias carried the fish, which would have been too heavy for him except that Rafayel made local adjustments in gravity. A sparrow flew right through Rafayel. Only Nimrod noticed. They did not walk on Shabbat.

FLANDERS UNDER RAIN

I long ago lost a hound, a bay horse, and a turtledove, and am still on their trail. Many are the travelers I have spoken concerning them, describing their tracks and what calls they answered to. I have met one or two who have heard the hound, and the tramp of the horse, and even seen the dove disappear behind a cloud, and they seemed as anxious to recover them as if they had lost them themselves.

22

Log cabin, Troll Wood Troop, Danish Free Scouts. Olaf, a fall of hair over one eye, sitting on a picnic table, legs crossed, had told them about Janusc Korczak and King Matthæus.

A long silence. Harald's arm across Allen's shoulders. Benjamin asked about Poland, the Nazis, the war. Aage asked why the sky is blue, and why it's bluest in August. Rasmus said that it was bluest in October, and wanted Olaf to tell them again about the inner parts of girls, exactly what was going on there. Isak wanted to hear more about the Education No Thanks kids in Düsseldorf, who ran a bicycle shop and defied all authority, settled enemies of capitalism, the family, and girls. Ejnar invited everybody to join him in a swim in the inlet, before the Swedes poured ice water into the ocean, as was their wont about this time of day, and was seconded by Marcus, who was already naked. Hjalmar offered to march them to the inlet with Haydn on his horn, Hommel on his drum.

Allen was most interested in a naked Olaf, about which he'd heard so much from Harald.

——It is sort of unbelievable, he whispered in Harald's ear.

—What's unbelievable? Marcus asked, loud.

—Who else, Ejnar crowed through the shirt he was pulling over his head, marches to a swim with a French horn and drum as spiffy as the Queen's Guards? Style is what we have, that's what.

—Watch, Harald said to Allen.

He bounced, with turns on his heel, over to Olaf, who lifted him onto his shoulders, with an awesomely squeezed hug on the way up. Harald was radiant, Olaf complacent.

Later, winded and dripping, Hjalmar and Hommel wrestling like puppies in the sand, Olaf said that he and Harald and Allen were going to walk back to the cabin the long way round, through the woods on the slope. Was Allen, Olaf asked when they were having a pee in the wood, comfortable with the outing, with the troop, with Harald?

—Oh yes. Sure.

—Allen only looks timid, Harald said. His heart's a lion's, a lazy lion's.

—Thanks, Allen said. Badger will like that.

—Who's Badger? Olaf asked.

—Allen's dog. Is he here, Allen friend?

—Not yet.

—How, Olaf asked, could a dog get here if Allen didn't bring him?

—Easy, Harald said. I've been on long bike rides with Allen when Badger was along, though all I could see, not being as spooky as Allen, was the empty air. I sometimes think, though, that I've felt Badger's Alpo breath and got a whiff of his dogginess. And Allen smells like Badger if you get him before a bath.

Olaf, confused, had other things on his mind. He had taken a course in modern art with Allen's mother at the university.

—And your father edits a classics journal, doesn't he?

—I think so, Allen said. Something like that. Wait till I tell Mummy one of her students is Harald's scoutmaster.

—She'll have to sit down, I imagine, Harald said.

BADGER

Of pests, the flea the fly the tick the leash, none stings like want, when

you are not there, where you are not then. The box on rounds the two
legs roll in, its stink is not worse than being here when Uln is there.
What are mustard, Ejnar? And Swan Wings with the ozone midnight
smell and Tobias who smells like Harald and Nimrod their dog whose
real name is Wind and with them a Fish. With ducks there are three,
duck and drake and the drake's drake friend Anders. Not natural for
them not to fight but what do ducks have for brains? Uln smells good
when he's with Harald, and feels good, so we like Harald.

24

Allen's suspicion that people created themselves was the only way he
could explain Olaf. His parents could not have designed him. Parents
don't think that way. God? But why would God, whose thoughts are
pure, have curved Olaf's upper lip just that way, with the tuck and
dimple at the corners, and shaped him all over in such a cunningly
sexy and perfect a style that everything about him was the way Allen
also wanted to be. Truth was, and why do people not say this, Olaf
made himself. You have to know what you want to look like. Nature
complies.

——It sounds right, you know? Harald agreed. You've found something out. But Olaf's body comes from swimming and running and
the gym.

——Understood, friend Harald. But his smile and the look in his eyes
and his friendliness don't. How did he get those? And everybody has
a cock, all boys I mean, but Marcus's looks like a grub and his balls are
peanuts.

——Olaf's seventeen, Marcus ten.

——Can you believe that Olaf's looked like Marcus's when he was ten?
Never. I'd say it was the size of a *polser* and stuck out, like yours, admired by all. Olaf thought his cock into the handsome monster it is.

——I know that he had a friend when he was little. He told me. Never
needed to say they wanted it. They knew at the same time. Dropped
their pants together, as if there'd been a signal. I think Olaf's been sad

since then. The friend got a whiff of girl around fourteen and has been on them, in them, since, humping away, with just enough wits left to stagger around between fucks. Olaf says girls are all wrapped up in themselves, hard to make friends with.

THE RED VILLAGES OF THE MEDES

Rafayel discovered that he could talk to Nimrod more easily than to Tobias.

—The grief of the fish, he said.

—Dun clouds on a Friday, Nimrod said. A flame is fat with sinking while it is slender with rising.

—The wife of four is three.

—Nine is the grandmother of numbers.

—Walking, Rafayel said with wonder in his voice, walking. There were trees of crows at Charleville, a winter of crows. Or will be. Tenses are not for angels. A boy named Jean Nicholas Arthur. Like Tobias. Like Uln. I walked, will walk, walk with him toward black trees in a winter field, the angelus chiming from the square tower of a small church, the rim of the world red where it was rolling away from your star. He spoke of the Prince of Aquitaine, whose heart was widowed and dark, and cried *Give me back Pausilippe and Italian sea!* and the crows cried in their hundreds *The sun is dead!* The wind carried their caws.

—The wind, Badger said.

—The wind, said Allen.

—One hundred crows!

—What does a dog know?

—Ask Nimrod. He knew that Rafayel was not people, by his smell. No oniony armpits, only celestial electricity, rich in ozone. Thorvaldsen, now, would have taken Rafayel to be a higher rank of bishop, and from Sweden. He would have stropped his leg. He would have sat across from him on an episcopal cushion, pretending to be of equal rank among ecclesiastical cats.

SCORESBYSUND

The stranger facing Allen was blond and trim. His intense gaze made
the blue discs of his eyes seem slightly crossed. His shirt sleeves were
rolled above his elbows. His jeans were pleated with creases across the
top of the thighs and at the knees. Twenty, friendly, made in Scandinavia.

27

—Of course I made myself! Olaf said. Allen's right as rain. How plain
I used to be, I won't say. Around three, it must have been, sucking my
thumb, knock-kneed, and given to whooping cough, nose drip, and
pyromania, I began to rethink myself. By six, still a thumbsucker, I
had a vision. I knew that I admired some people and found others revolting. Being a philosopher, I knew that the people I didn't like were
being repulsive on purpose. There was a girl with a kind of pearly mole
just inside her nostril. She had made it grow there, to annoy her parents, and me. She liked to puke in Kindergarten, without warning.
Nurse asked her one hundred times at least to point to her mouth
when she was going to barf. She never did. Oh, the happy beam in her
eyes when she had spattered her coloring book, my blocks, Nurse's
shoes. So it followed that the people I loved had made themselves
adorable. By eight I was in love to the point of being legally insane
with a twelve-year-old who had big brown eyes and a mop of curls,
and long legs, and petted his crotch in public. I would willingly have
died if I could have *been* him, if only for one day. I did the next best
thing: I set out to wish myself, will myself, magic myself, to be him.
This worked. It worked so well that when I met Hugo at twelve, he was
in love with me, I discovered with my heart floating up to my mouth.
That should happen to everybody at least once. We became each other. Wore each other's clothes. There's a pair of little denim pants I have
packed away, thin as gauze and threadbare, which we both wore.

WIND AROUND A CORNER, FULL OF LEAVES

I long ago lost a hound, a bay horse, and a turtledove, and am still on their trail. Many are the travelers I have spoken concerning them, describing their tracks and what calls they answered to. I have met one or two who have heard the hound, and the tramp of the horse, and even seen the dove disappear behind a cloud, and they seemed as anxious to recover them as if they had lost them themselves.

29

The first night Allen spent at his house, Harald as soon as his folks left for a dinner party walked around naked in the back garden, level sunlight making gold fire in his hair.

PARK WITH FIGURES

A young man lay as if fallen from the sky onto the grass of the Rosenborg greensward, arms and legs spread, his shirt rolled under his neck, jeans open and briefs pushed onto his hipbones.

—I would like, Badger said, to be the drum major in front of the Queen's Guards when they're marching to *The Stars and Stripes Forever*, and I'd love to roll in horse flop and not get lectured on it. Also, I'd like to visit a jungle, for the tremendousness of it, you know? But you're looking at that boy with hair all but down over his eyes and his underpants bowed out in front. Butterflies, monkeys, frogs, shelf fungus, green fleas, sponge trees, blue parrots, yellow parrots, red parrots, and vines as long as Jylland if you straightened them out.

—The principle of essences, Allen said, is identity: each essence's being is entirely exhausted by the character which distinguishes it from any other essence. It's for Harald we're here, O Badger.

—Taking things in, Badger said, that's what's important. Your mother said so. Said that if she could teach her children to miss nothing of what the world has to give, she would be doing her duty. Her example, you remember, was a pear tree in bloom. We're being admired.

—I am, anyway. What do you suppose she means?

—Got me. The rock dove flits starbright through the oleanders.

—Amber gleam, Allen whispered, of the wild partridge in umber gloom. I can recite poetry, too. He is staring at me, isn't he?

—A pear tree in bloom. *Ork jo.*

——White, fragrant, green, by a brick wall, beside a roof, thatched or tile, pears to come, if fuckered properly by bees. Lovely in sunshine, rain, moonlight. Crisp blossoms in profusion, small, tender, white.

——Painted by Stanley Spencer.

——Christian Mølsted.

——Charles Burchfield.

——Samuel Palmer.

——Hokusai.

——I forget that I'm invisible, not here to be seen.

——Brave's the word.

——Don't you think your admirer's a bit rough, from the Christianhavn docks, wouldn't you say?

——I would say that, yes.

——Dirt under his fingernails. Good-looking, though. Flat bone down his nose, plumb from where his bronze eyebrows almost join, to the square tip. What does Telemann *mean* in the slow movement?

A RUCKLING OF DOVES

The high wall around the yard was grown over with Virginia creeper, which a breeze tickled. Trees beyond the wall, lazily liquid in the fitful wind that precedes rain, were so tall and densely green that the yard was a square space in a thick forest. Allen studied a compass, an ordnance map. He made a study of the sky, Baltic blue marbled yellow and green. The house was still, empty. The ladder was against the wall. A wheelbarrow. A rake. A hamper basket.

He knelt to untie his sneakers, stood on one leg, and then the other, to pull off his socks.

Harald toward dawn in the tent had said that the rain, with them so warm and close, was the finest sound he had ever heard.

The clouds were drifting from the east. He tugged his jersey over his head and rolled it into a baton.

Next it rains, she had said, if you could believe girls. He believed Hanna. She had freckles, wore glasses, and knew things. She was witty, but nice, about Harald. So that was all right.

He took off his shorts and wrapped them around his rolled jersey.

Red underpants. Did the sun make fire in his hair as it had in Harald's? You are the earl of the elves, Hanna had said. Not passed on to Harald, who would flip his fingers. Lord of the forest. Telemann, the slow movement, and rain on the tent.

THE SEDGE TO THE SEA

How did Badger know where he was going, that he could accurately run ahead? Harald liked to be sniffed by Badger, reveled in it. Boys, Edna said, are so thick, you can't find a place where you could shove in a pin. And Badger was comically confused when Harald passed over the frayed, worn denim pants Olaf lent him with the injunction that if he lost them, or tore them, he'd wish he was somebody else in another country. But had wanted us to wear them.

—But we do understand, Harald had said, ever so seriously.

—I hope so, Olaf said. I'd hate for me and Badger to be the only ones here who see what's going on.

—I'll tell you, Allen said. It's like the day I finally took Badger into town with me, so his curiosity could be satisfied. He was out of his mind happy, looking at everybody, everything. And when he saw how I make a territory on Strøget, all mine, all ours, he almost wagged his tail off with pleasure, and when I set up the music stand and played, he too was playing the cello, and acknowledging every attention, beating time with his tail to a music none of us will ever hear.

—Don't we? Harald said.

—If, Harald, Olaf said, you hadn't said that, I would have been disappointed the rest of my life.

INTO NØRREPORT

I long ago lost a hound, a bay horse, and a turtledove, and am still on their trail. Many are the travelers I have spoken concerning them, describing their tracks and what calls they answered to. I have met one or two who have heard the hound, and the tramp of the horse, and even seen the dove disappear behind a cloud, and they seemed as anxious to recover them as if they had lost them themselves.

Postscript

When I rolled up my sleeves, took a deep breath, and began to try my hand at fiction back in the 1970s, my hope was to make a few imaginative structures about various people and events in the fabric of history that were, at the time, unfamiliar enough to be interesting and consequential enough to be known— the Russian genius Vladimir Tatlin, the discovery of the prehistoric painted cave at Lascaux, the traveler Pausanias walking around Greece in the second century of our half of time. I tried to be as inventive as I could, obeying the injunction "in letters of gold on T'ang's bathtub" to "yet again make it new" that Thoreau quotes in *Walden* and Ezra Pound used as a battle cry.

There are now eight collections of these "imaginative structures," or stories (a doctoral thesis at the Sorbonne calls them "fractal assemblages"), sixty-two of them in all, one of which runs to 130 pages, and another to 235. The shortest is half a page.

Each book was meant to be the last; *Da Vinci's Bicycle* ends with a farewell to writing, and *Apples and Pears*, the fourth (a treatise in narrative on Charles Fourier), was an inventory, I thought, of everything I'd squirreled away in my notebooks.

Par qui vos livres sont-ils lus? Cocteau asks at the end of *Léoun*. The answer on bad days is *nobody, yet*; and on good days *more than I deserve*. Cocteau also asks, *Existe-t-il un monde où je pourrai me taire?* Making things is so human that psychology and philosophy have gotten nowhere in trying to account for it.

It is not wise to look too hard at what's going on when we read and write, for in both we are dithering around on the boundary between the demonstrable world and the inviolably private world of our minds. The realm of the physical and the realm of essences, as Santayana explained; Rilke's taking in and giving out (if we're poets). Inside Lascaux the painter was saying, "This is a tarpan, and here is a cow." Whereas Homer could ask a muse to help him, we must invoke the imagination, or our aesthetic will, or some fashion in what's getting published. Whatever we invoke, we are dependent on the reader's attention.

Attention. A contingent of the Peace Corps once had the bright idea that a film made in the African village to which they were bringing enlightenment and hygiene would make wonderfully clear that puddles breed mosquitoes and that mosquitoes distribute malaria. Everyone got to be in the film; important elders had lines to say about standing water. The film was shown one evening to the whole village. At one point their solemn watching was broken by screams of excitement and wonder. "Ntumbe's chicken!" they all cried. Could they see the film again? There were inattentive children who had not seen Ntumbe's chicken. Please show Ntumbe's chicken again!

The Peace Corps was mystified. But, sure enough, at the top of a few frames only, in a scene where a conscientious mother was sweeping away a puddle of rainwater, a chicken could be seen crossing the camera's line of vision. The film was thereafter known as "Ntumbe's Chicken." These nice young Americans can tell their outlandish tales about the *keke* all they want to, but to have Ntumbe's chicken, strolling and pecking, in a moving picture, what more can one ask of art?

For thirty years I have been writing stories in which Ntumbe's chicken has riveted the attention of too many of my few readers. The academy has even evolved a school of criticism to teach people to see nothing but Ntumbe's chicken (or its absence).

These twelve stories are the ones I choose to salvage from *Tatlin!* (1974), *Apples and Pears* (1984), and *The Drummer of the Eleventh North Devonshire Fusiliers* (1990), where they were the outworks to the long and densely collaged novelle "The Dawn in Erewhon," "Apples and Pears: Het Erewhonisch Schetsboek, Messidor-Vendémiaire 1981," and "Wo es war, soll ich werden," all three of which were derived from Charles Fourier's *Théorie des quatres mouvements et des destinées générales* (1808) and Adriaan van Hovendaal's *Higgs Reizen in Erewhonland* (1964) together with his *Blue and Brown Baltic Notebooks* (1978–80). Another age, beyond our end-of-the-century comstockery and Liberal puritanism, may find these works interesting, *aber freilich nicht wahrscheinlich*.

It was long after writing my *Konstruktivist* story about Vladimir Tatlin that I met a man who had known him well and could find out the color of his eyes (gray) and what his emotional life might have been ("there were women"). When Mario Muchnik was translating "Robot" into Spanish, it occurred to him that he might drive up to Montignac from Barcelona and discuss the story with Jacques Marsal himself, which he did, spending "a magic day" comparing fact with fiction. "It was like walking into your story."

None of the other stories can be walked into except through texts by Poe, Kafka, Plutarch, and Bashō, whose *Oku no hosomichi* alternates with other travels in "Fifty-Seven Views of Fujiyama."

Lucretius asks if we can imagine going so far into the star-seeded emptiness of space that a thrown spear would bounce back. These stories are about limits and boundaries, and are themselves bound by my limitations. The illusion that all imaginative writing must create is that the thrown spear finds a hole in the stars and sails serenely through. Fiction is not a mirror but a waking dream. "1830" is a lie Poe told Rufus Wilmot Griswold as the bourbon sank in the bottle.

"The Bowmen of Shu" begins with a letter from Henri Gaudier-Brzeska, written from the trenches in 1915, that John Cournos showed me one evening in Haverford, taking it from its envelope, while remembering introducing Gaudier to Pound fifty years before. "The Gingham Dress" I heard with my own ears. "Tatlin!" began as a painting, "Herakleitos" as a translation for classroom use, "The Aeroplanes at Brescia" as a scholarly article, "Juno of the Veii" as part of a book on Plutarch that I never finished. "Fifty-Seven Views" is all that's left of a *Robert Browning Overture* that I may yet write. "Badger" comes from reading *Calvin and Hobbes* in Danish newspapers, "Colin Maillard" from a photograph by Bernard Faucon.

Instigations, however, are deceptive guides into imaginative structures, and the maker of the structure may be as deceptive a guide. The imagination sees with the eyes of the spirit; the maker, finished with his making, must then see what he has done, like the reader, with corporeal eyes. Thoreau on an afternoon in 1852 when he had been looking at birds, trees, cows, squirrels, and flowers for hours raged that he had no words for the *music* he felt in every muscle of his body.

To see that Thoreau could achieve a spiritual music in words you have only to look at any page he wrote. His frustration is the habitual anguish of all writers. A congeries of essences must find a form, and the form must be coherent and harmonious.

A witty Frenchman has said that I am a writer who disappears while arriving. I would like to misunderstand him that I come too late as a Modernist and too early for the dissonances that go by the name of Postmodernism. All writers being creatures of language and the past, I look back (however inaccurately) to Lucian reading his dialogues in Greek to Roman consular families in Gaul, to Ausonius trying to see the Garonne in the Moselle, to Walter Savage Landor writing his imaginary conversations in Fiesole.

Printed in the United States
by Baker & Taylor Publisher Services